T0244642

Groundwood Books is grateful for the opportunity to share stories and make books on the Traditional Territory of many Nations, including the Anishinabeg, the Wendat and the Haudenosaunee. It is also the Treaty Lands of the Mississaugas of the Credit. In partnership with Indigenous writers, illustrators, editors and translators, we commit to publishing stories that reflect the experiences of Indigenous Peoples. For more about our work and values, visit us at groundwoodbooks.com.

WHO WE ARE IN REAL LIFE

Content note: This book contends with themes of homophobia and abuse. Take care when reading.

WHO WE ARE IN REAL LIFE

VICTORIA KOOPS

Groundwood Books
House of Anansi Press
Toronto / Berkeley

Published in 2024 by Groundwood Books / House of Anansi Press
groundwoodbooks.com

We gratefully acknowledge for their financial support of our publishing program the Canada Council for the Arts, the Ontario Arts Council and the Government of Canada.

Library and Archives Canada Cataloguing in Publication
Title: Who we are in real life / Victoria Koops.
Names: Koops, Victoria, author.
Identifiers: Canadiana (print) 20230453953 | Canadiana (ebook) 2023045397X |
ISBN 9781773068893 (softcover) | ISBN 9781773068909 (EPUB)
Classification: LCC PS8621.O6645 W56 2024 | DDC jC813/.6—dc23

Edited by Emma Sakamoto
Cover illustration by Bhavna Madan
Interior illustrations by Freepik (poppy and dagger) and lineartestpilot @ vecteezy.com (d20)
Designed by Lucia Kim

Printed and bound in Canada

Groundwood Books is a Global Certified Accessible™ (GCA by Benetech) publisher. An ebook version of this book that meets stringent accessibility standards is available to students and readers with print disabilities.

Groundwood Books is committed to protecting our natural environment. This book is made of material from well-managed FSC®-certified forests, recycled materials, and other controlled sources.

For Bill
Who didn't know the first thing about *Dungeons & Dragons*
or growing up queer on the prairies but would have read
every word in this book and would have been willing to learn.

DARCY IRL

Strength. Dexterity. Constitution. Intelligence. Wisdom. Charisma.

I repeat the abilities in my head as the flat fields of wheat streak past. Only the occasional dirt road or giant combine interrupts the yellow haze. People would be so much easier to understand if they were characters in a role-playing game with ability scores.

A jock would have an off-the-charts Strength ability, like a natural twenty at least, and an Athletics skill too. A theater kid would have great Charisma ability, plus Charisma-based skills like Performance and Deception in the upper teens.

I give my one mom, Monica, an eighteen in Charisma and a sixteen in Wisdom and Intelligence. Her Constitution, Strength and Dexterity are all between ten and twelve, average at best. In game, she'd be a traveling artisan, selling beauty remedies and homemade tinctures from the back of a covered wagon. In real life, she's a short, round woman who needs a step stool to cut, dye and style hair at her salon.

Her own hair is curly, like mine, but instead of almost-black-brown, Monica has dyed her head a silvery purple. Over the course of my sixteen years, her hair has been red, blue, green and now silver.

Carrie, my other mom, has an epic Intelligence score of twenty — the highest base ability score possible — given that she's been through all that med school. If she were a character in an RPG, she'd obviously be a healer. I play a healer too, a hedgewitch named Poppy, but my character is a magic user, and Carrie is more likely to play a combat medic. I can't imagine Dr. Evans in the front seat there — with her smooth blond ponytail, superclean nails and stoic brown eyes — waving a staff around to cast a spell.

Side note: I'm ignoring both of The Moms right now. I have music blasting, RPG stats rattling around my head, and I haven't said a thing for five whole songs.

"Darcy!" Monica's voice pierces my favorite Weird Al playlist. She's impressive like that; she has a yelling proficiency, and proficiencies always help. During character creation, the roll of the dice determines a character's base abilities, but proficiencies are earned with practice.

"What?"

Monica sighs.

"Try not to use that tone, Darcy," Carrie says, her very British accent softening and rounding out my name. She left England fresh out of boarding school and hasn't gone back since, but despite nearly three decades abroad, she still sounds as though she's auditioning for some BBC period drama.

"We've already been through this, love." Carrie waves her hand at the last-minute boxes and winter coats shoved in the back seat with me. "This is happening, so enough is enough."

I blow a curl from my forehead. Monica's eyes cut across the front seat to Carrie.

"Darcy," Monica says, but before she can launch into a full lecture, Carrie takes up the parental reins again.

"We know this has been hard on you," Carrie says, as though she's trying to avoid a fight.

She takes Monica's hand and looks at her with a familiar tenderness; Monica returns the gaze with her own private smile. I've seen that same exchange countless times, the same meaningful expression shared every single time.

Love. True love, if you believe in that sort of thing. Which I might?

I think about my boyfriend, James. Or maybe not. I'm not an idiot. I've seen the way James looks at me, and it's not even remotely similar to the way Carrie stares at Monica.

"Hello?" I wave my hands to get their attention. "Eyes on the road, please."

Carrie tears her focus away from Monica, while Monica turns back around to face off with me.

"They made an offer we couldn't refuse," Monica says. The muscles around her mouth tighten. "You know your mother has always wanted her own practice. She'll be the head physician at the clinic."

"Yeah, I know." I shrink back. There's no point in fighting this late in the game. I know when I'm defeated. I imagine Monica going to battle with a red dragon. She's armed with nothing but a pair of scissors and her magic ability to guilt-trip. She disarms the dragon with one look. Her silver hair blows in the wind. The beast lowers its head and fully submits rather than face her wrath.

"Well, you haven't been very cooperative lately," Carrie

says. Her voice is still fluid, even with the pointed tone. She's not angry though, just concerned.

"I just miss James," I say. Deflection, my go-to strategy.

The Moms don't groan but they don't need to. The tension in our clown car ramps up as soon as I mention my boyfriend's name. They hate him. I mean, they've never said as much, but I know they do. Honestly, that's probably why he and I are still a thing.

An accordion echoes from my headphones. This is my favorite part of this song. I grab my phone to turn up the volume, but Carrie changes the subject.

"Aren't you even a little excited to meet new people?"

"No?" I fold my arms across my chest. "I had perfectly good friends back home."

Home.

The place we left behind. Our little house in the middle of the thrumming city. The drive isn't long, only an hour or so, but with no license, everyone from my previous life might as well be trapped in the Upside Down.

I sink in my seat. "I don't need new friends."

The back of Carrie's head thumps against the driver's headrest. She probably thinks that I don't notice but she doesn't know that my Perception skill is super high. I see everything.

My abilities IRL would look like this: Intelligence seventeen, Wisdom sixteen, Charisma fourteen, Dexterity fourteen, Constitution eleven and Strength ten. Perception is a Wisdom-based skill, and because my Wisdom ability is one of my best, I would have great modifiers applied to every Wisdom roll. On top of that, I'd have a handy Perception proficiency too, to add an extra boost to my chances of success.

After all the math is done, I'd have a decent plus-five

modifier added every time I roll for Perception. Not too shabby for a nearsighted sixteen-year-old.

If life were an RPG.

"We're going to have a new home," Carrie says.

I lean an elbow against the window and rest my chin in my hand. "Sure."

On the other side of the glass, fields continue to streak past us.

"Do you have everything you need for school tomorrow or will we have to look through your boxes?"

"Excuse me?" I launch myself forward over the center console of Carrie's car. My head pops out between The Moms to look back and forth at their faces. "What do you mean, am I ready? Tomorrow's Friday."

"Put your seat belt on!" Monica says. "Has it been unbuckled the whole time?"

"I can't start school on a Friday!"

"Seat belt! Now!"

I open my mouth to yell back at her, but the look in her eyes reminds me of that red dragon. Instead, I lean back and make a show of buckling up, succeeding my Survival Check.

Monica's eyes linger, narrow, then she turns to the front again. "Thank you."

"Who starts school on a Friday?"

"You do," she says. Carrie nods along.

I glare over top of my glasses. The Moms take unfair to a whole new level.

I skip back to the song I missed. I'm happy to fume, listen to my music, and stare at the nothing landscape, but Monica twists around in her seat. Again. She waves a hand in my face.

"What now!"

She makes a motion for me to take the earbuds out. I was wrong. Monica wouldn't fight a monster; she is one. And I'm trapped here with her.

"Thank you," she says, as I remove the headphones. "Now, could you please turn that down? I don't want to be able to hear Weird Al for the rest of the drive."

I do what she asks. She smiles, what's meant to be a nice smile, I suppose, though it comes across looking like a harpy's grin.

Then, I put my earbuds back in and lean my head against the car window. I refuse to make eye contact with Monica. Finally, she turns back to Carrie.

If they want quiet, I can be quiet.

Unity Creek is, like, four main roads and a bunch of back alleys. We drive down Main Street, and The Moms point out my new school, a sprawling dungeon made of concrete. After we've turned down a couple more pothole-ridden side streets, we pull into our new driveway.

The house is one of those old brick ones that you don't see very often, the kind that would have been owned by some loaded old guy back in the day. The Realtor told us that the character home was built by Unity Creek's first mayor, who happened to be the minister of agriculture or something.

I hate to admit it, but the house is nice. Even nicer than when we came for a tour. All the renovations this summer — the freshly painted trim, big red door and new windows — have given the old building a face-lift.

It's all so damn pretty now.

I hop out of the car and slam the door behind me. Carrie and Monica follow and direct the white-uniformed movers who were hired to bring all our stuff from the city. They march past me like out-of-shape stormtroopers. I'm completely ignored. Why would they care about the fat girl in a denim jacket and high-tops, perched on the veranda?

Each worker carries a labeled box. Each box has a number, a room destination, and the contents, written in Monica's almost illegible handwriting. I notice a box labeled *34, Darcy's Room, Books*.

I follow my book box inside, hoping it's the right one. The mover man walks through the front door, past the open-concept kitchen, and weaves his way to my new room. I skulk in behind him. He knows the house better than I do, which is kinda creepy.

He chucks the box on the floor and it lands with a thud.

"Hey! Be careful, those are expensive!"

The mover lifts up his hands like I have a loaded crossbow leveled at him. "Sorry, but they're just books, kid. A little bump won't hurt them."

I glare at him until he leaves the room. My room.

"Just books, my ass."

The walls are freshly painted a faint taupe color, and white curtains were hung before we got here, but otherwise the bedroom I'm supposed to feel at home in looks completely sanitary. Brown moving boxes have been stacked in a pile against the wall.

I peel back the packing tape with a satisfying rip and imagine unlocking a loot box. My reward for a long and perilous journey awaits.

The smell of paper welcomes me before the box is even

completely open. I yank back the cardboard flaps. Something icy thaws in my chest as I dig through the box. It's about half-filled with the hardcover novels I get for Christmas and birthdays but never read. I toss those on the floor. The rest are the books I've been desperately missing since they were packed two months ago: *Player's Handbook. Dungeon Master's Guide. Monster Manual.*

I stroke their spines. "Hello, beautifuls."

ART IRL

I bounce from the skills list to their corresponding abilities and erase previous ability scores. Do I want a plus-eight on every Stealth roll? I'd have to spend all the points in my Dexterity ability to do that.

"I took a feat this level," Alex says from behind the library counter. He's supposed to be working, but he's trying to help me level up my character. To be fair, only one person has come into the small town library to pick up books this entire shift.

"Yeah, you've mentioned that once or twice."

He flips through the *Player's Handbook*. Feats are special level-ups; flavorful, but not really practical. No matter how many times I explain that to Alex, he always suggests that I take something ridiculous, like Tavern Brawler or Lucky, whenever we level up. I'd rather spend my point increase on something useful.

I've played the same tiefling rogue, or variations of that character, since we started playing *Dungeons & Dragons* after school in grade seven. That was more than four years ago now. Roman is charismatic and dashing, a real silver-tongue, and the de facto leader of our party. Pretty much everything I'm not.

"You should take a feat this time, too. How about Sharpshooter?"

"Roman doesn't even have a ranged weapon." I take the *Handbook* from Alex's hands. "I'm just going to take the ability score upgrade like a normal person. That'll put my Dex at a twenty."

"Where's the fun in that?" He pulls out his phone. In T-minus five seconds he'll be distracted by TikTok.

Five. Four. Three. Two —

Alex slams his hands on the library desk. "Did you hear about the new doctor?!"

I pitch my pencil in surprise. The graphite HB lands somewhere in the rows of dusty books, lost forever in the abyss of obsolete encyclopedias.

I stare murder at Alex. He's my best friend. He might even be my only friend, but half the time I want to throttle him.

"What the hell?"

He smiles, a devilish smirk that only fuels my annoyance. The expression looks like Kastor, the wizard Alex plays in game. IRL, Alex is average height and medium build, with light brown hair that's always covered by a beanie. Kastor is so old that even Alex doesn't know the wizard's true age. Really, that's just lazy character creation. An old man with amnesia and the strength of a teenager? Please.

He shakes his head in mock disapproval. "Hell? Watch your mouth, Preacher Boy. What would your father say?"

"He's not a preacher. Besides, hell isn't a swear. It's biblical."

"And the difference is?"

"Lots." I push back my chair. "Did you know that even linguists and historians don't know the etymology of the f-word? There are theories that it might be an acronym but others think it simply means 'to strike.' Hell, on the other hand, has a very clear definition, and Dad says that if it's in the Bible, it's fair game."

"Nerrrrrd!" Alex hollers from the front desk as I root around in the stacks for my pencil. The stupid thing probably rolled under a bookshelf or something. Hopeless.

"You're one to talk."

"My grandma says your dad has more influence in this town than the whole church board combined."

I find a dollar, but no pencil. I give up. "Not true."

Alex laughs. He sounds like a donkey when he laughs. "Where is Father Bailey these days, anyway?"

Dad's in Dallas this week. His last email said that he should be home by the weekend if all the talks go well, or maybe the weekend after that. He didn't even bother to erase the corporate signature at the bottom of the email: Chief of Legal Counsel, Marcus Bailey, LLM. He also reminded me and my sister to go to church on Sunday.

I sit back down at the circulation desk. "What's the deal about the doctor? Did you meet him?"

"Her. They hired a female doctor."

"And this is news because?"

"Have you heard anything about her? Anything at all?"

"Alex, I need to finish leveling up my character for tonight's game."

"Okay, okay," he says. His whole body is vibrating.

If Alex was a superhero, which he is most definitely not, but if he was, he would be the Flash. Me, I've always liked

Aquaman — from the comics, not the movies — but apart from our shared first name, we don't have much in common. I've never even been to the ocean.

"She's a lesbian!" he shouts. "As in, she sleeps with other women!"

He waits for a reaction, but I'm stuck on why he'd think this is more important to me than leveling up my character.

"So?"

"So, she moved here from the city. We saw them moving into the old Mayor House just down the street from us today. There were the two lesbians and a daughter. I think she's about our age. Do you think they used a turkey baster?"

I don't say anything.

"Anyway, my grandma and I went to say hi. The doctor introduced all of them. When we got home, Grandma said the clinic must be desperate. I got a look at the daughter too. She looks like a totally normal teenager."

I try to focus on the character sheet in front of me.

"Can you believe that we have a gay doctor?"

"I don't really get why this is such a big deal to you." I pack up my character sheet without looking up. We always leave a little bit early on Thursdays to make it to Game on time. "Go lock the door, we're wrapping up this quest tonight, and Michelle will kill us if we're late."

I make a mental note of the changes I want to make to Roman's character sheet as we pull into Michelle's driveway. Life's been so much easier since I got my license. Walking to Game every week was a total drag, especially because my dad is never around to drive me or my sister anywhere. Not that he would if he were around — he doesn't 100 percent approve of *D&D*.

WHO WE ARE IN REAL LIFE

Alex and I head to the side door of Michelle and Tyler Anderson's house. A gust of wind rips through my hoodie, a reminder that summer is gone. Winter is coming.

We knock, but only to be polite, before walking in.

Various greetings echo up to us from the basement. We kick off our shoes and go down to join them.

Michelle and Tyler and their friend Robert are all crowded around a gaming table Tyler made for Michelle last Christmas. The chestnut table is solid with a slim LED TV mounted flat in the center. Michelle sits behind a laptop, her orange cat's-eye glasses on the tip of her nose as she pulls up this week's map. On her right, Tyler is lining up a row of painted miniature heroes and monsters. He picks out a female paladin with elf ears and sets her in front of him: his character, Moira of Tyr. Across from him is Robert. IRL, Robert's a mechanic, but in our campaign, he plays as Bearpuncher the barbarian.

Alex and I sit in our usual spots, and after a few minutes of rustling backpacks, sliding papers and clattering pencils, everyone is ready. Well, mostly.

Alex is still telling Robert about his newest Kastor-inspired antic, so I jab him in the arm. He stops, mid-explanation. Michelle smiles at the two of us and points to the deep green forest map that illuminates the screen between us.

"You guys ready for this?" She selects a red dragon from the line of miniatures in front of her and places the figurine on the digital map.

"Bring it on," Alex says.

I slip into character. Roman takes over. "We're ready."

The End

The forest was burning. The tiefling rogue Roman swiped a bead of sweat from his horned brow. Smoke burned his eyes.

In this moment, his life wasn't measured in years or days, or even in minutes. Survival meant clinging to his next heartbeat, jumping behind a burning tree for cover. If he wanted to live through this, he needed to resist the exhaustion in his bones.

Fire licked up the trunks of old pines and gnawed at the deadfall surrounding him. From his hiding spot, Roman glanced toward the source of the inferno — a red dragon — and what he saw made him curse in an ancient, gnarled language.

The dragon's long neck whipped side to side, and with each angry movement, the monster pushed Roman's friends closer to the burning woods. Soon the others would be trapped between the dragon's jaws and a wall of fire.

He sprinted from the shadows, dagger in hand. As Roman collided with the dragon's extended neck, the tip of his blade found a soft spot — an exposed knot of muscle where a larger blow had knocked away the dragon's scaled armor — and he thrust with all his remaining strength. The dragon's cry of pain rattled the trees and shook the ground.

"The river!" Roman shouted, his voice lost in the mighty roar. He was already scrambling back toward the water, and as he ran, he waved his arms. If his friends couldn't hear him, he prayed they would see him.

He crashed into the forest river, and dived. The water was freezing against his soot-streaked skin. He broke the surface with a gasp, and before he could open his eyes, he heard the clanking of armor. Pushing wet hair back from his face, Roman watched the others follow him out of the smoldering woods.

Moira — a half-elf paladin from across the sea — pulled an aging human wizard with her into the river. Kastor Wolfgang Tom Tiberias Gambon looked as though he had one foot in the grave, his head lolling onto Moira's shoulder. Roman bit the inside of his cheek. As she ran, Moira cast a healing spell, and Kastor's eyes fluttered open.

"Where's Bearpuncher?" Roman called.

Moira shook her head, the incantation on her lips dying.

Roman scrambled to his feet, heart hammering as he searched for the last of their party. When Bearpuncher the Barbarian — a hulking, seven-foot wild man — emerged with his arms pumping at his sides and a battle-ax in one fist, Roman sagged with relief. Unfortunately, time slipped again and there was no pause to celebrate.

Behind Bearpuncher, the dragon pursued. Unhinging a mighty jaw, the beast bared row upon row of sharp, jagged teeth. Roman saw the spark of flame snap and crackle in the dragon's gullet. Another stream of deadly fire would pour from the dragon's mouth; Bearpuncher would become a pile of ash in moments.

"Go for the eyes!" Roman called, his throat raw.

Moira whispered the incantation for another spell, and this time a brilliant white light flashed before the dragon's eyes. The monster reared its head and writhed as though it could shake the magic away.

Roman surged from the riverbank, water sluicing off his leather armor. He reached for his only remaining weapon, a rapier given to him by his father. The blade sang as he unsheathed the thin sword.

Roman snarled, "Now, Bearpuncher!"

Yellow eyes snapped toward Roman, his command drawing the dragon's attention, just as Bearpuncher nodded and turned his back to the monster.

Roman glanced over Bearpuncher's shoulder, focusing on the flat ridge between the dragon's eyes. Just then, the beast opened its mouth once more. If Roman didn't succeed, his friend wouldn't see death coming.

Bearpuncher took a knee, his axe discarded on the ground, and laced his meaty fingers together.

The catch of fire breath crackled in the dragon's throat again.

Roman tilted forward, running harder, faster than was natural for any human. But he was no human, and the infernal heritage in his bloodline burned hot, as if to fuel him. Roman's foot landed in Bearpuncher's waiting hand, and he heaved Roman into the air.

Roman landed on the dragon, his rapier sinking deep into the corner of the monster's eye.

The death throes that gripped the dragon would have sent

anyone else tumbling, but not Roman. His muscles protested and sweat slicked his hands, but still he held fast.

It wasn't until the rest of his company — Bearpuncher, then Moira and Kastor — surrounded him, that Roman realized the dragon had ceased to thrash.

His arms shook as he released his hold on the dead monster, his smile just as shaky. "Now where is that prize we were promised?"

In moments, the entire party was tossing gold coins from the dragon's cave into the air.

"With these winnings we can finally afford transport out of Durgeon's Keep," Roman said, as he assessed the mountains of treasure.

"We could afford a luxury caravan past the Durgeon Forest altogether!" Kastor whooped, restored to health after several healing draughts. His mustache quivered with excitement.

As the group counted the loot, Moira folded her arms. The look she shot Roman pierced deeper than any of his wounds. Shame flickered in his belly.

"May I remind you of our contract?" she said. It was a question, but not. "We're being paid to return the head of the dragon, and all this treasure, to Lord and Lady Daeroot. We're adventurers, not common thieves."

Roman swallowed. "The Daeroots have never laid eyes on the dragon or the treasure, they won't miss a few pieces."

When that did nothing to soften Moira's scowl, Roman sighed and turned away from her toward a pile of treasure on the other side of the cave. She wasn't wrong, but she also didn't know how to take what she needed. She had never been left without, forced to survive in the streets of Durgeon's Keep. Elves like Moira were a novelty, but Roman was a nightmare, and had been treated as such since leaving the castle two years ago.

A glint of fading sunlight caught a sharp edge on top of the pile of gold. When he was closer, Roman saw the elegant stiletto, flung carelessly as if it were a trinket. He picked up the beautiful weapon, and as soon as his fingers closed around the hilt, a buzz thrummed up his arm. The tingle was familiar: magic. With a twirl and flick of his quick fingers, Roman slid the powerful blade into his cloak. A fine replacement for the one he had lost in the burning forest.

The rest of the day was spent loading a cart with as much loot as they could carry and carving the dragon's head from its thick neck. When they had all they had been sent to collect, they rode along the Hebenon River — the same river that had saved them from being burned alive — back toward the only seat of power in the Barony of Blackwood, the grim city of Durgeon's Keep.

The lingering light of sundown cast a warm glow down the river and illuminated clusters of pink Hebenon blossoms along the riverbank. Roman glowered at the path ahead.

Going back into the city was risky. He knew as much, but they still needed to deliver the treasure to the Daeroots and collect their payment. It was the only way they would have enough funds to secure the services and silence needed to escape for good. A headache began between Roman's horns. If they were caught, if he were recognized —

"The end?" Bearpuncher asked, the simple question pulling Roman back from his worries.

Roman snapped the reins against his mount's shoulders; the horse jolted forward.

"No," he said. "This is just the beginning."

DARCY IRL

I stand the loser after an epic with The Moms. In the morning, my eyes are itchy from crying and I have one of those headaches that starts before you wake up.

I stare at my makeshift bed, a mattress on the floor, where I've laid out my various outfit options. Luckily, all my favorites were packed in my pink suitcase at the very last minute.

I've been staring at the clothes for a long time. You only get one chance to make a proper first impression, and I don't want the locals mistaking me for one of them. That rules out all plaids. I toss a flannel shirt onto the floor.

I pick up a black turtleneck dress. Perfect.

After wiggling into the dress, I step into the bathroom and glance in the mirror. The bedhead life is real this morning. I manage to pull my unruly hair into a bun, which is only a little better. My dark mane is halfway between wavy and curly; difficult to manage is an understatement. Most days, a messy bun is good enough. Today, I scowl at my reflection and try to convince myself that I don't care what my new classmates think of me.

I yank the bathroom door open and stalk toward the kitchen.

Monica's been busy. Right now she's making oatmeal, her favorite breakfast, but the rest of the kitchen is almost perfectly tidy and organized. You'd never know we've lived here less than a day.

She even unpacked Carrie's little tea plants and lined the pots up on the windowsill.

The only giveaway is the pile of unopened cardboard boxes stacked behind the couch. They all have *Salon* scrawled across the top.

I sit down at the kitchen island and point to the boxes. "I thought you were setting up the salon in the basement?"

Monica's back is to me but her shoulders rise as she spoons the oatmeal into a clay bowl I made at summer camp three years ago.

"I will." She slides the bowl toward me. Then she fills a matching bowl for herself. "It's not like I have any clients out here yet, so there's no rush. Besides, we have some renovations to do downstairs first. Can't be cutting hair without a sink and basin."

I spoon oatmeal into my mouth, only half listening. I spent hours in Monica's hair studio when I was little. I'll never sit in the back of that salon again, painting my nails while Monica finishes a shift. I knew I'd miss James and my friends, but the tiny downtown building that always smelled like ammonia? Weird.

"You look like that girl from the Addams Family. What's her name?"

Carrie walks in, a tie undone around her neck. "She's too young for that, darling." She bends to kiss Monica on the cheek, then steps back and spins, "What do you think?"

Monica's lips pinch into a small smile and her eyes get soft.

"I think you look great. But maybe something more feminine for your first day?"

A look passes between The Moms.

"I'll go change, then." From down the hall, she calls, "Where did you pack my work dresses?"

"They're in the brown suitcase!"

I scrape the sides of my bowl and finish my breakfast.

Monica smacks the island countertop. "Wednesday!"

"It's Friday, Monica."

A shadow darkens her face. She hates when I use her first name.

"I know that. I mean, you look like Wednesday Addams from *The Addams Family*, with the black dress and those boots. You know, I bet you'd like that series. We have them on DVD if you want to watch them."

I hop off the island stool.

"No one watches DVDs anymore." I don't tell her that I've already seen all the episodes and movies. Twice. Not to mention the new Netflix series entirely dedicated to Wednesday Addams. "I gotta go. Don't want to be late for my very first day."

Monica hands me a paper bag without a word.

"What's this?" I ask.

"Your lunch. The school doesn't have a cafeteria so it's packed lunches for you, young lady."

"That's just perfect." I stuff the brown monstrosity into the bag at my hip.

The satchel is a hand-me-down from Carrie's university days. Vintage leather, worn and authentic. There's even an embroidered *E* for Evans on the side, which is cool, it being my last name and everything. Well, technically, Evans is only half my last name. I'm Larocque-Evans on paper.

I've loved this stupid bag since I was a kid. I squealed when Carrie gave it to me the year I started high school. Now a variety of trinkets decorate the leather bag, everything from a *Be Gay, Do Crime* button to a collection of *Sailor Moon* patches.

Swinging from the strap is a d20 on a keychain. I found the roundish, twenty-sided die in a mixed bin of dice last summer when I was working at our local comics shop in the city. I drilled a hole in one corner, then found these jewelry screws to fix the die onto a keychain. When I came in for my next shift with the new keychain, my manager asked me to make more to sell at the store. Now the little d20 goes everywhere with me on this bag that is a perfect reflection of who I am — so of course I never leave it behind.

Carrie rushes back into our new kitchen. She throws her briefcase onto the island, almost knocking over Monica's coffee.

"How's this?" Her hands smooth the front of an emerald dress that I've never seen before.

Monica steps back and examines the new dress. She walks past Carrie and brings back a pair of shoes from their bedroom. I recognize the black pumps I borrowed for the spring formal last year.

Monica hands the shoes to Carrie. "You look beautiful."

Carrie bends over to slip on the pumps. "You're a life saver," she says.

I dig out my denim jacket from my bag. "I thought you looked fine before. You always wear a tie to work."

"Thanks, love." Carrie kisses my cheek. "Are you ready to go? I can give you a ride."

"What? No! I can't show up with my mom on the first day of school. Do you want everyone to hate me?"

"It's either get a ride with me or walk," she says. "Or get your license. I could take you driving after work."

"I'll walk."

"All right. If you say so."

I pull on the grunge denim. "I do say so."

Carrie shrugs, then pulls Monica close. Monica giggles like a lovestruck teenager. They rub noses and that's about all I can handle. Any more and I'll barf.

I go to the door and call back, "I'm leaving." Between the kisses and giggling, they don't even notice.

Gross.

I pull out my phone and search for the school. A single pin pops up, fifteen minutes away on foot. Rain starts to splatter the sidewalk, because of course it's raining on my first day, and I'm seriously considering skipping school, but where would I go?

Carrie pulls out of the driveway. She eyes the gray clouds, then rolls down her window. "You sure you don't want a ride, love?"

I scowl and stomp down the front steps.

"Suit yourself," she says. "Have a good day."

Not likely, I want to say, but she rolls up the window before pulling onto the street. I look back down at the directions on my phone and notice the time. I'm going to be late.

ART IRL

I tap my pencil on the desk and stare out the window. Raindrops splatter against the glass, beading together and running down the cold surface in little rivers.

Inspiration strikes. I flip to a fresh page.

Wet hair. Smoldering. I scribble in the margin. Soon, an entire line follows. *Pushing wet hair back from his face, Roman watched the others follow him out of the smoldering woods.*

I start doodling Roman opposite the line of writing. I've sketched him hundreds of times, from the twisted horns at his temples to the blackened claws at his fingertips. He's wiry, tall like me, but somehow more graceful. In this sketch, I try to draw his dark hair wet and plastered to the sides of his face, his black eyes wide with shock.

"You must be Darcy!" Ms. Stacey exclaims from the front of the classroom. I jump; a thick black line jolts through Roman's likeness. When I lift my eyes, Ms. Stacey is beaming. "Come on up! Let's introduce you to your new classmates!"

Gazes shift, bodies swivel, as the entire class turns to look at the classroom doorway. So this is the girl Alex was telling me about yesterday. She's short with curvy hips. Dark hair creates a fuzzy halo around her face and thick hipster glasses sit crooked on her nose. A gold ring loops through the middle part of her nose, between her nostrils, and I can't look away. Can noses be pretty?

Really, she'd be cute if not for the scowl across her face.

She edges her way up to the front of the class, staring at the blank chalkboard ahead of her. When she gets to the front, Ms. Stacey puts an arm around her. You can almost see the girl — Darcy — stop breathing.

"Darcy will be joining our class today," Ms. Stacey says, and whispers rise from groups of bowed heads like smog. "She's new to town, her mom is the new doctor at the clinic, and I trust you will all work extra hard to make her feel welcome."

Darcy slips out of the awkward half embrace.

Ms. Stacey scans the classroom. There are only two empty desks. One is beside Hannah Lawson, the perfect blonde Betty type, and the other is beside me, the awkward nerd at the back of the class.

Please put her by Hannah. Please put her by Hannah.

Darcy stares at the back of the room with a warrior's resolve. Ms. Stacey puts a hand on the new girl's shoulder and smiles softly.

"You can sit by Arthur Bailey for now, right there in the back." Perfect.

Darcy looks grateful and rushes to the back of the classroom, a ratty, vintage bag held in front of her like a shield.

She sinks into the seat beside me and pulls her bag onto the desk without so much as a sideways glance in my direction.

Ms. Stacey starts talking about literary devices, but my new desk neighbor folds her arms over that leather bag and buries her face in the crook of her elbow.

Usually I spend the majority of class writing down our game's latest adventuring session or peeking at my phone to see if anyone has posted in our group chat. Today, I keep stealing glances of Darcy.

She doesn't move for the entire class. She keeps her head down, literally, her almost-black hair bouncing to life as it dries.

The bell is about to go, but before the obnoxious ringing begins, Ms. Stacey tells us about a new project.

"I'm handing out your next assignment." She shuffles a stack of papers and begins walking between the rows of desks. "In lieu of a final this semester, you will do a class presentation on a storytelling method. I want everyone to find a partner."

Group work is the worst. If only Alex was taking English this semester.

"Each group will research and present on a different form of storytelling. Please go to the first page of your assignment syllabus and follow along."

She hands me a couple bundles of paper, the pages stapled together. Two packages. One for me and one for Darcy.

I shove one handout in with the rest of my unorganized notes and hold out the other to Darcy. She doesn't look up.

I reach out and tap her shoulder. She rolls her head to the side to look me over with one eye. As soon as she moves, I pull my hand back. She raises her eyebrow.

My whole body feels hot, so instead of saying anything or handing her the syllabus like a normal person, I push the papers under her arm and turn to the front, pretending that

I'm following Ms. Stacey's directions about how to approach the assignment.

"Any questions?" Ms. Stacey finishes.

No one raises their hand. Everyone is already making eyes at the people they want to partner with, some more obvious than others. A few of the girls push their desks closer together.

Ms. Stacey claps her hands. "All right! The rest of this period will be brainstorming with your partner. Please come up one at a time to tell me who is with who.

"Oh!" she adds. "Remember, the more creative the better!"

I scan the classroom for a partner, but my eyes end up, like they have for the entire period, at the girl beside me. She's not hiding her face anymore. In fact, she's staring right at me, too.

"Ugh." She sits up. Seated, she only comes to my shoulder.

I try to pretend I don't notice what she's doing and look around the rest of the room. Everyone else is pretty much partnered up, and the eager ones have started brainstorming with pens, paper and idea maps.

I pull my notebooks and papers into a messy pile. Maybe I can convince Ms. Stacey to let me do the project alone.

The bell rings and I'm about to push myself out of my chair, but Darcy stands up first. She blocks my way, preventing my escape.

"So, it looks like you're my partner."

I cower, trapped in my desk. She puts her hands on her hips.

When I finally get to my feet, she's dwarfed beside me. I'm at least a foot taller, but she doesn't seem small. I fumble to collect my thoughts. "What for?"

Again, she raises an eyebrow at me. I stare back.

Her hair is dry now and it curls around her face, escaping the elastic on top of her head. She's still scowling, but the glower doesn't reach her eyes, which are guarded but uncertain. She pulls on a corner of her denim coat, then on the hem of her dress.

"For the project," she says, her words measured. "Everyone else is paired up, so that leaves me with you."

The way she talks makes me feel like an idiot.

"Yeah, I guess so. I mean, we can work on it tomorrow. I bet Ms. Stacey will give us more time then."

"Or you can take me to the library after school and we can catch up there so we don't have to talk in class."

"What?"

"Never mind. So, library? After school?"

My brain doesn't have time to process before I agree.

"Do you have a car?" she asks.

"No." Her eyes narrow and she looks as though she might give up on me then and there. "But I can drive us! I have a truck."

"Perfect," she says, the venomous look dissolving faster than it developed. "I'll see you after school, then."

"Yeah. Cool. That's cool."

She steps aside to let me out, and I edge past her. The farther away I walk, the more relaxed I feel.

"My name is Darcy!" she calls after me.

I know that, but I face her anyway. She's smiling now, and the way her nose scrunches up makes me think that noses can be pretty after all.

"I'm Art."

I toss my collection of keys onto the counter when I get home. *Collection* is a generous word for what is really just a house key, the truck key and my favorite keychain, a black d20 with gold numbers that I bought in the city during the summer.

My little sister, Dawn, is doing homework at the kitchen table. She's been grounded, but even so, I'm shocked to find her here. Dad would never know if she were home or not, seeing as he doesn't get home himself for another ten days.

"What's up?" I throw my bag beside her on the counter.

"It's your turn to make supper." She chews on the end of her pen. A deep frown creases her freckled forehead. "Don't forget that I'm off meat."

"Right, how could I forget?" I made the mistake of saying she wouldn't last a week when she announced that she was going to go vegetarian. That was months ago now.

"How was school?" I ask.

"What do you think?" She motions to the math home-work on the table with narrowed eyes. "If I don't improve my grades, Dad threatened to pull me from the drama club and cancel my acting lessons. How am I supposed to rehearse for auditions under his totalitarian expectations?"

"My day was fine, thanks for asking." I pull on an apron. I'm about to tell her about my new English project.

Then, like lightning, I remember Darcy.

"I've gotta go." I grab my keys. "I'll see you later. You'll have to make supper. And please, no tofu!"

"Where are you going?" The door swings shut behind me.

No one is outside the school when I pull up to the door. I glance around. Darcy is nowhere to be seen. A string of swears rattles around my head, none of them strictly Biblical. I run into the school.

She's not there.

I run back to the truck and drive to the library.

Alex is standing alone at the counter when I rush in.

"Hey, man!" he says. "Nice apron."

"Has that new girl been here?"

"You mean the new doctor's daughter?"

I nod.

"No? Why are you looking for her?"

"Her name is Darcy. I was supposed to come here with her to work on a project for English class but I forgot to wait for her after school. I thought she might have found her way here without me."

"Damn, dude!" Alex smirks. "The new girl! With lesbian moms? Hot!"

I lean against the counter.

"It's not like that."

He winks. "Sure it's not."

I weigh my options. I could go to her house, Alex told me where it is, but that seems kinda stalker-y. Or I could go home, and tomorrow at school I could beg for her forgiveness. Alex rattles on about how he's going to ask Michelle about a new spell. He doesn't seem to notice when I leave.

If life were an RPG, with experience points and levels, I just failed my personal quest.

DARCY IRL

"How was your day?" Monica asks before I step through the front door.

I resist slamming the door behind me. Instead, I stomp to my room. I toss my bag down, rip off my glasses and proceed to change out of my wet clothes.

Tears prick the corners of my eyes. I swipe them away with the palm of my hand. This is stupid. I have no reason to cry. Suck it up, Darcy.

I feel like a freak. All the hushed whispers and backward glances. And then I got stood up. I waited almost half an hour for Art before giving up.

I'm standing half-undressed when Monica knocks. Just a whisper of a knock, just enough to let me know she's there.

"Changing!" I peel off the dripping velvet dress and toss the denim jacket into the back of the empty closet, then rummage around for a pair of jeans and a T-shirt.

Monica opens the door a crack and pokes her nose into my room. She has a small jeweled stud in one nostril that glints in the light. We went to get our piercings together as a gift for my sixteenth birthday. She held my hand as the needle pushed through my septum.

I squash the memory and pull on my T-shirt.

"Darcy?" She keeps her voice soft, as if she's not really probing.

"Monica?" I toss back.

She takes a deep breath, and a pang of guilt ripples through me. That is, until I remember that she's the one who made me start school on a rainy Friday.

"How was your first day?"

I shrug.

She closes the door behind her, then sits on my mattress. She pats the spot next to her. "You can talk to me, sweetie."

I fold my arms across my chest to stop myself from falling into her lap. "Everything's fine. I have unpacking and homework to do, so if you could leave me in peace. I'm a bit busy."

Monica looks around my room. She must have been busy today, too, because most of my boxes are already unpacked. Even my bed is set up.

"Would you like some help with that?"

"You've done enough." I mean it as a thank-you, but the words come out too sharp.

Monica's eyes drift to the empty spot on the bed beside her, then she gets up to leave. She stops, one hand on the doorframe. "If you need me, I'm here."

Part of me wants to apologize. I step toward her, but she's already gone. I'm not one to chase, even in game, so I pull out my phone. I snap a picture of my half-unpacked room for James.

I guess this IS happening ...

Monday morning, I get to English class before anyone else. Late. Early. Clearly, I haven't perfected my walking routine yet.

Ms. Stacey looks up to see me lurking in the doorway. She reminds me of a sage — an eccentric scholar learned in ancient lore — with her thick black hair and pencil-shaped earrings. Her skin is dotted with freckles from her forehead to her chin. She looks young, but with my advanced Perception skill, I notice the delicate laugh lines around her eyes, even behind her gold wire glasses.

"Oh! Good morning, Darcy. You're early!"

Of course she's a morning person.

"Hi," I half whisper, half grumble.

"Feel free to come in and make yourself comfortable. I'm just doing some prep, but you won't bother me if you want to sit down."

I don't wait for her to ask a second time. I turn and flee from the scene, messenger bag in tow. I hear a bemused chuckle on the heels of my retreat.

I stop at my locker and pretend to be really interested in setting it up as people trickle into the hallway.

First are the overachievers, like the blonde girl from English class. Heather? Hailey?

She stops at her locker, just a few down from mine, and swaps her pink backpack for a stack of bright notebooks and a couple of paperback books. I notice *Lady Knight* on top of the pile, and a teeny bit of my resentment melts away.

Anyone reading Tamora Pierce can't be that bad. No matter how blonde and perky.

H-girl glances over at me. I panic and scowl, before turning to shove more books in my locker. She doesn't come over, mercifully. Instead, she beelines for Ms. Stacey's room.

Next to arrive are the freshmen who don't have a driver's license yet. Their parents are obviously dropping them off before work. Half of them scurry past on the farthest side of the hallway, totally afraid of me. The other half press in close, invading my personal space to get a better look.

I want to snap around and lunge at the curious ones. Maybe roll for Dexterity and get in a side kick.

A couple of boys pass.

"I'd totally do her," one says.

"Nah, too fat."

"Dude, those are the best ones. Low self-esteem."

"Her mom is the lesbo doctor."

"Do you think she's one of them too?"

"Probably."

"That's hot."

I spin around. "No. To everything you just said. Absolutely not. You don't have the right to talk about me, my family or anyone else like that."

The group of boys turn to stare at me. I raise an eyebrow and they scatter, scrambling away as fast as they can.

"Oh, that's fucking fantastic!" I flip them off. "Run away, then! Good riddance!"

I lean into my locker, my breathing heavy. The damage is done and the AoE — Area of Effect — is the entire hallway; everyone erupts into muffled whispers.

I clench my jaw. So much for staying off the radar.

A slow clap starts halfway down the hall. "Slay!"

The speaker, a tall boy with a sharp jawline and long, dark hair braided in twin ropes over each shoulder, slinks down the middle of the hallway, and students part as though he's on a runway. He's striking, but I can't tell if that's because of his flawless skin and influencer-level style, or if it's the confidence radiating off him. My brain goes offline while I try to process what I'm seeing. The person walking toward me is Queer with a capital Q.

He doesn't stop by my locker to introduce himself or slow down, just keeps on walking. I can't look away, unable to reconcile that someone so obviously Out lives here in Unity Creek. I thought for sure that my mothers would be the only openly gay people, but maybe I was wrong?

He glances over his shoulder, raises a dark eyebrow, and says, "You're staring."

I bury my head in my locker, mortified. Making a big show of grabbing a textbook I don't even need, I sling my heavy messenger bag over my shoulder. For good measure, I twist my hair up and stab a few pens into the bun. Then, I slam the locker door shut.

A tall redhead, with just enough freckles on the bridge of his nose to play connect-the-dots, stands on the other side of my locker.

"That's Wyatt Cyr," Art explains. "He's a year older than us. I can introduce you to him if you want, he's the director of the drama club."

I jump in surprise and exhale a string of profanities in his face.

He runs a hand through his already messy fire-engine-red hair. "Sorry."

I wish I could slam the locker door again.

"What do you want?"

He tilts his head down the hall in the direction of the stupid boys. "Just ignore them. They're in my sister's class, and from what I hear, they're all idiots."

"You saw that?" I try to keep the panic out of my voice.

His smile is nice; shy and crooked. "Yeah. I think everyone in the hallway saw that."

I push past him, heading for English. "What do you want?"

"I just wanted to say —" He falls in beside me. He takes a deep breath. "I'msorryforwhathappenedlastweek."

I halt. His whole face flushes. That's a lot of red for one person.

I laugh. I can't help it.

Then his brow furrows and he shoves his hands in his pockets. He mumbles something else and brushes past me.

My hand shoots out to grab the elbow of his sweater. I'm not a total asshole.

"Art, just wait. I'm sorry, I shouldn't have laughed."

He takes a deep breath. "I just wanted to apologize for not picking you up after school on Friday. I'm sorry. I forgot, and by the time I remembered, you were already gone." His voice is automatic, robotic in a way that betrays his discomfort, but his gaze becomes unflinching. He looks at me as though he can will me to believe him, to feel his sincerity.

And damn it if that level of attentive focus and genuine remorse doesn't do something to me. I let go of his sleeve, unsure how to process exactly the way he's affecting me. "Oh? You're apologizing for that?"

Then he's back to himself. He runs another nervous hand through his hair and looks away. "I mean, I'm trying to."

"Art, it's fine." I pull on my bag strap and hike it higher on my shoulder, suddenly embarrassed by the way my insides have turned all melty. "I figured you just forgot about me and I walked home. No big deal."

"Still," he says. "I'm sorry. You must think I'm the worst."

He looks so dejected. I press my lips together, shift my book bag around in front of me and dig in it. I rip the corner off some random assignment and pull one of the pens from my messy bun to scribble on the paper. I shove the note at him.

His eyes dart from me to the paper in my hand. "What's this?"

"My number." He hesitates. I push the paper at him. "Take it. That way we don't have a mix-up like yesterday."

He opens a notebook, one I didn't notice tucked beneath his arm, and I catch of glimpse of a campfire doodle between the pages as he tucks away the scrap of paper. When he notices me noticing his drawing, he snaps the notebook closed and looks everywhere I'm not. Such an awkward cinnamon roll.

The bell rings for first period. Students scramble to get to class, pushing in around us. I stumble out of the way of a particularly large boy with a pretty girl beside him. Art moves to steady me. He grabs my shoulder so I don't knock into the lockers.

Still pressed against him, I say, "Hey, watch it."

The couple apologizes before continuing down the hall.

"Are you going to pick a fight with everyone this morning?"

"I might," I say, defensive. "If you don't watch it, you might be next."

This time his smile takes over and he's laughing. He covers his mouth to hold it in, but instead explodes and doubles over.

"Wasn't that funny," I say under my breath.

"Here," he says, still smiling. "I'll walk you to class. I'm going that way too."

"No kidding." I smother the little flip in my stomach as Art falls into step beside me. Get a grip, Darcy.

The Barge

Dense forest crowded the banks of the Hebenon River, slowing what would have otherwise been a short ride home. Pines towered along either side of the riverbank, and as the others rode on — laughing and dreaming of warm beds and hot food — Roman's gaze drifted toward the thick trees. He'd been raised on a steady diet of fairy stories, told to him by an unending cast of elderly nannies. Hidden in the woods there were trolls, hobgoblins, sprites, imps, forest folk, elementals, beasts and other creatures. There was a reason so many had fled from the forest toward the perceived safety of Durgeon's Keep.

It wasn't until the silhouette of the Keep emerged on the horizon, St. Oswin's Tower defiant against the wastelands beyond, that Roman began to relax. They were almost out of the forest now. The trees had been pushed back from the Outer Wall on all sides, and a small tent city crowded the entrance to the gate.

They called it the Ditch, the bleak lowlands between the

forest and city, where the poor were discarded. Nothing grew in the Ditch, Roman knew. Nothing, save the population of displaced people and the Hebenon flowers along the river-bank. With pretty pink petals, the flower bloomed beautifully, but after a season of growth and death, the petals would fall into the river and poison the water. The tainted water flowed from the river into the marshes, killing all other life. A pesti-lence sent by the All Father, if the priests were to be believed.

To Roman, the flowers had always been another reason the common folk overcrowded Durgeon's Keep. With very little clean water in the Barony lands, the only fresh water in the area flowed from a fountain in St. Oswin's Tower. From the fountain, a newly constructed aqueduct distributed the water throughout the city.

These architectural wonders provided Durgeon's Keep, and even the Ditch by way of the city gate, with unpolluted water. The tower and aqueduct were so crucial to survival that most city folk only whispered about the Baron's brutal construction methods.

That night, five souls shrouded in cloaks gathered in St. Oswin's churchyard.

Everything — the churchyard, the tower and the fountain within — had been built on the backs of slaves. All of whom worshipped the Old Gods; all of whom refused to renounce their beliefs when the Baron converted the entire city to the High Church.

Roman shuddered. Bones and blood had been built into the walls of their reservoirs.

In the quiet dark, Roman stepped forward. He lifted his hood to reveal his twisting gray horns; a sign of his identity and infernal heritage, along with his ashy skin and clawed hands. From the shadows melted the rest of his friends, each of them stepping into the weak light of his covered lamp.

All business, Roman tossed a bag of gold at the feet of the fifth person. "This should be enough."

A massive hand reached down and closed around the pouch. The man belonging to the hand — a barge master named Beckett — weighed the coins. "And the rest?"

Roman motioned to Bearpuncher, who deposited a large sack of cheese, salted meat, mead and medical supplies.

The rogue hadn't asked questions when one of his contacts told him Beckett's terms: gold and supplies in exchange for safe, secret passage down the river, out of Durgeon's Keep. Truthfully, Roman had been relieved when the supply list had only included mundane items like food and bandages.

Beckett opened the sack and peered inside. Satisfied, he hoisted the supplies over his shoulder, then smiled at Roman.

"Best be on our way, then," he said, his accent the abrupt and choppy Common found in the slums. "Lots to do if we're going to get you where you need to get."

Pulling his hood back over his horns, Roman nodded toward the other adventurers. They had placed their safety in his hands, and he felt the pressure of that trust as he fell into step behind their new captain.

Roman knew the city — every darkened door, abandoned alley and cracked culvert — but even he had difficulty following Beckett as they scurried through the streets like rats. The barge master twisted and turned through the night. He doubled back on himself and slipped between run-down buildings without logic or sense, until he led the group onto a wooden dock. Roman looked up and down the street, confused. He'd thought they would appear two blocks down from where they stood.

The Hebenon River flowed into the harbor, bringing both commerce and sickness in its wake.

Beckett nodded at a plain river barge. He planted his hands on his waist and lifted his chin with pride. "That's her," he said. "My barge, the *Baroness*."

The river barge sat low in the water, nearly flat except for a humble tent made of timber and oilcloth nestled in the middle of her deck. Roman recognized a long handle at the back of the ship as the tiller. He exhaled with respect. The sheer size of the pole explained the barge master's thick arms.

Kastor bounced past Roman toward the ship and skipped up the gangway. Not for the first time, Roman wondered at the old wizard's youthful countenance. "What a beautiful craft! Look at the length of that pole. Is that how you drive her? What freight do you transport? How much does it weigh? I don't see a sail. How do you propel her?"

Roman cringed as the wizard's voice echoed across the water. Before he could speak, a restrained laugh rumbled from Beckett's chest. In two steps, the barge master closed the distance with Kastor.

"I'll give you the grand tour," Beckett whispered. "After we're clear of the city."

Green light pooled over the edge of the *Baroness* and bathed Roman in a sickly glow. He held up a hand to cover his eyes, as he squinted past the strange light.

"Keep it down," said a man from above.

Beckett chuckled, drawing Roman's attention once more.

The grin that dawned on the barge master's face was bright enough to light up the entire dark night. Roman had never smiled at anyone like that.

Beckett offered his arm to Kastor and guided the old man onto the *Baroness*. Then Roman followed with Moira and Bearpuncher behind him. Once on board, Beckett put an arm around a reedy man in a floppy hat. "This is Penn, my first and only mate."

Penn held a covered lantern, where the green witch light flickered and cast a glow over his pale face and trim beard. After locking eyes with Roman, Penn turned to Beckett without a word of acknowledgment. "Were you followed?" he asked the barge master.

"No," Beckett said. "We moved through the alleys and took so many turns, I nearly lost the way m'self."

"Have you told them about the cargo?" Penn asked, his eyes narrowing in Roman's direction. Roman stilled himself and stood a little taller. Unimpressed, Penn raised an eyebrow at Beckett.

"Not yet," Beckett replied.

"But you trust them?"

The barge master followed Penn's appraising eyes and looked toward Roman and his friends. *What does he see?* Roman wondered. *Misfits? Mercenaries?*

Roman raised his chin. "You can trust us." His voice sounded more confident than he felt. "We simply need transport out of the city, and our contact said you are the best at what you do."

"The Path needs their coin." Beckett huddled closer to Penn. "And the supplies."

Without another word, the first mate ushered everyone

beneath the oilcloth canopy. He descended a flight of stairs located under the tent and motioned for Roman and the others to follow.

The witch light Penn held burned brighter in the belly of the *Baroness*. Penn hooked the lamp on a rafter, then murmured to the flame, and the light dimmed. In the cramped, dark corners, Roman began to imagine their journey away from the city. Would they have to contort their limbs to hide between crates full of merchandise and cargo? How long would it take for the *Baroness* to escape the reach of Durgeon's Keep?

Roman didn't want to think about all the reasons he had for running, he just wanted to leave. The hesitation on Penn's face began to grind against his nerves.

"Well?" Roman asked.

A moment passed in perfect silence before Penn relaxed his shoulders — and Roman marveled at the way their surroundings suddenly shifted and changed. If it hadn't happened in front of him, he wouldn't have believed the transformation. Dark, empty corners melted away, crates and boxes disappeared, and in their place, the hold was full of desperate people.

Sallow faces stared up at the newest stowaways.

Roman wheeled around to face Beckett. "What is this? Who are these people?"

"They worship the Old Gods." Beckett shrugged the sack of supplies off his shoulders. "They're slaves."

ART IRL

Alex doesn't usually work Friday evenings but of course he's sitting there when Darcy and I walk into the library. I mutter an Elvish curse under my breath.

"What?" Darcy asks.

"Nothing."

After I tried to apologize and made a huge fool of myself the other day, Darcy and I set up a time to work on our storytelling project. I don't know about Darcy, but I'm almost always free on Friday nights. I'm not popular enough to be invited anywhere and if I'm not writing, drawing or playing video games, I'm doing homework.

Pathetic.

Alex jumps up to the counter. He tosses aside his *Player's Handbook*. "Hi, Art!"

I almost shush him but before I do, he winks at Darcy.

"Hey there, New Girl," he says. The way he's smiling reminds me of those grade nine boys the other day. My eyes slide to Darcy's face.

She folds her arms; she's wearing a varsity sweater with *Hexside* scrawled across her chest. Not that I've been looking at her chest.

A rush of heat spreads across my face and through other places. I look down at my lap, horrified. How could my body betray me like this?

Dammit. I refuse to be the creep who gets a boner at the public library.

"Hey, man, are you okay?" Alex asks.

I toss my bag onto a table in the corner, then sink down in my chair, praying the entire time that Darcy doesn't notice anything unusual.

"I'm fine. Uh, Darcy, have you met Alex? He's in our grade but he's taking English next semester."

"We have math together."

"Nice to formally meet you." Alex shoves his hand out for a handshake. Darcy stares at it but doesn't move a muscle. "What?" he asks. "They don't shake hands where you're from?"

She pushes up her glasses before extending her hand.

"There." Alex shakes her hand like a mad man, kind of how Kastor would shake someone's hand. "That wasn't so bad, was it?"

I don't know why I'm so embarrassed; I just want to get Darcy out of here. I gesture to the empty chair across from me and level a pointed look at Alex. "We're here to work on a project in Ms. Stacey's class, Alex."

He winks at me this time instead of Darcy. "Suit yourself." He picks up his *Player's Handbook*, his expression too knowing as Darcy walks toward me.

She settles in the chair across from me. There are only two tables in the small library, and we're at the farthest one.

I'm about to ask if she wants to use the single library computer when she pulls out a laptop.

She tilts the computer screen open. "Wi-Fi password?"

"Last time I checked it was this."

I write *Kastor_is_Betterthanyou* on the corner of my notebook and hand it to her. She looks up at me with an eyebrow raised.

I press my lips together. "Inside joke."

She shrugs and types out the password. Then she frowns from behind those huge black glasses.

"That didn't work." She pushes herself back from the table, half standing.

Torn between wanting to prevent her from interacting with Alex, and having to stand again, I force myself to think about the least sexy thing I can come up with — Dad's legal textbook — and jump to my feet. "I'll go find out what it is, don't worry about it."

The stupid grin on Alex's face makes me grit my teeth. "What's the Wi-Fi password?"

"Here you go, man!" He slides me the new password on a folded piece of paper.

ROM@Nsucks

I snort. "Thanks. Very original."

I turn around and catch Darcy staring at us. She doesn't look away, just continues to stare, unapologetic. I shuffle back and hand over the new password.

"What does that mean?"

I open my mouth to explain, but she answers for me.

"Inside joke." She types it in. "Right. Now we have Wi-Fi."

I sit down across from her and pull out my notebook.

"So, I was thinking we could do something about

black-and-white films." She opens up a new window, then she types in a few search words.

"Sure."

Her eyes flick up from the computer screen. "Sure?"

I blink. What did I do?

She jabs the backspace button. "Obviously, you don't like that idea."

I hold up my hands like she has me hostage. "Wait, I was agreeing with you."

"It's the way you said it." She leans back in her chair, the leather cushion creaking beneath her, and transforms into some sort of crime lord. I can imagine running into her in some seedy tavern with her goons on either side. "What's your great plan, then, genius?"

I swallow. "I dunno."

Darcy leans an elbow on the table. She presses her fist against her cheek. "Let me know when you come up with something better than silent films." She pulls her messenger bag closer and fiddles with a keychain hooked to the strap loop.

I do a double take, then I check my pockets. My keys are there, just like always.

"Hey!" I point at her keychain. "Where did you get that?"

"From Fantasyland —"

"Fantasyland Comics! In the city, right?"

Alex makes a noise. I look over at him. When I catch him staring, he scrambles to flip through an open sourcebook in front of him, as if he weren't listening. I'm so excited that I don't even care he's spying.

"Yeah?" Darcy says.

I pull out my keys and push them across the table to

her. My d20 keychain looks like a long-lost twin beside hers, except that hers is colorful, with swirls of pastel blues, pinks and purples, and mine is solid black.

She picks up mine. "Did you know that d20s are called icosahedrons?"

Of course I knew that. "Did you know that a full *Dungeons & Dragons* dice set includes seven types of dice?"

And that's how everything changes. Darcy looks up from our keychains. A small, bashful smile tugs at the corners of her mouth.

She plays with my keychain. "So, are you a gamer?"

The way she asks is less of a question and more of a hope. No one outside of our regular Thursday night Game group is ever interested in what I do. I beam at her.

"Yeah! I am! Tabletop role-playing games mostly, you know like *Dungeons & Dragons*. The dice are used to determine if the player characters — the PCs — are able to achieve their actions. Each character has these ability scores that correspond with the d20, and they roll the dice to see if they succeed or fail —"

Darcy laughs. She waves a hand to stop me. "Art, I know *D&D*. This is so embarrassing, but I made that keychain."

"For real?"

"Yeah. I worked at Fantasyland Comics last summer. I might have sold it to you."

I blink. "There's no way we've met before. I would never forget you."

Her eyebrows shoot up. I've done it again. Somehow I keep putting my foot in my mouth. She looks away and tucks a piece of hair behind her ear. I want to crawl under the table. I try not to groan as I change the topic. "So, do you play?"

"Yeah, or I used to, back in the city. Then we moved here."
She hands back my keys. "I didn't think anyone here would
even know about RPGs."

"Oh, well, I probably know too much about them." I take
my keys back and our fingers brush. "Wait, can't you play
online with your old group? I've never done it, but I could
help you get set up, if you want."

"That's sweet of you to offer. But I can't. I mean — I could.
I love video games, especially RPG-based games. Have you
heard of the Dragon Age series? If you haven't you should
check it out." She wiggles closer in her chair. "Everyone will
tell you to start with *Origins*, but it's so old, and I personally
love *Inquisition*. You sort of remind me of this one character,
Cullen. I've played the game, like, eight times and I keep
telling myself I'll romance someone else —"

My keys clatter against the table. When she realizes her
implication, Darcy's eyes go wide and her mouth snaps shut.
I expect her to start laughing at me or to tell me she didn't
mean it, but when she doesn't, I don't know how to respond.
Apparently, neither does she because she continues to stare
at me in horror.

Finally, I offer her a slow smile, as if I'm approaching my
sworn enemy with a peace offering. I flip over the first paper in
front of us and scribble down *Dragon Age: Inquisition*. I choose
my words carefully. "Good to know, I'll definitely look into
it now."

"Sorry," Darcy says, "I can get carried away talking about
this stuff."

"No worries. Me too."

She scrunches her nose. "Anyways, to say I'm obsessed
would be an understatement. I just get so involved, and now

my moms have these super strict rules. I'm not allowed to play longer than an hour a day. You know, screen time and all that."

I hesitate.

She notices. "What? You're staring."

"So, it's true, then?" I don't know how to ask about her moms.

"Is what true?"

"You said moms. As in plural." I rub the back of my head again, and this time I avoid her eyes. "Alex was telling me about it, and I guess I just didn't really believe him. You know how small towns can be. Gossip."

Darcy's eyes narrow.

"I don't see how that's any of your business." She looks fiery, any softness gone, as if she might cast Lightning Bolt on me. "But if you must know, yes, I have two moms and I'm not embarrassed about it so if you have a problem with that —"

I wave my hands in front of me in a panic. "No! No. It's not that I have a problem, it's just, different. I've never known anyone, you know, gay."

Darcy rolls her eyes. "That's absolutely not true. What about Wyatt?"

I play a rogue in game, and I recognize a trap when I see one. Anything I say in response is going to sound, at best like an excuse, and at worse like bigotry. "I'm sorry."

She closes her laptop, then stands. "Not good enough. Look, Art, you seem kinda cool, but I'm bi. I have two moms. I don't want to be friends with someone homophobic."

"I'm not!"

She folds her arms. "Are you straight?"

I run a hand through my hair. "Well, yeah."

"Have you ever heard of internalized homophobia?" This isn't going well. When I don't respond right away, Darcy sighs. "That's what I thought. Bye, Art."

My hand shoots out, but then I hesitate, alarmed by how desperate I am to stop her from walking away. I don't want her to think that I'm totally ignorant. My fingers brush her wrist, and when our skin touches, she freezes. I search for the right words.

"I swear, I want to learn," I say finally. "I would like to be friends and I'm sorry. I can't imagine that moving to Unity Creek has been easy for you or your moms."

Her eyes narrow and for a horrible moment, I'm certain she's going to walk away. Instead, she sinks back into the library chair. "Apology accepted," she says, an edge to her voice. "For now. And don't think I won't hold you to that promise. I'm sending you a bunch of links and research later. And you have to watch the latest season of *Queer Eye*."

I have no idea what *Queer Eye* is, but that doesn't stop my sigh of relief. I nod, my red hair flopping in my eyes. "Thank you."

"Okay. So, tell me about this game you play in?"

Thank god, a safe topic.

"Well, we meet every week on Thursday nights, and we've been playing the same group for years. In fact, we're just about to start a new quest."

Darcy leans in as I begin explaining our game. I start with Michelle's homebrewed setting.

"Wait, so these flowers taint the water and there's a legend about some giant snake that hasn't been seen in a generation that could purify the whole land?" Darcy scrunches her nose.

"Yeah, I mean, it might sound lame —"

"No, no! It's not lame, I'm just curious. Sounds suspicious."

I chuckle. It does sound like foul play and if I had to guess, I'd put money on Michelle using that piece of lore in our new quest line. I like this girl.

Alex comes over. "Did you tell her about my awesome wizard?"

"Wait, you play too?"

"You bet, we've been gaming with the same group since we were in grade seven. Michelle and Tyler ran a program here at the library. Tehnically, Art and I weren't old enough to join, but they took pity on us because neither of us has a mom."

I stop smiling.

Darcy looks over at me. I already hate that look, half expectation, half pity.

I run a hand through my hair. "Alex plays a wizard named Kastor."

"Kastor Wolfgang Tom Tiberias Gambon."

For the first time, Darcy smiles at Alex. "And let me guess, Art plays a lawful-good paladin with golden retriever energy?"

Alex bursts out laughing.

"Actually," I clear my throat. "I play a tiefling rogue named Roman. And he's badass."

"Angsty. He means Roman's angsty," Alex says.

I continue, as if I can't hear my best friend. "Our friend Michelle is our game master. Her husband, Tyler, plays an elven paladin name Moira. The last member of our party is a friend of Tyler's, Robert, who plays a barbarian."

"You're a rogue?" Darcy asks, skeptical.

"Only in game."

We talk a bit more before Alex remembers that it's closing time. "Sorry, guys, I have to kick you out."

"Shit." Darcy checks her phone. "I need to get home. Monica already sent me three texts. I'm so dead."

A gust of wind, the kind that promises sleet or worse, whips against the library windows. Darcy's lips pucker as if she's eating a sour candy.

Alex's house is only a few streets away, which means that Darcy's house isn't that far either. Then inspiration strikes.

"Can I give you a ride?" I ask.

I'm almost positive she'll say no, but some wind rattles the library awning. She steps back. "Actually, that would be nice."

Alex locks the door behind us. "Don't worry about me. I'll call my grandma to come pick me up."

I'll text him later to thank him. For now, I open the truck door for Darcy.

We're quiet the entire way to her house, except for her last-minute directions.

"Turn left here," she says. Then adds, "I think."

I don't have the heart to tell her that I know where she lives. Alex's house is just down the street, and everyone in town knows how to find Mayor House.

She slides out of the truck with a little "oof" noise.

"Thanks, Art. I'll see you."

She walks away, strands of dark hair escaping from the messy ball of hair on top of her head, her bag over a shoulder, and those jeans hugging her hips. I stare, then immediately freak out. I scramble to start the truck. My foot pops off the clutch. The manual transmission lurches and makes a grinding whine, then it stalls.

"Dammit." I glance out the front window. She doesn't look over her shoulder.

I turn the keys in the ignition again, my fingers brushing the d20 keychain. Of all things, role-playing games.

Then it hits me.

I roll the passenger window down. The old thing takes a fair bit of elbow grease and my arm is sore by the time I get the window down far enough to yell, "Hey! Darcy!"

She's rummaging around in her bag. When I shout, she looks up. "What did you say?"

I roll the window down the rest of the way. "I know what we can do for our English project!"

"Yeah, what's that?"

"Role-playing games!"

"Role-playing games?" She nods as the idea sinks in, then she squeals like a *Critical Role* fangirl meeting Matthew Mercer at Comic Con. "That's brilliant, Art! I love it!"

The door opens behind her, and a woman appears, about Darcy's height, with light purple hair. She says something to Darcy that I can't hear. Darcy's whole frame goes stiff. I'm not sure if I should wave or drive away, but then the woman disappears back into the house. Darcy relaxes. She waves at me then follows one of her moms inside.

DARCY IRL

Art is not what I expected. I've already sent him book lists, movie recommendations and articles about being an ally to people like me by the time we reach my house. When he suggests we do RPGs for our English project, I totally geek out on him. Just then, the front door opens.

Monica is standing there in a bathrobe. "Where have you been?"

The accusation in her voice brings me back to the present, and it's as if I land flat on my ass, square IRL.

I wave goodbye to Art and hope he can't hear Monica. Her eyes flick from me to the truck. She squints, then her mouth tightens. She disappears back into the house. "Come inside. Now, Darcy."

I follow without a word. Even with the door closed behind us, I can hear Art's truck drive away.

"Where were you?" Monica asks. I pull off one combat boot and toss it to the side. It lands with a thump. "Excuse me? I think you mean, 'Sorry for not telling you I'd be out late, Mom.'"

I say nothing. There's no way I'm apologizing for doing homework at the library.

Monica continues the onslaught, her voice a sharp axe cutting the air. "Explanation, Darcy."

She corners me in the foyer. I throw up my hands in surrender.

"I just went to the library with my English partner to do some research, sue me!"

I try to walk around her, but she blocks my move.

"I don't like your tone." She searches for my gaze and traps it.

This is usually the turning point in our arguments: either I back down now or stand my ground. I'm not in a submissive mood today, so I stare daggers back at her.

That's how Carrie finds us. She opens the front door into my shoulder.

"Ouch!"

"Oh sorry, love!" Her ponytail is disheveled, and she has purple bags of sleepiness under her eyes. "What are you two doing?"

I try to back up. I might be able to make a speedy retreat to my room, but Monica points to the couch. I stomp past her and throw myself down onto the cushions.

She fixes me with "the look." Then she goes to my other mother and drops her voice to a low whisper. "You're home later than usual."

I sneak a quick glance at The Moms. Carrie's mouth is a tight line; Monica's hand reaches out to squeeze her forearm. The way Carrie's almost invisible blond eyebrows knit together sends a shiver down my spine. Something is wrong.

Then they both summon some sort of inner Strength, like

they've just ingested a mana potion.

"So, what's going on here?" Carrie's accent sounds thicker now. That only happens when she's tired.

Monica puts her hands on her hips. "Your daughter disappeared after school and neglected to check in with me. I had no idea where she was!"

Carrie's pinches the bridge of her nose. She looks back and forth from Monica to me. "Is that all?"

Monica raises her eyebrows. "If that isn't enough for you, she was also with a boy."

"Hello? Did we all just forget that I'm queer too? So unless you're going to ban me from going out with anyone, that's an unfair, heteronormative argument." I turn to Carrie. "His name is Art and he's just a friend from school. Don't you want me to make friends? She pounced on me before I even opened the door."

Monica sputters, her hands fly through the air. "That's because you didn't check in! I was worried."

"Why?" My voice grows louder. "It's not like you cared when I took the bus home in the city!"

"There were rules in the city, too! You. Have. To. Check. In!"

Carrie interjects. "Monica is right, Darcy. Remember what happens when you break curfew."

"House arrest," I mutter.

"Temporary grounding." Monica's voice escapes between clenched teeth. "I don't see why the same rules wouldn't apply here."

"You can't be serious! What's the worst that could happen to me out here? I'll tell you. Nothing!"

"You don't know that."

"Come on! Carrie, help me out. I went to the library! You can't ground me for that!"

Carrie shakes her head. "Look, you two, I'm exhausted. I don't have energy to play referee."

I hesitate. When she says it like that, I feel like a kid. Monica pauses too. Then she pats Carrie on the shoulder. "We can talk about this later."

Carrie smiles, my signal that this is just about over. I get up to leave.

"I don't think we need to ground her, darling. But, Darcy, from now on you need to check in with us, just like in the city. We still worry."

Monica peeks out from behind Carrie's shoulder like some smug kill stealer. "Do you understand?"

"I understand."

I toss my bag on my bed, which is perfectly made thanks to Monica. For some reason, this just makes me angrier. She's so nice, too nice. All the time. Always so thoughtful, always the best mom, always worried about me. It makes me want to scream.

I pull out my phone to text James. He's always ready to bash The Moms. I notice two unread messages.

I swipe open my phone to check the texts. The messages are from an unknown number.

Hi. It's Art.

Did your mom put out an APB?

Some of the anger melts and my fingers fly across the screen to reply.

> No, but she almost ate me alive for giving her attitude.

> Lucky for me, my OTHER mother stepped in.

Lol. You have an attitude problem? No! Never!

I reread the text at least three times before I realize he's teasing me. Well, two can play that game.

> Of course not. I'm practically perfect.

I'm waiting for Art to reply when a banner appears at the top of my screen. I feel a small pang of guilt when I see James' name pop up.

> Hi.

Can't stop thinking of you. If you know what I mean ...

>

Help a guy out. Pics?

I've told you before ...
Not gonna happen

Come on, don't be like that
princess. I just miss you like
crazy, that's all

I roll my eyes and flip back to Art's text. I will him to
message me back.

He doesn't.

Irked, I toss my phone on the bed. I pull out a file folder of
character sheets from my desk. The very first page has pencil
smudges in the margins and crumpled corners; in the lower
left half there's a salsa stain that smeared some of the printed
ink, but even so, it's like seeing a long-lost friend.

POPPY is printed in bold letters along the top of the
character sheet. I haven't looked at her since before we moved.
As I reacquaint myself with the pink-haired human healer,
I think back to Art's animated expressions at the library as
he talked about his game.

I check my phone again. Still no message.

All this talk about RPGs makes me realize how much
I miss playing in a game. I pick up a pencil. It's been a while
since I've spent time with Poppy, so I grab a new salsa-free
character sheet. Might as well switch over her abilities and
skills. I might even bring her with me tomorrow to show
Art.

Muffled voices creep into my awareness.

"So they're asking to transfer?"

"Yeah, I was reviewing client files when a nurse came into
my office," Carrie's voice floats through the walls. We share

a wall, which means even though they're quiet, I can pick up snippets of their conversations.

I miss my old bedroom. It was in the basement of our city townhouse and the privacy was mutually beneficial.

"Apparently, some of my patients are uncomfortable with the idea of being treated by me."

"Female patients?"

My ears strain as I lean into their conversation. If this were an RPG, I would definitely roll Perception.

"See, that's just it. They don't want to be treated by me, but the only other GP in town is Dr. Raavi, and he's a man."

"So, it's a lesbian thing?"

Carrie is silent, but I can sigh with frustration and sink onto the bed. My chest tightens.

"We knew this might happen, Carissa." Monica's voice dwindles away to gentle reassurance.

I pull my headphones from my desk and grab my phone. Still no word from Art. I could text James back, but now I don't feel like dragging The Moms, so I put on some music. Then I crawl into bed.

I can't hear The Moms anymore. I don't really want to listen anyway. Tears burn in my eyes.

It's not right.

Rage explodes through my chest. We move all the way from the city — from a community that accepted and cele-brated our family — to this small backwards town, all because Carrie wants to make a difference. She's an excellent doctor, one of the best, and Unity-fucking-Creek doesn't even realize how lucky they are to have her.

I grab one of my many pillows and smother a frustrated cry. I mean, I knew things would be different here, but this?

ART IRL

I load up my virtual shopping cart with books from the list Darcy sent me — *The Mists of Avalon, Gideon the Ninth* and *Six of Crows* — and think of excuses I can use to explain to Dad why I spent over a hundred dollars with the credit card he gave me. At least the books will be easier to explain than the copy of *Dragon Age: Inquisition* that I just bought. A text buzzes, and I swipe out of the shopping window. I lie in bed and stare at my phone.

> Of course not. I'm practically perfect.

My fingers fly across the screen. My response sits there in the message field. The text glows back at me. I typed the words without thinking but there's no way I can send this to her.

> You might be perfect for me. ⬆

The Execution

"What are you playing at?" Roman snarled, his hand dropping to the stiletto tucked in his belt. Magic tingled in his fingertips as he gripped the blade.

Before he could lunge at Beckett, though, something — someone — smacked the back of his head. A weathered voice rattled off a string of agitated words in a language unknown to Roman. He turned, only to find a withered woman, with thin arms and a cane gripped in her wrinkled hands, waving frantically at him. A braid of stark white hair lay across her shoulder, and at her collarbone, Roman noticed a puckered scar peeking from a tattered homespun blouse. Immediately, he recognized the shape: the All Father's eye.

She smacked him across one of his horns while Roman stared at her, distracted.

Beckett chuckled, the sound resonant in his deep chest. He sidestepped Roman and set one of his large hands on the woman's thin shoulder. His voice dropped to a low and comforting whisper.

"What are you saying?" Roman's fingers tightened until the hilt of his dagger bit into his palm.

"He just convinced her to spare your life," Kastor said.

The woman turned her cutting eyes to Roman, but stopped waving the cane around, as Beckett continued to whisper in that strange tongue. Roman leaned forward, listening. He'd never heard words like that before. Definitely a different language but one peppered with familiar sounds, as though the Common tongue — the language of trade — had been dissected, reinvented, then braided back together.

He looked from where Beckett calmed the woman, to Penn, who had begun distributing food to the others. Then understanding loosened Roman's grip on the dagger; his knees turned soft.

"You're liberators. You're freeing them."

Beckett nodded. A strangled sound escaped Moira's throat. "But slaves are — they can't be — slavery was outlawed decades ago."

Roman flinched, then schooled his expression into one of ignorance. How naive Moira sounded. He both pitied and envied her.

"Only in ceremony," Penn spoke, a fire burning in his dark eyes. He handed a slice of cheese to a little girl. "The reformed slavery laws leave plenty of wiggle room for the nobles. Too many souls have been left in the Ditch, and it ain't long until they find themselves indentured to some fancy prig with too much money, or worse, hanged as heathens."

Penn spat the last word, as if it tasted sour in his mouth.

Roman tried to ignore the memory of his life before: the fine silk doublet he'd worn, the acrid reek of burning flesh, how he'd watched as the smiths branded the All Father's eye onto the collarbone of a screaming man. It was to identify the heathens, his father had explained, and remind them that the All Father was always watching. Roman glanced at the old woman. Shame crawled under his skin.

"Where are you taking them?" he asked.

"Somewhere safe," was Beckett's only reply.

Roman shifted his weight, and beneath his boots, the shipboards creaked. The sound filled the stifled hull. What does a person do when confronted with such horror? What would he do? The idea of running away, of leaving everything behind, chewed at his insides. He'd already done it once. Could he really run away now that he knew this?

He opened his mouth, a confession on his tongue, when the barge pitched to the side with enough force to topple the crates and boxes surrounding the passengers.

Beckett's frantic glance at Penn sent a shiver down Roman's spine.

"They found us," Penn said, eyes wide with fear.

"Stay here!" Beckett ordered, and in two giant steps, he bounded up the stairs. Ignoring the barge master's order, Penn followed close behind.

From the belly of the barge, the smell of smoke and sound of disembodied shouting filled the air. Roman glanced at the terrified faces surrounding him and his party. Beside him, Bearpuncher rolled his shoulders back. "Fight?"

A smile twitched across Roman's mouth, and that's all the encouragement his friends needed. They rushed up the stairs.

Above deck, flashes of fire cut through the moonless dark. Fireball after fireball volleyed toward the ship, catching ropes and timber ablaze.

Beckett's face twisted in a desperate shout. "Now, Penn!"

Green light burned Roman's eyes, and he stumbled around blinking until the dancing white spots receded to the edge of his vision. With his sight back, Roman opened his eyes just in time to witness Beckett pull Penn into a bone-crushing embrace. Beckett buried his face into the crook of Penn's neck, his voice low and gravelly. "You have to leave. Get them out of here."

Every long muscle in Penn's body tensed, but then Beckett was releasing him and yanking a harpoon off the edge of the barge. The barge master catapulted himself over the railing to the dock below.

"We buy them time," Roman called to his friends. He ran past Penn, stopped at the edge of the ship's railing, then looked over his shoulder. The heartbreak on Penn's face scared him.

"Moira, you're with Kastor. Bearpuncher take out as many as you can." Roman locked eyes with Penn. "And I'll stay with Beckett."

A battle cry split Bearpuncher's throat as he disembarked. The sound snapped Penn out of his worry. He nodded at Roman, then raised his hands above his head. Green magic pooled in his palms, then with one fluid motion, Penn circled his arms backward. The river churned, frothy foam bubbling up from deep below, and with another mighty backstroke, Penn propelled the barge away from the dock. Away from the danger.

Roman backed up, then took a running leap from the moving barge. He landed in a graceful crouch, his palm flat against the wooden boards of the dock. As the *Baroness* made a slow escape, Moira, Kastor and Bearpuncher charged into the dark, while Roman slinked into the shadows in search of Beckett.

Roman's ear twitched toward the sound of a man gasping in pain, followed by a dull thud. Abandoning silence for speed, he dashed out of cover toward the sound. He prepared himself for the sight of Beckett's corpse, but when Roman rounded a corner, he found the barge master alive, blood splattered across his cheek. Roman slowed to a stop, his heart thundering.

"Get down!" Beckett hollered.

The rogue barely had enough time to drop to his knees, as the barbed hook of Beckett's harpoon disappeared into the night behind him. Roman rolled to the side, coming to stand beside Beckett with two knives in his hands, but he wasn't needed. Beckett pulled on the leather cord bound around his wrist, and Roman's eyes widened. Not only did the harpoon return, but with it, Beckett brought an impaled man from the darkness.

Blood soaked through the deep green tunic worn by the dying man. Without needing a closer look, Roman knew that the heraldry stitched into the man's chest would be a golden crown of thorns and pink Hebenon blossoms. The symbols and colors of Lord Sangray, the Baron of Blackwood and Lord Ruler of Durgeon's Keep.

His father.

He saw the recognition in the guard's eyes before he died. So they were looking for him.

Roman's muscles seized. He couldn't move. This attack was his fault. He'd led his father's honor guard here. Guilt cramped his stomach. Scrambling back, Roman heaved the contents of his last meal onto the docks.

He would be the reason they all died tonight.

A large fist closed around his shoulder. "We're losing, you need to pull yourself together and get out of here, lordling."

Denial weighed heavy on Roman's tongue, but before he had a chance to protest, Beckett raised his hand. "No use denying it. We know you. The Goddess sent us to find you."

Roman winced, heat burning his cheeks. His gaze dropped to his boots, messy with stomach acid and chewed food. A sob tightened his throat. "I'm sorry."

Beckett made a sound, something that started as a chuckle, but turned into a groan of pain. "Don't have time for that."

Then Roman was falling. He hit the river with a splash, and it wasn't until he broke through the water's surface that he realized Beckett had pushed him. Confused, Roman reached for one of the massive poles holding the dock above water. Slime coated the wood and his boots slipped beneath him as he tried to climb back up.

"Where are the other criminals?" someone shouted above his head.

Beckett's voice didn't waver. "On my ship. And if they're smart, they'll stay put."

Roman's teeth ground together as he clenched his jaw.

"There were others on the dock. Don't test our patience."

Nothing happened.

"Search the docks and arrest this man. I'm sure the Baron will want to question you himself."

The sound of footfalls thundered above his head, and Roman prayed to every god, both old and new, that the others had gotten far away. He pulled a deep breath into his lungs, then disappeared beneath the water. They had selected a rendezvous point the night before, just in case, and Roman needed to find his friends before the guards did.

He surfaced as close to the canal wall as possible and hauled himself out of the water. A restless quiet, the sort of unnatural silence that suggested hidden figures and watchful eyes lurking in the dark, had befallen the docks. The honor guard was good, but Roman had personally overseen their reconnaissance training. Navigating the alleys alone, he easily outmaneuvered the remaining search party.

At the rendezvous, Roman exhaled a deep sigh of relief. Three silhouettes huddled beside a rune carved into the crumbling plaster of an old warehouse. A matching rune glowed on a bone necklace tucked beneath Roman's tunic. To everyone else, their hiding spot would appear like any other empty alley; they were safe. For now.

"You're soaked," Kastor said.

Moira looked over Roman's shoulder. "Where's Beckett? Weren't you with him?"

Roman shook his head. "I couldn't — he pushed me off the dock when the guards surrounded us. They took him."

Early the next morning, Roman hid beneath his mantle and avoided the curious stares of the people he passed through the gathering crowd. He came alone, sneaking in through a hole in the Keep's wall, one he'd discovered as a child. At first, he thought he might be able to save Beckett, but when he arrived at the prison, the cells were empty. He made it to the courtyard just in time to see a ratty black hood pulled down over Beckett's face. The crowd swelled toward the gallows. Expensive silk skirts and crushed velvet coats sparkled in the early sun, as excited and bloodthirsty nobles jeered and pointed.

A somber man, dressed in black with a green and gold

scarf around his throat, opened a scroll. The mob quieted as the executioner's voice boomed through the square. "For illegal smuggling, thieving and crimes against the Barony, including conspiracy, heresy and treason against Lord Sangray Blackwood, I hereby sentence Beckett Riverman, the barge master, to death by hanging."

The trap under Beckett's feet sprang open; he dropped, legs thrashing. In twelve heartbeats, Becket's boots ceased their frantic jig. Roman clenched his fists. He couldn't afford to fall apart in public, nor did he want to experience the emotions threatening to undo him. Instead, he choked back the grief, the sense of guilt, and pushed down his rage until he couldn't feel at all. Another death ordered by his father; another life Roman might have spared.

ART IRL

My phone buzzes across the table. Once, twice, and on the third time, Michelle stops her role-playing. "Are you going to get that?" she asks over top her orange glasses.

Michelle has a "No Cell Phones" policy. Each week we store our phones in a small treasure chest. The first person to reach into the gold box and grab their cell has to buy pizza for the next week. Usually, that's not a problem for me. Alex, on the other hand, buys pizza at least once a month.

But tonight, I kept my phone close. Somehow, I thought that might keep Darcy close too.

I hesitate.

"Just grab your phone, Art. The vibrating is really distracting."

"Looks like you're on for pizza next week," Alex says.

Two texts and a picture sit in my messages from Darcy.

I'm so jealous! I really miss playing.

Have fun at your game!

She's attached a picture of herself. Her large eyes staring over the top of the *Player's Handbook*. That does something to me, something I don't want to examine too closely at a table surrounded by my friends.

An idea takes shape.

I look up from my phone and take everyone in. Robert waves his arms as he describes what Bearpuncher does with his turn. Tyler leans his elbows on the table with his fingers tented, while Alex flips through his sourcebook, muttering something about some obscure rule that will give him an extra attack.

She'd fit in here; more importantly, I want her here.

The sound of chairs sliding backward usually makes my heart sink, but not this time. This week I'm almost happy to be done. I pull out my phone and text Darcy.

Hey! I'm back!

Alex pops up beside me. "Who are you texting?"

I shove my phone deep in my pocket. "Just a friend."

Robert zips up his jacket. "Just a friend?"

"More like a girlfriend," Alex says.

"Wait, Art, you have a girlfriend?" Tyler stops cleaning up papers and dice. "That's new."

Michelle joins the interrogation. "When do we get to meet her?"

I glare at Alex.

He shoves his hands in his pockets with a goofy smile. "She's the new girl in town, really edgy — super hot. All mysterious and moody, ya know?"

"Really?" Michelle laughs.

"Her name is Darcy." I regret what I've said when I'm met with a chorus of ooooh-ing. I have to raise my voice to be heard over the group. "I mean, she's not moody. And she's not my girlfriend. We're just English partners for an assignment."

"Hang in there, bud." Tyler slings an arm around Michelle's shoulder. "The whole idea that the geek never gets the girl is bullshit."

My phone buzzes and everyone leans in to watch me respond. My fingers twitch toward the device, but I resist responding. For now.

Robert bumps my shoulder with his. "You shouldn't ignore your girlfriend, dude."

Roman would relish all this attention, but IRL, I blush a deeper shade of red.

"Go easy on him, Alex," Robert says. He heads upstairs. "I'll see you guys next week! Good luck with your lady friend, Art!"

I shove my character sheet into a sourcebook and grab my dice bag. I shrug on my sweater and pull out my keys. I still have to drive the world's worst best friend home.

"Let's go, Alex."

Alex bows to the Andersons. "Good evening, madam, sir."

Both Michelle and Tyler chuckle.

"Oh, Art! Hold on a sec." Michelle slips out from under Tyler's arm.

"Yeah?"

She hands me a small stack of paper — the Game recaps from our previous sessions. "I just finished reading them. Art, these are really good. I love how you described the burning forest."

Our stories, but my writing.

It all started with a character journal. In the beginning, Michelle suggested taking notes. She offered Inspiration to anyone who worked their notes into the game narrative, and I was eager to do anything for an extra advantage on my rolls. Eventually, my journals evolved into more. Something between a fantasy novel and self-insert fan fiction.

I take the papers and tuck them away with my character sheet. "Thanks."

"There's something else," she says. "I was wondering if you might like to take a stab at GM-ing?"

Me? A Game Master?

"You don't have to make a decision right now, just think about it, okay? We've got lots of time before we finish in Durgeon's Keep, and it wouldn't be a permanent thing."

No, no, no. Not me. No. I gape and sputter a protest, but Michelle talks over me.

"Just think about it, okay? Maybe you could start sometime in the new year? I'd get you set up and would be there if you ever needed help, but you'd be so good. I know it!"

I press my lips together.

"And I haven't had a chance to play as a PC since we started. We could alternate, and it would be so nice to have someone else to switch with."

As she talks, her words come faster and faster; her face and hands are animated the same way she gets when she describes the most exciting encounters in game.

Torn, I run a hand through my hair. "Okay. Sure, I'll think about it. Maybe?"

I'm halfway out the door when my phone vibrates again.

Darcy. Right!

"Oh, hey, Michelle!" I call down the stairs. "Would it be okay if I invited my friend to join us for Game?"

Her smile widens. I've seen that expression on her face before, usually before our party walks into a trap.

"The girlfriend?"

My cheeks get hot. "She's just my English partner."

"Sure, whatever you say. Has she played before?"

"Yeah, she's totally cool."

Michelle looks at Tyler. "Why not?" he asks. "It might be nice to get some new blood in the party."

"That's true. Sure thing, Art. Go ahead and invite her."

A little jolt zips through my rib cage and into my chest. "That's great! She'll be so excited."

"Give her my number and let her know that she can text me with questions."

"Thanks so much, Michelle!"

On our way to Alex's house, we drive past Darcy's place. I try to keep my eyes on the road and ignore the house with the shutters, veranda and red door, but I can't help myself. I look back in the rearview mirror. The house is dark except for one light in a room on the front of the house. I wonder if that's her bedroom. If she's still awake.

We almost get to Alex's in absolute silence. I hope he'll just get out when we pull up to his house.

Not a chance.

He unbuckles his seat belt. "So? Darcy?"

"What about her?"

"Dude! What do you mean, 'what about her?' Are you going to get on that?"

"What? No!" I curse genetics for my pale skin and red hair. Just like my mother.

The pang in my chest doesn't surprise me. Sometimes I can't stop those sharp fragments of memory: her copper hair, how much she loved Halloween, the way she read stories with all the voices. I don't like to think about her often, for obvious reasons, but it's been a while. There used to be a time when I cried for her every night. I would crawl into bed with Dad. He always let me stay.

I wonder how different life might be if she were still here. How different I might be.

I push those feelings away and face Alex. "Do you always have to be a jerk? What's wrong with you?"

"I dunno." Alex brushes off my question. "Guess I'm chaotic evil."

"Stop. You're better than this," I say. My fists tighten. "And Darcy isn't a punch line, okay? No more turkey baster comments, no talking about 'getting on' her, and you're coming over to watch *Queer Eye* with me this week."

The smile fades from Alex's face. For once he seems to stop moving and goes very still. "I hadn't thought about it like that. Yeah, okay. I'm sorry, man. I'll do better." A moment passes, then he adds, "You've got it bad for her, don't you?"

I lean my forehead against the steering wheel with a groan. "Alex, we only met a couple weeks ago. I barely know her."

He tilts his head. "I mean, you know she's into RPGs. You have that in common and it's not like there's a ton of gamer girls in Unity Creek."

"I don't know."

"Well, it's okay if I ask her on a date then?"

I sit up and stare at him. "What? No!"

"See! You do like her!"

I feel like I arrived at a boss fight with a plastic knife.

He's relentless and I'm not prepared to have this conversation. I reach across him and push open his door.

"Good night, Alex. See you at school."

"Come on!"

"Bye, Alex."

He flips me off on the way to his house. I laugh, remember Darcy in the hall. Maybe I have a type? I shake my head and check my phone.

2 New Messages.

One message is another picture from Darcy. The little preview looks like it's another photo of her, and I feel blood creep up my neck.

Then I glance at the second message. It's from Dawn.

> Dad's home. Where are you?

DARCY IRL

The biggest truck I've ever seen in my life barrels past me. The pickup swerves into a slushy puddle as it rips by, and half-frozen water sloshes up onto my boots.

I lift my middle finger in the air and dub the driver King of the Rednecks.

"Hey, asshole!"

The chilled morning air nips my nose. I regret that I didn't grab a scarf this morning. It's a weird time of year. I freeze on my way to school, but on my way home, I have to shed my coat and mitts and sweater. There's just no winning.

I pull up my collar, then shove my hands in my pockets. Another gust of wind blows stray leaves across the sidewalk and onto the road. The gutter, where the street ends and the sidewalk begins, is clogged with orange, brown, yellow and red. Dirty water floods the pavement. Charming.

I watch where I'm walking, but Art's last text burns behind my eyelids.

Hey! I'm back!

I responded to him last night, and he read the message, but then, nothing. Absolute radio silence. Frustration twists through me. Followed by annoyance with myself. I fortify my Constitution. He doesn't owe you anything, Darcy. Besides, why do you care? You've got a boyfriend.

The thought of James just makes me angrier. I kick a rock. The stone lands with an underwhelming splash in the gutter.

For the rest of my walk to school I convince myself that I am only curious about Art's game. I'm so bored, out here in the middle of nowhere, that I have to live vicariously through this lanky nerd from English class.

I slide into first period, my nose dripping and cheeks burning, and see Art settled in his usual spot. His binder is tossed on top of the desk beside him and he's staring out the window again.

"This spot taken?" I ask. He startles out of a daydream, and despite my numb nose, warmth rushes through my chest.

Art grabs his binder. "No, not at all."

I want him to tell me why he didn't text back last night. He doesn't offer an explanation. Instead, he shifts in his seat. "I was saving that spot for you anyways."

I forget all about being left on read. I settle into the chair beside him. "It's bloody cold outside."

"Did you walk to school?"

"Always do, I don't have my license yet."

The bell rings. Ms. Stacey springs into action. "All right, settle down, everyone!"

"I could always pick you up," Art says under his breath. He faces the front of the class, but his eyes slide over to me.

"Really?" The squeal is out of my mouth before I can take

it back. A couple of classmates turn around to stare at me. I glare at them — that is, until Ms. Stacey claps her hands and looks over at me and Art.

"Something exciting happening back there?" she asks with a hint of laughter in her voice.

I sink lower in my desk. Art puts his head down, his shoulder shuddering with silent laughter.

I elbow his arm. "No, no, nothing exciting."

He snorts so quietly that I'm the only one who can hear him. Appeased, our English teacher turns back to start class with a swish of her tangerine skirt. I close my eyes. What is going on with me?

Today, Ms. Stacey instructs us to go to the school library and pick out books that will support our storytelling project.

I pull the first book I see off the shelf. Art is meticulously reading the backs of several hardcovers when I stroll over.

"So, how was Game yesterday?"

He drops the book he's reading and hurries to pick it up. "Good, good."

"Cool."

He nods along, but his eyes shift from my face to his shoes. Could this be more awkward?

"Hey, I was thinking that we, maybe, if you want, could hang out? At the library after school?"

The way he talks, it almost sounds like he's asking me on a date.

"That would be awesome!"

"Really?" Art looks up from his shoes.

"Really," I giggle. Then halt, horrified. I don't giggle.

"I'll meet you at the front doors after the final bell and we can drive over. I won't forget this time. Promise."

I allow myself an ironic chuckle. "I'm holding you to it. You're zero and one."

He doesn't laugh with me. Slow and intentional, he places a hand over his heart. "You have my word, m'lady."

I open my mouth, but how do you respond to that? Then Art's solemn expression melts and he starts to laugh.

I sputter at him. "You're ridiculous!"

"You should have seen your face."

"Life isn't an RPG, you giant dork."

"I know." He pulls another volume off the self and reads the back cover, then pauses. "But can you imagine if it was?"

It's warmer after school, just like I predicted, and I'm too hot in my jacket. I sling the denim coat over my arm while I wait on the front steps of the school for Art. The sun is shining, and it feels more like summer than it has all week. I stand on my tiptoes and look for Art's bright hair in the flood of teenagers escaping from the school. No glinting redheads in the crowd.

What I do see makes me freeze.

Leaning against a polished motorcycle at the edge of the parking lot is a familiar silhouette of black leather and ripped jeans. Girls whisper into the backs of their hands as he smirks at the crowd.

I wave at the dark-haired not-stranger. "James?"

He flashes me the smile that usually makes me weak in the knees. Around him, gaggles of girls turn to stare. I look down at my burgundy cardigan. I wish I'd worn my Wednesday Addams outfit. James loves the way that black dress hugs my curves.

All eyes are on me. The attention almost feels nice,

especially because the hot guy is walking up to me, not them.

In one swift movement, James sweeps me into a crushing kiss.

It's the type of kiss you see in the movies, the kind of romantic gesture that makes people stare. And I know he's enjoying the spectacle. I squirm out of the embrace.

"Hey, baby." His voice is magnetic. He smells like leather. "I missed you."

I blink a few times. "What are you doing here?"

"I came to rescue you." His fingers lace through mine. I fall into step beside him as we walk toward the bike.

"Rescue me?"

"Yeah." He pulls out a second helmet. My helmet. I'm reaching for it when I remember Art.

"Oh, shit." I drop my outstretched hand. "James, I made plans to study with a friend."

He shoves the helmet into my hands. "So, cancel. I didn't ride out here to be stood up for a study date."

"It's not a date." My voice sounds just a little too defensive but the tone is lost on James. He swings a leg over the bike and looks at me, waiting.

I dig around my bag for my cell phone. As I text, it occurs to me that Art might be outside already. I pull the helmet on in a panic, not loving the idea of Art seeing me with James.

James revs the bike to life. I hit send.

> Hey Art. Something came up. I won't be able to make our study session.

> I'll explain later. Bye. ☺

I hope the little wink softens the blow. But, I mean, it's only fair. He stood me up first.

On the bike, I wrap my arms around James. I squeeze a little bit, and without another word, he speeds out of the school parking lot.

I cast a smile at the other students, but a glimpse of messy red hair behind the steering wheel of a familiar truck catches my eye. I panic and hide my face in James' back.

"So, how's my girl?" James asks. His fingers dig into me. He pulls me close enough that we're practically grinding on one another behind some gas station out on the highway. I wish I could say that this is the first time I've made out with him behind a dumpster.

I think about Art's shy smile and recoil from James as he leans in for more kisses. He doesn't seem to notice.

I can't think clearly when he's this close. I place both my hands on his chest and push.

He's handsome. Like — Netflix-Original-adaptation-of-a-romance-novel kind of handsome. With a sharp jaw and tousled hair, he's the living embodiment of the Dark-Haired Love Interest, and if he were a movie star, he'd have thousands of fangirls going crazy for him.

The cynical part of me reminds myself that he probably already has a following of crazed fangirls.

"This move is going to kill me. Everyone here is so —" I twist out of his embrace and lean against the plaster wall. "So country."

"That's why your knight in shining armor came to rescue

you." He holds out a smoke for me as he lights one up. "Want one, princess?"

I try not to cough as he exhales a twisting ribbon of cigarette smoke.

As a rule, I don't smoke unless I'm drinking. I shake my head. "No, thanks."

He takes another drag with his eyes on mine. I shiver under his cool, unimpressed stare. Then, he taps the cigarette out.

"You're cold." It's a statement, not a question.

"I guess so." I look at the sky to avoid his gaze. The weather, like the mood, has changed. The summery sunshine from earlier has been replaced by weak winter sun, struggling to shine behind gray clouds.

"Let's go back to my place."

Another uncomfortable shiver zips up and down my spine. I bend forward to stare at our boots. Mine are soft suede today, and James is wearing a pair of combat boots. I have an almost identical pair at home.

"Come on, princess." His breath smells like sweet tobacco and icy-fresh mouthwash. "Come back with me. You can spend the weekend at my place, and I'll bring you back on Sunday night. We can hang out with the gang. Everyone misses you."

My imagination doesn't have to wander very far to fill in the blanks. Despite what everyone else assumes, James and I haven't gone all the way. We've done a lot, and I mean, almost everything else, but for some reason we've never actually done It. Not for lack of trying on his part or wanting on my part. Except now, now I'm not sure I'd want to at all.

"That's tempting." I try in vain to keep my voice from shaking. "But I can't."

James tenses. "Why not?"

I sigh.

"Why don't you just come over to my house?" My head is aching from the smell of gasoline. "I can show you the new place."

James' movie-star face twists into a scowl. A very swoon-worthy scowl, but still, a scowl.

"I can show you my new bedroom."

He flashes a self-aware grin. The tension passes and his shoulders relax. He pulls me into a hug. "You know Monica and Carrie would kill me if I snuck into your bedroom."

"If you had a vehicle with doors, we could just go park somewhere and make out in the car like normal teenagers."

"Blasphemy," he says to the motorcycle. "She didn't mean it, girl."

"Whatever." Suddenly, we're back to normal. "Hey, let's go grab a bite."

In the city we would have gone to find a dive bar that was maybe just a little bit relaxed with ID'ing their patrons. Here, we find Yee's Cozy Kitchen on the main drag. It's a Chinese restaurant, complete with red paper lanterns in the window and zodiac place mats on the tables.

"I guess this is the best you got." James holds the door open for me.

I waltz past him and as I do, he squeezes my butt. I freeze, repulsion crawling up inside me, but I push that aside and remind myself that he's my boyfriend. He can do things like that, right?

A young girl, like younger than me, comes to seat us. She has long dark hair that's pulled back into a ponytail and she's wearing a little half-apron over her jeans. "For two?"

We follow her to a corner booth in the nearly empty restaurant. There's a family with two very tired-looking parents and three loud daughters sitting in the other corner of the café. My butt has barely touched the seat when our waitress asks for our drink order.

I stammer and flip over the menus to locate the drink options.

"She'll have a green tea, loose tea if you have it, and I'll take a Coke," James says. He cuts in with such elegance that I can almost ignore the fact that he just ordered for me.

She jots that down on her little notepad. When she's out of earshot I lean close to James. "Could you not?"

"Not what?"

"I can order my own drink."

"Didn't you want a green tea?"

I do, but that's beside the point.

With no better argument, I fold my arms across my chest. "It's a matter of principle."

"Whatever."

Our waitress comes back with a tiny silver teapot, a ceramic mug and a can of Coke on a large round tray. She leans over, her T-shirt revealing just a little too much, and my eyes flick to James. He's staring at our waitress with a newfound appreciation.

This is also normal. I'm used to girls giggling at his good looks and him flirting back with his eyes.

I kick his shin under the table, and he refocuses on me. He smirks, totally unashamed, and shrugs. Our waitress straightens.

"Hey," she says, her voice quiet, almost nervous. "You're Darcy Larocque-Evans, right?"

My worst nightmare is coming true in front of my very eyes: living in a town where everyone knows your name. Judging from the snippets of talk I pick up when The Moms think I can't hear, I know exactly what she's heard about us too.

"Yes?"

She bounces on the balls of her feet. Not exactly the response I was expecting. What's her deal?

"My name is Rainbow. Rainbow Yee. I, we go to school together."

"Okay?" She looks like she's going to faint as she holds the serving tray in front of her.

"I'm in Dawn's class. Art's sister."

I perk up. "Dawn? I forgot that Art has a sister."

A broody scowl flashes across James' face. I catch his expression from the corner of my eye, and if looks could kill — I shudder. His voice is metal on stone. "Who's Art?"

ART IRL

I lope out of school like a Sasquatch. I'm all arms and legs and giant strides. The sun reflects off the hood of my truck, making it look like a silver chariot. Even the slushy puddles that squish beneath my runners don't bother me. I crane my neck to look for Darcy in the crowd.

Then my phone buzzes.

2 New Messages. They're from Darcy.

> Hey Art. Something came up.
> I won't be able to make our
> study session.

> I'll explain later. Bye. ☺

I stare at the winky face, feeling conflicted.

One time at Game, there was this temple we'd been hired to guard. The local lord was concerned about bandits stealing the treasures within and commissioned our group to protect the sacred place. We blew it up. Well, not we, but Alex did, and voided our contract. I was furious with him, both in game and IRL, but in the rubble of the explosion we found loot. Kastor gave Roman a tricorn hat with these huge feathers as a peace offering. The plumed hat was Magicked, a wondrous item that would otherwise have been left buried in the church.

Now Roman can disguise himself at will. In the end, what made me mad worked out in my favor.

It's kinda the same thing now. I read Darcy's text as I walk to my truck. Then I shove my phone into my back pocket. Fine. It's fine. We still have tons of time to work on our project. No big deal.

I slump in the front seat and pull out my phone.

I look at the little winky face again. It has the same effect as wearing that awesome hat in game. In a matter of seconds, I go from grumbling to grinning.

It's universally acknowledged that winky faces are the flirting emoji.

Is she flirting with me?

I pull out of the parking lot and flip on my signal light. A black motorcycle cuts me off; the bike roars like a hell hound. I slam on my brakes and the truck jerks to a stop.

That's when I see them.

There's a guy in a leather jacket driving and a girl holding on to him. I'd recognize that messenger bag anywhere. Darcy clings to the guy, her arms wrapped around his waist, her face buried in his neck.

And just like that, all thoughts of flirting emojis vanish. The sun moves behind a gray cloud, casting hazy light on everything. I wonder if it's going to snow.

I know I should go home. Dad didn't say as much, but after

coming in late last night, I'm more or less grounded. Though, the thought of going home — to a house that might as well be empty and to a dad I can't ask for advice — while Darcy rides around town clinging to some other guy, grates on me.

As if possessed by a rebellious monster, I crank the wheel at the last possible second and swerve away from home. Driving faster than usual, I remind myself that Darcy doesn't owe me anything. We're just friends and that's okay. The thought provides no comfort, and by the time I park outside the public library, I feel foolish. In what realm of existence did I think that the enigmatic Darcy would be interested in someone like me?

I slam my truck door behind me before marching inside. Stomping the entire way, I push aside the glass door, shuffle my way across the welcome mat, then walk up to the circulation desk.

Florence, the real librarian, is working instead of Alex. For as long as I can remember she's been the librarian here, with a beaded chain dangling her reading specs around her neck like an equippable item.

Dawn and I used to come here a lot, right after Mom died. Alex's grandma was our babysitter back then, and she would bring Alex, Dawn and me here when Dad was gone on weekends. We pulled nearly every book off the shelf and dragged out the storytime puppets every time. Miss Flo never once yelled at us for making a mess.

"Hello there, Arthur." She squints at me then pulls the glasses up to her nose. "What can I do for you today?"

I lean against the desk. "I'm just here to use the computer."

She takes my card and scans the plastic barcode, while making small talk. "And did you hear about the new doctor in town? I can't believe they hired someone with that lifestyle. I'm just not comfortable going to our clinic anymore. I'm going to have to transfer to the city. Such a shame."

I try not to grimace at her. Is this how Darcy feels? All the time?

I take my card back. "I don't know about that, Miss Flo." The older woman looks over her glasses at me. "You can log in now, Arthur. The computer is all yours."

My phone buzzes. I glance at the lock screen.

Marcus (Dad) Bailey
Text Message

I ignore Dad and go to my assigned computer. Normally, I wouldn't think twice about the exchange with Miss Flo. I've known her for most of my life. She's just old-school.

But being old-fashioned doesn't seem like a good enough reason to, what? To gossip about Darcy's mom? To drive to the city every time you need a doctor?

I log on to the computer with the intention of doing some research for the English project, but my thoughts are pulled off course by Miss Flo, Darcy's mom, Leather Jacket Guy and Darcy. I don't like the idea that my English partner is blazing around on the back of some jerk's motorcycle.

That's not fair. He might be a great guy. And I'm just some nobody who goes to school with her. *What were you thinking, Art?*

That's when I do something really, truly pathetic. I look up Darcy online. I search for her across every single social media platform.

It's a mistake.

I scroll through picture after picture and status after status of her with some guy named James. Judging from the way he is kissing her cheek at a party, red plastic cup in hand, I'd say that he is most definitely her boyfriend.

The worst part is that in almost every picture of this James guy, he's either cosplaying or playing video games or rolling dice. In one photo he's wearing a Demogorgon shirt that I've seen Darcy wear to school. I push myself back from the computer. Guess I'm not the only geek in her life.

I try to distract myself with writing out a scene from the last campaign session, but the words don't come. After a rough few hours, I finally write Beckett's hanging, which does nothing to improve my mood. I click back into my Instagram account and find Darcy again. Should I add her?

No, that would look desperate.

A sweet voice breaks into my obsessive thoughts. "Arthur, dear —" Miss Flo taps the gold watch on her wrist "— we're closing."

"Sorry." I scramble to exit the web page. "I'll just head out, then. Thanks."

I'm surprised by how dark it is already. Little flakes of white float to the ground and disappear before touching the pavement.

I pull into our driveway. The garage door gapes open. Dad's SUV is parked in his permanently reserved, but usually empty, spot. Before I even have time to shut the truck door, Dawn flies from the house. She springs across the concrete like a barefooted sprite in a blue sweater, her strawberry-blonde hair loose and wild.

Before I really know what's happening, she tackles me. She buries her face in my chest.

"He's mad," she sniffles.

I don't know what to say. I pat her head, my arm moving stiffly from the elbow like a robot.

Dawn pulls away and stares up at me. Her eyes are misty, but there's this sharpness in how her eyelashes flick upwards. She has Dad's eyes.

"Where were you?"

"I — I went to work on homework," I say. The lie tastes sour, and from Dawn's expression, she doesn't believe me anyway. I run a hand through my hair. "At the library."

"You were supposed to come home after school, and now he's mad. He keeps stomping around."

I try to edge into the house the way Roman would, quiet and sneaky, with Dawn close behind me, but either I fail my Dexterity roll or my father has an insane Perception skill.

"Arthur. Come here."

I set down my school bag before I step into the den.

There are a lot of different types of dads in the world. There are dads who play catch with you in the backyard, who teach you how to take apart an engine; there are stay-at-home dads; dads who let you put barrettes and clips in their hair; and dads who encourage you to follow your dreams. My dad is none of those dads.

My dad stands in the middle of the living room, dressed in an expensive pair of trousers and a white-collared dress shirt, with a tie loosened around his neck. The only indication that he's off work today is the suede jacket that has replaced his suit coat, which is tossed on the counter.

Marcus Bailey is the type of man who commands whatever space he occupies. He has a strong jaw and dark hair, with silver running through it at the temples. He's broad in his shoulders and incredibly fit for a man in his early fifties. He's practically King Arthur of Camelot in a business suit, the presiding noble of our small town. Local royalty.

In other words, he is everything I'm not. I'm almost two inches taller than him, but I feel dwarfed as I inch closer.

"Sit," he orders.

I do as I am told.

DARCY IRL

Before I gather myself enough to answer, James asks again. "Darcy, who is she talking about?"

Fear strokes a line down my spine. "No one," I say, my voice hesitant and small. Even I'm not convinced. "Just some guy in my English class."

Too much time passes before a cold smile spreads across my boyfriend's face. I open my mouth to assure him that Art is just a friend, but he turns his attention back to Rainbow. "She'll have beef broccoli with extra broccoli."

When Rainbow returns with our meal, she sets down fried rice and cashew chicken in front of James and a dish of mostly broccoli in front of me. Then she steps back and holds her serving tray in front of her.

"You should totally join us for lunch sometime, Darcy. Dawn and I usually eat on the stage with a few of our friends. Have you met Wyatt yet? I think he's a year ahead of you."

I dish rice onto my plate and think back to that first Monday in the hallway, when Art mentioned that it was

Wyatt who clapped for me. Then I glance at James. He pierces me with his stare.

Slowly, I shake my head. "I haven't had much time to meet anyone, yet."

"You met Art," James says around a mouthful of chicken. I shoot him a desperate, please-stop look, but he remains frigid.

Anger chews through the worry of offending James. If that's how he's going to be, then two can play that game.

I set down the serving spoon and lean my elbows on the table. "You know what, I'd love to join you for lunch. Maybe Dawn can tell me what her brother's been saying about me."

From the corner of my eye, I see the way James's hand tightens on his fork, teeth gnashing on another piece of meat. Rainbow bounces away, and I turn my attention back to my food.

James and I don't say another word for the remainder of our meal. That is, until it's time to go and he puts on this big show of paying for everything. I pull out my wallet to add some cash and he's all, "Don't worry about it, princess. It's my treat. I'm your boyfriend after all."

I slam the glass door on my way out of the restaurant. It doesn't really slam; the door hinges wheeze closed behind me with a tinkle of gold bells. Regardless, I march out of Yee's Cozy Kitchen. James follows a couple seconds behind me.

"You were way out of line, James —"

He grabs my shoulder. I didn't realize he was so close behind me. With a hard pull, he spins me around. His hand clenches into a fist around my bicep.

I look up at his face, to demand he let go of me, but when I meet his gaze I feel stuck. There's always a scene in those teenage romances when the angsty love interest reveals their tortured soul.

This might have been that moment, except it's happening in real life, and IRL James scares me. I try to pull away, but his fingers dig harder into my arm. "Hey — you're hurting me."

"You don't walk away from me," he says, his voice a malevolent curse. He did play a necromancer in our last campaign.

Tears prick the corners of my eyes.

When my voice comes out, it doesn't even sound like me. "I'm sorry."

I figured out James's stats a long time ago. Charisma is his highest and it's maxed at a natural twenty. That's without proficiencies or modifiers, and I'm pretty sure he has some crazy bonuses when rolling Charm against teen fangirls — girls like me.

His grip softens. "I just miss you so goddamn much."

"Sure." I look at the skiff of snow on the ground. James leans forward and kisses my numb lips.

He drops me off at home, and apparently, I'm still not used to small towns. One of our neighbors, a man named Mr. Watkins, is outside shoveling his driveway. He eyes James and the motorcycle as I walk up the path to my house. Then he waves at me and calls, "Good evening, Miss Evans."

"It's Larocque-Evans, actually, Mr. Watkins." I glance over my shoulder at James. He has another smoke in his mouth.

A faint smile touches the older man's lips. "Yes, that's right. Well," he coughs, one gloved hand on his shovel, the other covering his mouth. "Have a good evening, Miss Larocque-Evans."

I dash up my front steps. The door is open, spewing out the reek of paint.

Before I can wave goodbye to James, I hear his bike rev down the street.

"Darcy, is that you honey?" Monica's voice calls from the basement.

"Yeah."

"Where were you? You missed supper. Did you have another study date with that boy?"

The way she says date makes me swallow. I wish I had been on another study date with Art. The realization is dizzying.

I ignore her questions. "The front door was open."

"That's fine," Carrie says, her voice coming from the basement too. I'm thinking about going down to them when they both materialize at the bottom of the stairs wearing paint-splattered work clothes.

"What are you two doing?"

"Painting," Carrie says.

"Where were you?" Monica asks as she wipes her hands on her jeans. There's no distracting her.

"Nowhere." I lock the front door. "Just out."

I go to the kitchen and deposit my leftovers in the fridge.

"That's not an answer, Darcy!"

"Just leave her be, Monica," Carrie says.

"I don't like her attitude."

"She's fine. Give her some space, darling."

They keep whispering back and forth. I grab a sparkling water from the fridge before retreating to my bedroom. I may have won this battle, but I have enough XP in Monica/Carrie warfare to know that I have a long way to go before I win the whole campaign. Still, the small victory feels good.

Alone at last, I peel off my cardigan and look at my arm in the full-length mirror. The other day I hung up some twinkle lights around the frame, and now they sparkle back at me, casting soft light on the pale purple marks that are quickly darkening to a bruise.

My arms still hurts on Monday, as I walk up and down the hall looking for the elusive stage door. I walk by it three times before realizing that the door tucked around the corner from the girls' bathroom is in fact my destination. Just a painted blue door, with no writing or room number. I try the handle, but the door doesn't budge. Locked.

I wonder about knocking, but before I work up the courage, someone reaches around me and hammers on the door. "Hey! Let us in, assholes!"

I side-eye the knocker. They're taller than me, but who isn't, and not what I expected to see at this school. Blood orange pixie cut, three different layered blouses, and the chunkiest chunky jewelry I've ever seen. I look up at them and take in their long eyelashes and sharp jawline with just a hint of stubble. I'm trying to decipher their pronouns, when I notice a lanyard around their neck. It's tie-dyed gray and purple, and there's a card on the end that says *She/They for today.*

My mouth falls open.

A rueful smirk lifts one side of their mouth. "I'm Mackenzie, or Mack when I'm feeling boyish. You must be the doctor's daughter, right?"

The stage door swings open before I have a chance to confirm.

On the other side, Rainbow stands with her mouth pressed

into a tight line. She brightens when she notices me standing beside Mackenzie. "Hey, Darcy!"

"Hey." I half wave, my lunch bag in hand.

"Dawn, you're killing me!" someone whines from behind Rainbow. She rubs her temples, then steps aside to let Mackenzie and me pass.

"What's the tea?" Mackenzie asks under their breath as we walk up a short flight of stairs onto a hardwood stage.

"Wyatt is being Wyatt. He's convinced that some senior has been flirting with him, but Dawn saw the guy and his girlfriend making out in the park last weekend."

Mackenzie shakes their head. "If only we all had Wyatt's confidence, this would be a very different school."

"I'm not trying to upset you. I wasn't even going to tell you, but I didn't want to see you get hurt." That must be Dawn. Her voice carries with a matter-of-fact tone. She sounds so sure, so different from Art.

"I swear he's been queer signaling. He wore a floral button-down yesterday. And a bow tie!"

I'm the last to walk up the stairs, but as soon as I get to the top the fighting stops. Wyatt and Dawn stare at me, I stare back; there's just a lot of staring.

Wyatt — who's wearing a floral button-down himself under a tight wool sweater — looks me up and down. Sure enough, I recognize him from the hallway. The one who congratulated me for calling out those creeps, the one Art offered to introduce to me. I freeze under Wyatt's obvious assessment. He nods thoughtfully.

"Darcy!" Dawn says. She barrels into me before I have a chance to really look at her, but I think there's a flash of ginger hair. "Oh, my goodness, it's so good to meet you! Finally!"

I look around at everyone else — Wyatt shrugs; Mackenzie isn't paying attention, their nose in *Heartstopper: Volume 4*; and Rainbow smiles her sunny smile. No one comes to my rescue.

"Nice to meet you too?"

As if remembering this is the first time Dawn and I have actually met, she pulls away. "Oh, my god, I'm so sorry."

Now that she's not glued to me, I can see the similarities between her and Art. They have the same hair, wild, somewhere between wavy and staticky, although Dawn's red is more strawberry blonde. She's also tall like him and can see clear over my head. Her face is covered in freckles, just like Art—everything looks so familiar. Everything but her eyes. Instead of storm gray like her brother's, Dawn's eyes are a warm bronze color, somewhere between green and gold. And where Art's gaze is shy and bashful, Dawn stares at me, openly curious and excited. I like her already.

I smile at her, and that's all the reassurance she needs. Dawn loops her arm through mine and sits me down beside her on a black wooden box.

"I love your piercing. My father would never let me do something like that. I can't believe you came to eat lunch with us. Art is going to be so jealous. You really are as pretty as he said."

Dawn may look like her brother, but she talks about twice as fast and three times as much. I blink at her rapid-fire commentary, my brain sifting through everything she's saying.

"I'll invite him next time," I say, my voice rather blunt. Then it's as if my mind catches up and I finally hear the last thing Dawn said. "Wait, he said I'm pretty?"

The color in Dawn's face rises, her freckled cheeks reddening. "I don't think I was supposed to tell you that."

"Obviously not," Wyatt says, his voice dry.

As much as I would love to ask Dawn a million questions about Art — and I think she'd answer them all — I don't want to embarrass her. Or her brother for that matter. I turn my attention to Rainbow. She sits at the only desk on the stage, with Wyatt sprawled on the floor beside her.

"So, is this a club or something? Like, a QSA?"

Back at my old school, we had a Queer-Straight Alliance that had a similar vibe. A pang of longing shoots through me. Loneliness, I realize. I miss knowing where I fit, miss my friends.

Mackenzie looks up from their graphic novel. "No, we're not a club."

I pull out my lunch, unpacking the stackable container with intense focus to hide my embarrassment. "Sorry, I shouldn't have assumed."

They all share a meaningful look. I blink around in a vain attempt to read the room.

Dawn sighs. "How about some real introductions? You've met Rainbow."

Rainbow waves a pair of chopsticks at me. "And you assumed correctly, Darcy. I like girls."

"And that's Wyatt."

Wyatt raises his hand, as if he's about to deliver an oath or pledge. "Wyatt Cyr, Cree and two-spirit, also director for the school drama club."

Dawn points at Mackenzie, and they set down *Heartstopper*. "I don't love labels, but you're new, so here it is, I guess. Like I said, Mackenzie or Mack. I'm gender fluid, because gender is a construct, hence the name tag. I think I'm demisexual, although I've never really liked anyone enough to want sex, so there's a possibility that I'm actually ace." Mackenzie shrugs. "We'll see."

"And I'm Dawn," Dawn says. The lights buzz above us, but she doesn't elaborate further, and no one else offers any more explanation.

I drop my fork.

"Darcy?" Rainbow asks. "You okay?"

I take my first real deep breath in weeks. My shoulders drop. I relax into the temporary reprieve, like a player character taking a short rest. I return Rainbow's concern with a smile of my own. "I'm Darcy, as you all know, obviously," I say. "And I'm bi."

I brace myself for the inevitable questions that I've become used to answering as soon as I come out to new people. Things like, "Wait? You're not a lesbian like your moms?" or, "I thought you only dated dudes. Doesn't that mean you're straight?" But no one here second-guesses me or tries to explain my sexuality as if I don't know myself.

Yup. These are definitely my people. I have to tear myself away from the group when the lunch bell rings. Rainbow and Dawn linger with me in the hallway after Wyatt and Mackenzie head to class.

"It was so nice to meet you," I say with warmth. And I mean it.

Dawn's eyebrows lift and she presses her lips together, as if to stop a laugh. She elbows Rainbow, "We gotta go. Now."

Rainbow looks over my shoulder, which draws my attention in that direction too. A familiar redhead navigates through the crowd toward us. I wave Art over, then turn back to Dawn and Rainbow. The two girls are halfway down the hallway with their heads bowed together, giggling.

I feel Art's presence stop behind me. "Well, that's terri-fying," he says, as he watches his sister and friend. "How did Dawn corner you? What did she say? You know what? Never mind. I don't want to die from embarrassment."

Knowing he thinks I'm pretty makes me smile from the inside out and the urge to tease him is almost irresistible, that is, until I remember the faded, yellow bruises on my biceps. My smile drops as I remember James' grip on me.

If Art notices, he doesn't comment. Instead, he runs a hand through his hair and glances down the hall. Students have more or less disappeared into their classrooms, and we'll both have to hurry to our next class if we don't want to be late.

But all thoughts of fourth period social studies fly from my mind when Art leans closer. "Hey, Darcy. Would you like to come to Game with me on Thursday?"

ART IRL

A radiant smile illuminates Darcy's face. "Yes!"

I step back, surprised by her enthusiasm. Wow, okay. "Well, we play every week on Thursday nights, does that work for you?"

"Yes! Yes! Of course." She wraps herself around my arm, her face tilted up to me. "I need to know everything. What level are you all? Does your GM know you're inviting me? Is it an official campaign or homebrew? Can I play an already-made character? Details, Art. I need details."

I rub the back of my head, laughing. "How about I give you Michelle's number and you can ask her about character creation. Although, if you have a character already, I'm sure she can insert you without much of a problem."

"There's no way I'll be able to focus in class now. You've ruined me," Darcy says with a laugh.

"We could go somewhere else?"

A look of surprise, followed by a wry smile stretches across her face. "Are you suggesting we skip class?"

"We're already skipping," I point out, not recognizing myself. Who is this daring person? I shrug. "Might as well do something fun."

"What do you have in mind, m'lord?"

I hesitate, suddenly aware of the press of her body against mine. Everything in me wants to whisk her away somewhere private, somewhere intimate. Burning, I push away the thought of having Darcy alone and all to myself.

"What about a side quest?"

Her fingers loop through mine. We pass painted cinder-block walls, lockers and classroom doors as Darcy drags me down the hallway. We burst through the front doors, then she plants her feet, hands on her hips, and shouts, "Quest accepted!"

We laugh all the way to my truck, and somehow, without really deciding on a destination, we're driving to the city. What's a side quest without shopping?

The drive feels shorter than an hour as I answer Darcy's questions about Game. We're level twelve; Michelle is excited to welcome another *D&D* fangirl; the campaign is a home-brewed setting.

"You have a character that you used to play, right?" I ask, as we pull into the outer edges of the city. "Will you tell me about them?"

"Her name is Poppy. Poppy le Fey," Darcy says. "She's a witch."

The more she tells me about her PC, the more excited I am to have her join the campaign. She doesn't stop talking about Poppy until we're downtown.

I loop the block twice under the pretense of finding a suitable parking spot, but really I just don't want to interrupt

Darcy. She waves her hands, her voice bouncy and animated, as she explains the origins of Poppy's ivory plague mask.

"And then she took the bone dust and made an offering to the —" Darcy's hand shoots in front of my nose, the movement cutting off Poppy's backstory. "There's a spot!"

Unable to pretend anymore, I pull in beside a parking meter and try to suppress my disappointment. I could listen to her read the longest fanfic on AO3 — a seven-million-word saga set in the Terminator universe, a fandom I know next to nothing about — if she were this passionate.

Darcy looks across the street. "This is perfect."

Her approval dispels my reluctance to leave the truck. I unbuckle my seat belt with an exaggerated bow of my head. "After you."

Fantasyland Comics doesn't smell the way you'd imagine a comic shop would smell. It's not a dirty hovel that reeks of body odor. Instead, it's a bright little shop, low and squat, crammed between two tall brick buildings downtown. The door is painted green and has a large gold knocker on it, reminiscent of a hobbit door. Inside, the shop smells of books and ink, of zesty floor cleaner and nutmeg.

"Can I help you?" An employee in a beanie leans forward from behind the counter. They have full tattoo sleeves decorating their dark skin and an awesome mustache, but their face is almost too soft and round to be considered masculine. Pinned to their nondescript black T-shirt is an employee name tag that says *Morgan*. Beneath those silver letters, *They/Them* is written in purple marker.

"Morgan!" Darcy says, her cheeks rosy from the walk. We had to park three blocks away and the wind bites. She pokes her head around me and waves at them.

They stand up, grinning. "Darcy! How's it?"

Darcy bounds into Morgan's open arms for a massive hug. The two make small talk in bubbly, high-pitched tones. Morgan asks about the move.

Darcy sighs. "Don't get me started on that." Then, as if she remembers that I'm standing there too, she looks back at me. I rock on my heels.

Darcy bounces over and links an arm through mine. "This is my one and only friend in the boonies. Morgan, meet Arthur. His friends call him Art."

"You don't want to know what my friends call me," Morgan says with an easy smile. They extend a hand, and we shake. Then Morgan motions behind the counter to a cauldron. "You two want a Witch's Brew? It's pineapple juice, ginger ale and lime sorbet with a healthy amount of dry ice added."

"That's what all those bottles are for!" Darcy nods behind Morgan. A variety of glass decanters and plastic cups rest next to the cauldron.

"Yeah," Morgan says. Their eyes raise to the ceiling. "October promotion, free Brew with the purchase of fifty dollars or more, or four dollars a cup."

"Felicity," Morgan and Darcy say in unison.

"Here," Morgan pours two glasses, then adds a bit of dry ice to each. The liquid begins to smoke and bubble immediately. "On the house."

In the end, we earn our promotional drinks, and bring more than fifty dollars of sourcebooks, dice and RPG accessories to the checkout counter. The holy grail of the loot is a Hellfire Club T-shirt. I've never seen *Stranger Things*, but the way Darcy's face lit up when I stepped out of the changeroom made it impossible to leave the shirt behind. If Dad ever sees that devil-faced logo, though, I'll be grounded for life. I make a mental note to hide it in my truck.

"I got this," I say at the counter, our purchases heaped between us and Morgan.

Darcy shakes her head in protest. "No way."

"It's not a big deal." I pull out the credit card Dad leaves with us.

I am about to pay when Darcy's hand shoots out. She eyes the Visa logo. "Does your dad pay for that?"

"It's our only source of money when he's away on business."

Darcy raises an eyebrow. "Using your dad's card while skipping?" she says. "Noob mistake, Art."

She pulls out a Sailor Moon wallet and hands Morgan cash. "Remember, I worked here all summer, and The Moms still give me an allowance. I've got this."

"I'll pay you back," I say, but she just waves her hand in a 'don't bother' motion.

"It's my treat."

The green door closes behind us with a chime. "Arcade?" I ask.

"Definitely."

DARCY IRL

We get back to town later than we planned, but I don't mind. In fact, I'm wishing we had more time together.

Somewhere in the span of the drive we started holding hands. The way his thumb rubs the inside of my wrist is nice. I relax; that is, until James texts me.

Hey babe

Guilt settles like a stone in my stomach. I should text James back, but I don't.

Art pulls onto my street and I see flashing lights outside a little brick house. My house. There is a police car parked on the curb — in the same place James dropped me off the other night. Where Art probably would have dropped me off tonight.

"What's going on?" His voice sounds distant and echoey, even though he's right beside me.

I barely hear him over my own worry. Where are my moms?

"Art, pull over."

I have to squint to see them but there they are, huddled together, talking to an officer. Next to them is Mr. Watkins, also speaking to someone in a blue and white uniform. I tumble out of Art's truck before it stops moving. Art catches up to me in a few steps.

Carrie sees us first. She squeezes Monica's arm, then my stay-at-home mom runs to me. She's wearing pajama pants and a tank top. Her arms wrap around me in a tight hug. I can see Carrie speaking with the police. She pauses the officer by holding up her hand, all business and professionalism, until she turns to walk over. She's still in work clothes, her scrubs tucked into big winter boots. As soon as her back is to the police, her face becomes dangerous.

"Where were you?" Carrie asks. She sounds scared, not angry. Her expression protective, not violent.

Monica pulls back and the hair dye and shampoo scent that seems to cling to her skin pulls away too. She holds me at arm's length, her hands on my shoulders.

"We were —" I stammer. I can't tell them the truth, so I stumble to come up with an appropriate cover story. *Working on homework* is on the tip of my tongue when Art cuts me off.

"We went to the city. I thought it might be fun to skip school and take Darcy to Fantasyland Comics, then we went to the arcade and saw a movie. I'm sorry, it's my fault she's late."

Carrie looks surprised, as though she wasn't expecting that level of honesty, and Monica looks disappointed.

"That's not what happened at all!" I'm not going to let them paint Art as the bad guy when he's so obviously lawful good. "Well, I mean, it's kinda what happened, but it wasn't his idea. I'm the one who made him skip class and take me to the city. The rest of it, the arcade and movie, that was all me too. I was showing him the sights. What's going on here? Why is Mr. Watkins talking to the police?"

I'm blabbering, I know. I want them to like Art but I also want to know what's happening. It all blurs together as the panic rises.

Carrie shakes her head. A little smile cracks her grim appearance. Monica looks to the heavens.

"Well, you're safe now, that's what matters," Monica says. She fixes Carrie with a pointed look. "Mr. Watkins is giving a statement."

A police officer breaks into our little circle. "Ma'am," he says. "We have a few more questions, if you don't mind. About the attack."

"Not at all," Carrie takes a deep breath and follows the police back to the house.

"Attack?" I wheel on Monica. "What attack?"

"Just some vandalism." She squeezes me closer. Her voice wobbles. "Someone threw a brick."

We walk toward the house. Art follows. I think he's carrying my messenger bag.

The police have taped off our front window. A jagged hole has shattered the double sheet of glass. One officer is reconstructing the scene with Carrie, who is pointing and describing what happened. The other officer has left Mr. Watkins and is walking toward us, a bag in her hand.

"What's that?" I point to the clear bag. There's something rectangular inside.

The officer hesitates. "Evidence."

"Is that the brick?"

"Yes."

"Can I see?"

Ms. Police Officer waits for my mother to answer.

"Oh, honey," Monica says. "I don't think that's a good idea."

"I want to see."

Monica indicates her consent with a nod.

The officer holds the bag up for me.

It's just a brick, I think. Just like any other brick. Red. Rectangular. Heavy-looking. There's nothing special about this brick. Then she turns it around. Someone has written a word on the side in angry black marker. This brick says *DYKES*.

Tuesday and Wednesday are a blur. News spreads fast in a small town and soon everyone knows what happened at our house. I stay home from school and Art brings me home-work. I think it's just an excuse to see me, but the butterflies disappear when I ask him what people are saying at school.

"You don't need to hear that," he says.

By Thursday, curiosity gets the better of me and I go to school. My locker neighbor, Hannah, the girl who reads Tamora Pierce, whispers that she heard what happened and she's sorry. As if she's responsible, and I mean, she could be for all we know. The police have been zero help trying to figure out who did it, even with Mr. Watkins' account. Apparently, he heard the sound of breaking glass, then a truck engine revving, but by the time he made it outside, the street was empty. He came over later with a pie from the grocery store and some ice cream.

Other than Hannah, who obviously isn't the person who vandalized our house because she's so damn nice, everything seems to be pretty normal. That is, until lunch. Art and I are sitting together, which we've done for the past couple weeks, to work on our storytelling project. We already confirmed our topic with Ms. Stacey, so it's been full steam ahead on the RPG presentation. We have character sheets spread out beside our packed lunches and we're discussing how to lead the whole class through character creation. We've been debating how many sets of dice we'll need to roll everyone's ability scores.

We open our lunch bags: he has leftover pizza, and I'm eating one of Monica's pasta creations.

I push back my chair to go warm up my pasta. "Microwave?" I know I don't need to ask — he eats cold pizza every week — but today we're going through the motions.

He shakes his head, and I allow myself a small smile.

I'm standing by the microwave, waiting my two minutes, when a scrunched-up napkin lands in front of me. I look around, but I just see the bodies of anonymous, shuffling teenagers. No one stands out.

I open the napkin, and I don't need to look twice before crushing it in my hand. Anger, then panic threaten to cut off my air. I suck in a desperate breath.

Hold it together, I think. *If they see you cry, things will get worse.*

The microwave dings, and I grab my lunch with the napkin crumpled in my fist. I keep my chin up and march out of the cafeteria.

I walk down the hall and straight into someone's chest. I don't even realize that tears blur my vision until two firm hands steady my shoulders. I look up and it's Alex.

"Whoa. Watch where you're going, New Girl. Almost knocked you on your ass."

I chuckle but the sound is dry. For his part, Alex doesn't buy it. He squeezes my shoulders. "You okay?"

From the corner of my eye, I notice the girls' bathroom, and beside that, the stage door. I nod. "I'm fine. Just going to the stage."

Alex lets me go, and I bolt to the blue door. It's locked. I bang on the wood until Dawn opens the door for me. I barely make it through, before I fold into her arms and sob.

Mack, Wyatt, Rainbow and Dawn surround me on the stage. Dawn and Rainbow rub my back, while Mack and Wyatt whisper in low tones across from us. They have a crumpled napkin flattened between them. I didn't even notice dropping it when I hugged Dawn.

"We should tell the principal," Wyatt says. "This is exactly why we need a QSA here. Fucking homophobes."

Mack shakes their head. "We've been trying that since freshman year. Wyatt, you know what's going to happen."

"Darcy?" Art calls. I bolt to my feet and try to swipe the tears and snot from my face.

"We're up here," Dawn answers.

Alex follows Art up the stairs, and I'm both annoyed and grateful that Alex obviously went and found Art. The latter of the two boys finds me in the group, my eyes puffy and red, my nose still dripping, and he crosses the room in just a few long strides. "What happened? Why are you crying?"

I shake my head, not trusting myself to speak.

"Here." Mack hands Art the napkin. I cringe, I don't want him to read the ugly words scribbled on there.

Die DYKE.

Art reads the napkin once, twice and a third time, and with each pass, his eyes grow harder, more furious. By the time he looks back up at me, his face twists with anger. "Who did this to you?"

"I didn't see," I say.

"Well, we've got to do something. I can't believe this is happening. Maybe the principal can look at the hallway cameras?"

"I don't think the school has hallway cameras," Alex whispers.

Mack stares at Art, as if Art's just grown a second head. "It's not that simple."

"Why not?" Art folds his arms. "Seems pretty simple to me. This shouldn't even be a discussion. That's a death threat!"

"How about because you're not the one in danger here?" Mack squares off with Art. "Why don't we start by asking Darcy what she wants to do, instead of going all white knight on her ass, Preacher Boy?"

"Hey!" Alex steps forward, until he's standing shoulder to shoulder with Art. "He's just trying to help, and only I get to call him that!"

Art looks beyond Mack, his eyebrows pinched and jaw tight. I try to hold his gaze, but my eyes sting. Part of me wants to do all the things. I want to meet Art's imploring gaze and assure him that I'm going to fight, that I'm going to take a stand, but I hesitate. Broken glass and police lights, speculative whispers and crumpled napkins; my chest tightens. Suddenly, I'm overexposed, splayed out and on display for everyone to see, as if standing up for my family, for myself, is a form of open-heart surgery.

My gaze drops to my shoes, and Art's response follows quickly after. "No, it's okay, Alex. Mack's right."

The stage floor creaks, then long, slender fingers smudged with graphite pencil slide into my hand. I look up, and Art's expression softens, his blue-gray eyes steady.

"I'd be lying if I said I wasn't angry. None of this is okay. And I hate that you might not feel safe enough to report what happened —" He stops, inhales a deep breath. Then he continues, voice low and meant only for me. "I'm sorry, that's not the point. What do you need? What can I do?"

There's something about the way his anger melts into tenderness that brings me back to myself. I lean into the warmth of his hand. "You're not wrong," I say. I glance at where Wyatt and Mack stand together. "I don't feel safe enough to bring this forward. And that's the problem."

Wyatt straightens.

"Unity Creek High School needs a QSA," I say.

After school, Art invites me to a little park, somewhere on the north end of town. We're almost outside of the town limits, but that's nice because it's quiet. There's a bright red swing set and an old wooden bridge.

Art stops his truck, and we walk to the bridge. There are deep cavernous walking trails below. The paths are little valleys, carved out of the earth by a backhoe rather than a glacier, but they're charming and twisted. I imagine the trails provide the illusion of wilderness to whoever walks through.

I fall in love with the untamed little park.

Art slides down the bank to the bottom of the trails.

There's a large tree with exposed roots that he uses to help himself climb down. When he reaches the bottom, about seven feet below me, he offers me a hand, and I slide down too.

"We call that one the Fairytree." He tilts his head to the tree beside us. "Or at least, that's what Dawn used to say when we were kids."

I smile and try to forget the brick and the balled-up napkin. It almost works. Almost.

"Come here," Art says, guiding me beneath the bridge. He let's go of my hand, but only to slide both of his palms up my shoulders, where he gently positions me to face his Fairytree. Goosebumps shiver across my skin, hidden beneath my long sleeves.

With me in place, Art bounds back to where we came. He climbs partway back up the ravine, overgrown grass whispering against his jeans, then he sinks down and disappears from sight. Hidden by the long grass and shadowy tree, he's just gone, and if I hadn't just watched him sit, I might have walked by without even noticing him.

"I used to bring Dawn here after our mom's car accident," he says from his hiding spot, his voice detached in a robotic way. "We'd play in the walking paths and under this bridge for hours. Dawn told me that our mom was taken by fairies. I couldn't tell her that Mom wasn't a changeling."

I abandon my post and climb back toward him. He's never talked about his mom.

"Do you think about her often?" I cross my legs on the cold earth beside him.

I realize that Art doesn't have a mother, and I have two.

"No," he says, his voice small. Then his chin bobs down. "And yes. She died right after Dawn turned six. I was only eight, but I didn't want to be known as the kid with a dead mom, you know? So it was easier to just forget, but sometimes I get these flashes. She had glasses like you."

I don't really know what to say. Any of the things I could say aren't right for this place, so I lean my head against his arm and I don't say anything. Our breath rises and falls like we're a collective thing, like the monster under the bridge. The kind, sad monster.

"I'm scared," I say, surprised by how easily the words roll from my tongue. "And I hate that I'm scared. I don't want to back down, but what if starting up a QSA isn't enough?"

There it is. And there are about a thousand ways he could react. Art twists a fistful of dead grass from the ground. "It's hard to think of you backing down from a fight. You're so confident."

If he only knew. My laugh sounds brittle, like the crunch of dead leaves. "What if I make everything worse?"

He lets go of grass and stares at the Fairytree. "What would starting a QSA mean for you? For Wyatt and Mack?"

"A safe place at school, protection." My reply is automatic. "The confirmation that queer students matter, that our safety means something. Not just to the straight allies, but to every-one here in Unity Creek."

"Exactly. That sounds like a noble quest to me. Isn't that what heroes do? Fight injustice?" He shifts in his seat until he can hold my gaze, his gray-blue eyes steady. "You're not going to make things worse. You couldn't."

I sit up straighter. It's as if he's tuned into a lower frequency than normal, a frequency focused entirely on me. Rather than twitchy and embarrassed, he's self-assured, determined, and I feel the difference in the deepest parts of me.

My body leans forward and more than anything, I want to kiss him.

Art's expression softens, no trace of panic. He lowers his head to me. My lips part, ready, but before we connect, my phone rings.

Annoyance floods through me, and I'm tempted to toss the distraction into the long grass, but Art has already scrambled away, his chest heaving and face red.

I fish my cell out of my coat pocket. It might be one of The Moms, and despite their cruel timing, I'm done with the silent treatment. After The Brick, they deserve better. I glance at the screen. The name on my display sends chill through me.

James.

I can still see Art's red taillights disappearing down my street when James appears and wraps me in a tight embrace. His lips crash down on mine. I struggle to pull away from him as red taillights disappear down the street.

I frown in Art's direction. I told him that my moms wanted me home for dinner before Game, rather than explaining the unexpected text, but now the lie feels like treason. And that rough kiss even more so.

James demands my attention by spinning me to look at an old car. "Like my new wheels?"

"What was that about?"

He smirks. "What was what about?"

A small breeze swirls the orange and russet leaves on the ground around our ankles. It's not as cold as it was the first time he came to visit but it's still chilly. I might just be a teen-ager, but Art's right, I'm also the hero of my story.

Whatever this is between James and me, it isn't what I want anymore. This is my personal quest, and it ends now.

"Don't be mad, Darcy. I was just excited to see you." He pulls at my hips. "Damn, you're freezing. Let's get out of here."

I bite my lip and silently rehearse what I want to say to James. I want to let him down easy. We don't make sense anymore. Breaking up will be better for him; he'll save gas and time. Besides, I know he'll have another girlfriend in a couple days anyway.

Reluctantly, I get into James's new wreck of a car. It will be easier to say what I have to say if we're alone. But then we pull up to Art's park, and I instantly regret going anywhere with James. I feel as if I'm cheating on Art.

I'm on a park bench with my IRL boyfriend. James looks at me with hungry eyes before leaning in for a kiss. His lips press against my ear, and I think of Art again.

"James, stop. We need to talk."

He sits up. His dark hair, styled high on top and cut close to his head on the sides, is just a little out of place. His eyes grow darker. "That doesn't sound good."

"I've been thinking —"

His lips crash onto mine, and my skin crawls as I try to squirm away. He holds me tighter. I try to push him back, but he grabs my wrist. His other hand is snarled in my hair. When he finally pulls away, I gasp for air. Tears sting my eyes.

But it's James who is crying. His forehead presses on my shoulder, and he sobs into neck. I don't know what to do anymore.

"I — I need to tell you —"

"Don't," he whispers. "I know what you're going to say. Darcy, I can't lose you. I don't know what I'd do if you left me, I just know it would ruin me."

"James," I try again. I ignore the sense of dread that is binding my shoulders like a shroud. "We don't make sense anymore. It would be better for both of us this way."

He surprises me when he springs to his feet. He's fast. Like, twice the average movement speed sort of fast. "No, I don't want to hear it," he says.

"I'm sorry."

"Stop that! We're not doing this." James marches past me and gets into his car. He speeds away and leaves me, and my attempted breakup, behind. Alone, I can't help but wonder if I've just made things a whole lot worse.

My phone buzzes and I brace myself as I check the notification. I expect to see a text from James, but the name that pops up is Michelle Anderson, Art's GM.

> Hey! We're about to start, are you still planning on coming?

> You bet! I'll be there soon!

I pause and send another quick text to The Moms.

> I'm going to hang out with Art and some friends.

> Won't be home until later. Love you. ♥

Monica reminds me that it's a school night and Carrie tells me to say hi to Art for them. I wrap my arms around myself. With James gone, I feel better already.

Then I pull up a map and realize that I have no idea where I'm going. You'd think that it would be easier to find your way in a town of only two thousand people, but no. Thankfully, Michelle's house isn't far.

Relief warms my arms and legs as I walk up to a little blue house with white trim. I don't need to make sure I'm at the right house because a huge *Welcome* sign is posted beside the front door. It's normal-looking enough, wooden and carved in elaborate pseudo-Elvish script, but beneath that it says *Roll Initiative*.

Yup. I've got the right place.

There are lights on upstairs, but I don't see anyone. As I walk toward the front door, movement from a basement window catches my eye. I pause and crouch down to look. Warm light casts a golden glow on the frosted grass, and I see a group of adventurers sitting around an elaborate gaming table, plates of pizza next to their dice and minifigures.

Art has told me so much about all of them that I have no problems identifying each one.

There's no mistaking the Game Master. Michelle is confidently at the head of the table, surrounded by game screens and papers. A pool of dice sprawls across the glass screen set flat in the surface of the table, just within her reach.

To Michelle's left is a man who must be her husband. I can't remember his name but he's leaning back in his chair. From his bemused expression, he is enjoying whatever chaos is unfolding in front of the party. Beside him is another man — Robert — I think, who has a big bushy beard and an oil-stained T-shirt. He's wearing plaid, and beside him is Alex. That's weird. I thought Alex and Art sat together.

My eyes drift toward Art. There's a flip of excitement in my stomach. His face is animated, and his hands fly round. He knocks back an imaginary drink.

My stomach tightens as James' words haunt me, *I don't know what I'd do if you left me.*

This is a bad idea. I should leave.

Just then, Art looks up, his eyes wide at first, but soon he's grinning from ear to ear. He breaks character, waves at me through the glass, and pantomimes. I shake my head that I can't hear him. He pushes back from the table.

Then he disappears from view, and a door opens. I hear my name.

"Side door," Art calls to me. That's what he was trying to say through the window.

I walk over to the side door, where six feet of lanky, awkward teenage boy is standing, his arm outstretched, holding the door wide to let me inside.

Without much thought, I fold myself into the space where his arm extends and wrap my cold self around him in a tight embrace.

Art's body is stiff at first, but after a half breath, he relaxes and ushers me inside. He closes the door behind us, then returns the hug. I exhale into his chest and my breath escapes, ragged with relief. I've never felt more safe.

We stand there, holding on to one another in the boot room, probably longer than we should. Then we go downstairs.

The Hedgewitch

"Another round!" Bearpuncher yelled.

"I've never heard him speak this much before," Roman whispered to Moira, his words slurring together. The taste of something clear and too strong was sour on his breath.

All around Roman, the crumbling tavern was spinning. Everything smelled of warm bodies and ale-soaked sawdust. A table of dwarfs boomed a drinking song, and somewhere, someone played a fiddle. Bodies pressed in around him; Moira to his right, Kastor on his left, and countless strangers behind him to order their drinks at the bar. The tavern squatted outside city limits in the Ditch, built into a literal hole in the wall.

Moira looked beyond him at Bearpuncher and tilted her head. A wave of shiny blonde hair slid over her shoulder like a curtain. "He knows how to talk fine, but Common isn't his mother tongue. He's not confident speaking in it."

"If you spoke Tribal, you wouldn't be able to get him to shut up," Kastor harrumphed. Foam lined the bottom of the old man's mustache.

Roman stared at the wizard in surprise. "You speak Tribal?"

"Tribal," he responded. Kastor held up five fingers, and counted aloud, "And Elvish, Celestial, Common — of course — and as you saw yesterday, Old Common."

Roman took a swig of his own drink, the spirits bitter on his tongue. Swallowing, he asked, "Old Common?"

"The language of the Old Faith," Moira said, her eyes downcast.

"The secret language we used when I was a boy." Kastor shook his head. "When the Baron outlawed the Old Gods, I never thought I would use it again."

Roman stared down into his glass, sober despite the alcohol swimming in his head. "I had no idea, my friend."

When Roman looked up from the glass, Moira was staring at him. Her eyes dark and assessing. "There's a lot we don't know about each other," she said. "We all have secrets."

Roman's tail twitched. He turned his attention back to his drink and downed the last of the clear spirit. Could she know? Had Beckett told her?

Bearpuncher clapped Roman on the back and shoved a pint of amber ale in front of Moira. "Drink!"

In the Durgeon Forest, the barbarian clans braved a life of uncertainty. There, in the remote and dangerous forest, death was not so uncommon, and a death in battle was the most celebrated of all. Since arriving at the tavern, Bearpuncher had outpaced even Roman's constitution with no indication of slowing down anytime soon.

Bearpuncher hiccuped in Roman's ear before tossing an arm around Moira. Roman tilted his head and wondered about their relationship. They made a curious pair, but for some reason, he couldn't imagine one without the other.

He lifted the pint toward his friends. "To Beckett," he said.
"To Beckett," they responded in unison, clinking their goblets together.

A heartbeat later, a small voice colored with a melancholy lilt added, "May Deyja carry his soul to the Aaderhall."

It was reflex, the way Roman's hand flew to the dagger on his hip. He pulled the blade out and focused all his attention on steadying his drunk hand. When Roman turned, his grip faltered from shock. His dagger slipped and fell in the sawdust with a dull thud.

Behind him, a large bird cocked its head to the side. When Roman moved to reclaim his dagger from the floor, the bird stepped back and very slowly raised two hands. Human hands, with small plump fingers and no feathers in sight. Roman hesitated, still reaching for the dagger, and squinted as he tried to make sense of what he was seeing.

From the neck down, the creature looked human — a human woman to be sure, with a full chest, short torso and large hips all covered by a bibbed skirt — but from her neck up, where her face should have been, was the head of a bird. He'd heard of the birdfolk but had never seen one before. He'd thought there would be more feathers.

She tilted her head to the other side. Most disorienting was the curved white beak that glinted like polished bone and looked deadly enough to rip through flesh. Roman shuddered.

"Easy there," she said, her voice like the sound of mourning doves. "I mean no harm."

With steady, sure fingers, she reached behind her neck. A moment later, she pulled off her beak. Roman gagged, and the liquor threatened to rise from his unsettled stomach. Then, she smiled.

And she wasn't a bird at all, but a girl. A human girl with a heart-shaped face, large green eyes and curved lips. Roman's stomach tightened again, but this time it wasn't because of the alcohol. He sucked in a breath; she was easily the most enchanting woman in the tavern. A braided crown of pink hair looped around her head and reminded Roman of the Hebenon flowers along the river.

He wanted to ask her name, but it was Kastor who spoke as Roman collected himself. "You a surgeon, girlie? I haven't seen one of those masks for the better part of a century."

So the beak had only been a mask.

Kastor shuffled off his seat, brushed past Roman, and reached into the girl's skirt pocket. He pulled out a jar full of something amber and viscous and held the glass before a lantern. "Honey and Yarrow Infusion," he read aloud, stroking his beard. "No, not one of those artless butchers, then. You're something more effective. A midwife maybe or perhaps a hedgewitch?"

All of that from one jar, Roman wondered, and as though Kastor could hear his thoughts, the old man tossed the honey and yarrow at Roman. He barely caught the jar with his sluggish reflexes.

"My name is Poppy," the girl said. She stepped toward him and reached for the jar. His pulse jumped to his throat when her fist closed around his clawed hand. "And that belongs to me, Roman."

Roman bristled. He released the honey mixture and stepped back. "How do you know my name?"

She tucked the jar back into a pocket, then put her hands on her hips. Her eyes slid down Roman's body, and he braced himself for the disgust he'd become accustomed to from strangers. Except, when Poppy's eyes returned to his own, her gaze remained unchanged. Determined, purposeful, but not horrified. "I need to speak to you," she looked around at each of Roman's friends. "To you all."

"And what does a hedgewitch know about the late Master Beckett?" Moira asked, her voice clear and unaffected by drink.

A shout from across the room, followed by the cracking of wood interrupted Poppy's response. She looked around, then raised her bird mask back over her face. "Not here."

Against his better judgment, Roman followed her out of the tavern and into the cool night. He'd already turned behind the tavern, when he realized that his companions hadn't been so eager to trust the strange girl. They lingered farther behind Roman, but he was relieved to see them follow too, if only to hear Poppy's explanation.

"I know what you did for the *Baroness*," she said behind the leather beak. "Penn was able to make the rendezvous and get those people to safety because of you. He sent me word, told me to find you."

Roman sagged beneath his guilt. "But Beckett —"

"Beckett died for the cause and he would do it again," she said, her eyes fierce. She leaned closer, and Roman inhaled sweetness and florals on her skin. Her voice dipped low. "I'm from Deyja's Path, the same organization as Beckett and Penn, and I'm afraid I need your help. Please."

Maybe it was the alcohol, or her sweetness, or perhaps it was the guilt threatening to drown him, but when Poppy asked, Roman knew that he wouldn't be able to deny her. He hadn't even hesitated when she had invoked the oldest of the Old Gods, something his father had outlawed years ago. And so, he nodded.

Poppy reached out her hand. "Then, welcome to the Path."

ART IRL

Michelle pinches her fingers together like a method actor. "And scene."

Then she ushers us all out of her house. Tyler waves over her shoulder. "See you next week. Nice to meet you, Darcy!"

"Rob," Alex calls, as he bounces out the door. "Can you give me a ride home?"

He winks at me, and that's how Darcy and I end up lingering beside my truck, alone.

"So," I say. I'm torn between asking if she's okay, bringing up our almost kiss, or asking who was outside her house when I dropped her off earlier.

"That was so much fun, Art!" she says. And she really does look as though she had fun; her eyes are wide and bright. "I thought I was going to have to give up gaming when I moved here, but that was amazing!"

I nod as she recaps the night's events.

"And that letter Michelle made for me, the one from Penn with a wax seal. I can't believe she actually made me a real letter.

Like, an actual parchment letter! I can't wait for next week!"

"Do you need a ride home?"

I enjoy listening to her describe Poppy's backstory on the way home, and I decide that it's none of my business who she met in front of her house or what happened. Still, I thought that there was something here, between us. She definitely leaned forward at the park, and what about that hug at Michelle's place?

"Art," she says.

"Yeah?"

"You passed my house."

I slam on the brakes. The truck lurches.

"Sorry."

I back up to her driveway and park at the curb.

"Hey." Her fingers brush the top of my hand. "Are you okay? You've barely said anything the whole way here."

I look past her at her brick house. A happy light shines on the porch, like a spotlight on the red door. Inside, it's dark. I smile at how easily she asks me the same question I've been wanting to ask her this whole time.

"Nah, I'm fine." I run a hand through my hair. "I just like listening to you talk."

Darcy nose-scrunches.

"— about Game," I clarify, as I look away.

"Oh. Right. Of course. I like talking to you about Game, too," she says, then grabs her bag and opens the door. My grip tightens on the steering wheel as I mentally kick myself. She hops out of the truck. "Well, thanks for the ride."

I sit there, the engine humming in neutral. As soon as she leaves the cab, I want her to come back. I wonder how her lips taste.

I've only kissed one girl, on a dare at summer camp, and it didn't really count. Kissing Darcy would definitely count.

She arrives at the front door. After a few moments, she's digging in her messenger bag and her lips move like she's casting a hex.

"You okay?" I call across the lawn.

She jumps and I wince. Idiot. I turn off the truck and run up to her.

She spares me a quick glance. "I can't find my keys."

I eyeball the doorbell behind her, and without even looking up, she answers my unspoken question.

"The Moms are in the city. Date night."

"Right," I say. "That's nice for them."

Darcy looks up over top of her glasses and waggles her eyebrows at me. "Apparently we inspired them. They didn't want to leave, but I assured them that I'd be okay."

I try not to stare as she keeps rummaging around in the messenger bag. Seconds tick by in awkward silence before I whisper, "Can I help?"

"Here." She shoves the old satchel in my hands. "Hold this."

I hold it open for her so she can pull stuff out.

First come her *D&D* sourcebooks, then a chain mail bag of dice. She pulls out a pocket folder with character sheets sticking out the top, then her school notebook. There's a granola bar, headphones, and at the bottom of the bag, I see her pastel d20 keychain.

I open my mouth to point out her keys, just as her fingers close around them.

"Huzzah!" She hoists the keys high in the air.

There's a jingle and a cracking noise. Keys vs. bone. The keys win.

Pain shoots up my face. I drop everything; my hands fly to my nose. I don't understand what's happening until I see blood dripping from my hands into Darcy's as she cups her fingers below my chin.

"Oh, my god," she shrieks. "Art! Oh, my god! You're bleeding. I'm sorry! I'm so sorry!"

Tears are already trying to wash away the thick river of blood. The pain seeps into my cheekbones and jaw. I try to tell her I'm okay, but she opens the door and pushes me inside.

"Pinch the bridge of your nose and tilt your head forward," she says as we cross the threshold of her house. She dashes deeper inside, and I edge my way into the living room.

I pinch the bridge of my nose and tilt my head back.

"No!" She brings me a roll of paper towel. "Tip your head forward. Drain the blood out. If you tilt your head back, you could choke. There's so much blood. Oh, my god, Art. I'm so sorry!"

She rips off several pieces of paper towel and shoves them at me.

"You need to sit down." She sounds less like Darcy now and more like Poppy.

I let her take me to the kitchen. There's an island counter with a bright bowl of fruit in the middle next to a hair magazine.

She pulls out a stool and helps me onto it. "Sit here."

I'm all limbs and awkward angles as I tuck myself onto the stool.

Darcy moves to switch on the light. I'm not prepared for the stark red of the blood against the white paper towel in my hands. I lean my elbows against the granite countertops.

"Take a deep breath," she directs, her hand on my shoulder.

I try to breathe through my nose and that's a big mistake.

"I think you broke my nose. I didn't know you had Tavern Brawler as a feat." I try to make a joke of it as I wince in pain. I expect her to laugh or at the very least let out a nervous giggle, but when I look up to her, her face is ashen.

"Do you really think it's broken?" Tears swim behind her glasses.

"No!" I snort. Wince. "No, no. It's fine. I'm just joking."

She doesn't laugh.

"Let me see."

She's definitely more healer than fighter.

She pulls the wad of paper towel away with a gentle hand. It's not just spotted with blood, it's soaked. I'm a little light-headed, but the blood doesn't seem to bother Darcy at all. Her hands move like an expert as she examines me.

"Where is Carrie?" she whispers under her breath as she studies me. My face is electric where her fingers touch my skin. The air around us is charged with anticipation, like the calm before battle. Darcy pulls away. She grabs a bottle of pills from a nearby cupboard. "You allergic to any drugs?"

I shake my head no.

She offers me three red tablets. "For the pain."

I gulp them down without any water. She's halfway through opening a cupboard full of sparkling glasses. She raises an eyebrow and closes the door, then comes back and leans against the countertop.

It reminds me of her leaning against that guy's car, and I don't know why I do it, those keys obviously rattled something loose in my head, but I say, "So about that guy —"

"What guy?" Darcy's head tilts to the side. There's a little dimple in her forehead when she frowns.

"The one who was waiting for you when I dropped you off earlier?"

The dimple on her forehead deepens and her eyebrows knit together.

"He your boyfriend?"

I must be going insane because there's no way Art Bailey asks these kinds of questions. That's more of a Roman move.

I'm dreading her response. I distract myself by shoving paper towel up my bleeding nose. Darcy hesitates for an eternity.

"No, not anymore."

My eyes snap up to her.

"Your shirt is going to stain." She looks down at my white cotton T-shirt. Drops of red dot my chest, from collar to stomach. "Let me help you with that."

Darcy presses a cold dishcloth to my T-shirt. She scrubs away at the blood, but it just leaches into the white cotton, going from red splatter to pink splotches. She pushes up her glasses and swears under her breath.

Time seems to tilt and I can almost imagine the distant clash of metal on metal as swords crash against each other; horses whinny and a fair maiden pulls me from the battlefield. In a dim tent she bandages my wounds with practiced hands, candlelight betraying her sharp Cunning and Wisdom.

"I give up." Darcy throws the dishcloth on my lap.

I tug on the paper towel shoved in my nose. "Well, at least the bleeding stopped," I say, as I start to wipe blood away from my face.

Darcy groans and covers her face in her hands. "I can't believe I hurt you. I'm so sorry."

My fingers wrap around her wrists and I gently pull her

hands apart, until I can see her face. "It's okay. I'm fine."

What would Roman do? Sweep her into a passionate kiss, probably. I'm swiping my tongue over my teeth, praying that my mouth doesn't taste like blood before I realize that I plan on kissing her.

Darcy blinks at me. "Why are you so nice to me?"

The electricity is back. It hums in my ear: *kiss her, kiss her*. My heart races and I think the blood loss is making my dizzy. This time, I lean in. Her fingers comb through my hair, barely generating any friction, then wrap around my neck. Her breath caresses my lips.

DARCY IRL

"Darcy!" Carrie yells. "Darcy, love. Are you all right?"

"Carrie, look! There's blood everywhere." Monica's voice is frantic from the entrance.

"Come on —" Art groans, as if being interrupted for a second time pains him more than the bloody nose.

I know we should jump apart. Or that I should get Carrie to take a look at Art's face. But I can't pull myself away from him. Not again.

In the end, my hesitation doesn't matter because Art musters the strength to slide away. He loosens my arms from around his neck and stands, the stool a buffer between us now.

Just in time too.

The Moms race into the kitchen, their attack readied, as if they expect someone to be holding me hostage. Carrie has a golf club. Monica has her phone, poised to dial 9-1-1. The whole thing would be hilarious if they didn't look so scared.

Blue and red police lights flash in my memory.

"I'm fine," I say as they burst into the kitchen.

"We're fine." I glance at Art. His chin is caked in drying blood. "Well, mostly fine."

Art snorts. Then he winces.

The Moms stare at us.

"Carrie." I point at her weapon. "The golf club."

She lowers the putter. Monica locks her phone. They share a look of profound confusion.

"What's going on here?" Monica tucks her phone in her pocket.

Art's eyes glint, and I wonder if he's more like his RPG character than I thought. His smile is private, a secret meant only for me.

I'm halfway through the swoon when I force myself to get a grip. I fix him with a withering cut-it-out look of my own. Red creeps up his neck, and he looks anywhere but at me. Back to his usual self.

"I was looking for my keys —" I pantomime the entire thing for Monica and Carrie.

"There was a lot of blood." I indicate the heap of crumpled, stained paper towels. "Do you think his nose is broken?"

Carrie rolls up her sleeves. "May I take a look?"

I'm surprised to watch her do almost the same things I did earlier. As she looks him over, she cleans away the blood with quick, expert hands. Monica pulls up another stool.

"So, Darcy," Monica says. Her eyebrows disappear into her purple bangs. "Aren't you going to introduce us to your friend?"

The word *friend* rolls off her tongue and confirms all my suspicions about her. She's most definitely a dragon. A protective, intelligent, cunning and curious dragon, set on making my life all the cringe.

I can't answer her. I'm thinking about how he leaned in and almost —

Art waves at Monica from behind Carrie. Even though he hates being the center of attention, he is rescuing me.

"We've met. The other night, well, the night with the police and everything." His dashing rescue attempt goes sideways, and he fumbles. I smirk.

Monica stares at him and her gemstone eyes narrow. Carrie takes a step back and looks at him again, this time as a mother instead of as a doctor.

"I don't think we were formally introduced that night. You're Art? The boy who took Darcy to the city?" Carrie asks. Her voice is unreadable, even with my wicked-high Perception skill.

It's a trap! If this were a dungeon, Art would have to roll to detect the hidden pit with spikes. My eyes widen, as I try to get his attention.

He sits up a little taller and looks Carrie in the eye. Standing, he would have four inches on her, but sitting they're almost the same height. "I am. Nice to meet you. Sorry about your carpet."

That was not what I was expecting.

The Moms look at one another; they're just as surprised as I am. Monica softens first and pats Carrie's shoulder. "It's our pleasure, Art. We've heard so much about you."

Carrie stretches her hands. "Well, the carpet will wash. Also, I'm happy to report that our daughter did not break your nose."

Monica offers him herbal tea.

"Thank you, but I really need to head home. My little sister will be wondering where I am."

"Well, that's very considerate. Hopefully we'll be seeing more of you, Art. You're welcome over anytime."

The Larocque-Evans women say goodbye to Art. The entire time, I strategize how to get a few more private moments with him. I can't decide if I want to apologize to him once more or continue with that almost-kiss. In the end, The Moms follow us to the front door. I rush him outside.

Halfway across the lawn, he spins around and waves. "Good night. See you tomorrow!"

The second after I lock the door behind him, The Moms launch into full-on interrogation mode. The surprise attack weakens my defenses, and before long I'm pouring out my guts to them.

Figuratively, not literally.

It's been too long since the three of us have had a good heart-to-heart. Even if we're only talking about a boy.

In the end, I tell them almost everything. I leave out any kissing stuff. Mostly because there was no kissing.

But I do tell them about the trip to the city, with all the details this time. They're not pleased about us skipping school, but they squeal when I tell them about holding hands with Art on the drive back.

I chew on the inside of my lip, sigh, then decide to come clean about the note at school too. As expected, they swing between worry and outrage. Monica insists on going to the principal as soon as possible, Carrie nodding along. I beg them to let me handle things my way; I even explain that I have new friends and we're planning on starting up a QSA. When that doesn't seem to distract them, I casually mention Art's Fairytree. Then they're all sweet smiles and fangirl-level excitement again. They are both definitely Team Art.

I don't mention James, or my almost breakup, and they don't ask.

It's past midnight when Carrie finally puts her foot down. "I'm on call tomorrow at the hospital and I have a long day at the clinic. Time for bed." She pauses. "I'm so proud of you, Darcy."

I smile at her. "I love you, too."

Monica hugs me, then shepherds me to my room. "Good night, sweetheart."

Tears prick the corners of my eyes, as the memory of Art's voice whispers in the back of my mind. *I didn't want to be known as the kid with the dead mom. It was easier to just forget.*

I'm so selfish.

My phone rings, and I grab it, half expecting to see Art's name on the caller ID. There are five missed calls.

The caller is James. I should just ignore him, it's so late, but then I think about Art and how I lied earlier. Maybe I can actually do this dreaded deed over the phone.

"Babe?" James says, his voice thick with emotion.

"James —" I whisper. The pause lasts so long that I have to say something more. "We need to talk."

James sucks in a deep breath. "Listen. Before you say anything, I just —"

His voice is shaking. That's when I realize he's been crying.

"I just want you to know that you mean the world to me. I love you. I'm sorry for everything. I know you hate me and I don't blame you. But, Darcy, if you give me another chance, I'll do better. I can be what you want me to be."

I throw a pillow across the room. How dare he! He has no right to profess his love. I open my mouth to tell him that he can go to hell, but his next words force me to stop.

"I couldn't live without you, Darcy. If I lost you, I'd die."

His voice is dangerous. I sink onto my mattress and realize I believe him; he would hurt himself to keep me from leaving him.

How am I supposed to respond to that?

My chest tightens as I listen to him go on and on about love. He keeps talking about how he'll do better. Someone else's voice, a voice I don't recognize, tells him I forgive him.

We fall asleep talking on the phone. James whispers sweet promises in my ear, and I try to sort through this mess. My phone must have died, because in the morning, the alarm doesn't go off. I wake up with a jolt and that sick feeling after sleeping too long.

I look at the phone. Black screen.

Monica is sitting at the island, a cup of tea in her hand, when I stumble into the kitchen.

"Why didn't you wake me up?"

She shrugs. "We had a late night, and I thought you could use the rest. Things have been a bit crazy lately."

If only she knew the whole story.

I glance at the clock on the stove. I completely missed first period. I wonder if Art texted me. My stomach tightens. I wonder if James texted me.

"I've got to get to school," I say. Monica raises an eyebrow and shakes her head with a bemused smile as I get ready in a rush.

She meets me at the door. "I'll drive you, baby. I have a meeting with Mr. Elliot anyways."

Any other morning that might alarm me, but this morning, I'm just trying to avoid thinking of James. His sharp smile and dark eyes. His broken voice.

I'm getting good at ignoring the feelings of guilt, especially after the events of the last couple days. It's simple: James isn't here right now, so don't think about him. I pretend my heart is a Mimic. On the outside, it looks like a heart, sounds like a heart and beats like a heart, but when I open it up, it's a dangerous monster. Better to leave the lid closed.

I get to school after the start of second period and don't see Art until lunchtime. He drops into the seat beside me. I try to look as if I haven't been scanning the crowd for his tall frame.

I go to open my mouth, unsure of what I'm going to say, but I gasp instead. Purple bruises cover Art's face like a mask. The splotchy skin shadows his eyes and creeps across the bridge of his nose. My hands fly to my mouth. The guilt that was slowly eating away at my edges now consumes me whole.

"Hi," he says with a shy smile. "What do you think of my battle scars? I got into a fight at the local watering hole with this Tavern Brawling shield maiden. That'll teach me."

"Oh, my god, Art!" People around us stare. I don't even care. "Your face looks so much worse than it did last night."

He looks down at his slice of pepperoni pizza. "Hey, you're not appreciating *Dungeons & Dragons* feat comment. I'm being funny."

"I am so sorry," I say overtop of what he's saying, and when he finishes I add, "About your nose, not the Tavern Brawler comment."

"You wound me, Darcy."

"Not funny."

The way his mouth curves into a private smile makes my heart hammer double time.

He nibbles a pizza crust. "A little funny."

I roll my eyes and I can't decide if I want to hit him again or kiss him. I need to figure out what to do about James.

"Hey, Darcy." Art runs a hand through his hair. "Would you like to go on a date?"

ART IRL

"Fee, fi, fo, fum," Alex caws. He scrambles and stomps on the bridge. Fallen leaves scatter around his boots.

My foot taps against the weathered wood. I crane my neck at every car that drives by. The next one might be her. Or not? What if this was a stupid idea?

I check my phone again. The last message is the series of directions I sent her. She hasn't texted me back.

> Adventurers wanted:

> Date Night, Fairytree Bridge. 6:00.

> Bring your sword or staff, costumes recommended.

I shove my phone back into my pocket and correct Alex. "That's giant speak. Not troll."

He stops. "You're a ray of sunshine today."

"Who invited you anyway?"

My best friend hunches over. He raises his arms and tickles the air with his fingers. "I'm just getting into character. You should be thanking me! I've got some serious talent."

"Yeah." I take in his outfit, red cap, denim vest and all. He's committed, I'll give him that. I mean, where did he even get that prosthetic nose from?

Alex pulls the pointy red cap off his head. "Hey, don't judge. You're the one who organized this whole live-action role-playing date. Don't blame me if she doesn't show up."

"She's coming." I crane my neck to look down the road again.

"That's what she said."

I'm about three seconds away from launching him off the bridge, when the sound of tires on gravel makes me look behind us at the little parking lot.

And there she is.

Darcy slides out of a silver car. She's wearing a pink wig. She clutches a smooth white mask to her chest. Behind her, Monica waves at me. Darcy whispers to her mother before closing the door.

She's not just beautiful, she's epic.

She ties the medico della peste mask onto the strap of her messenger bag, then pulls a staff out of the back of the car. She's wearing a long dress with a poufy skirt that bubbles out around her ankles. A linen apron hugs her curves, pulled tight around her waist.

She looks good with pink hair, exactly like Poppy IRL.

I look down at my hoodie and jeans. Between Darcy and Alex, I'm underdressed.

Darcy waves and smiles.

Behind me, Alex whispers, "Damn."

That shakes me out of my daze, and I remember how this is supposed to pan out. "Go away, idiot. You're supposed to be under the bridge, remember?"

My date giggles. I shoot one last desperate look at Alex. The words dry up inside me as I approach her, and I kick myself. Why is this so much harder than talking to her about Game?

Darcy tucks a piece of pink hair behind her ear. "Hi."

"So, you look —"

"Stupid?" she asks.

"What? No!"

She plays with the hem of her dress. Her mouth is set in an embarrassed half-smile, half-scowl. "I made it for a convention. My entire group in the city went as our characters that year."

I step closer. Then reach out and touch her elbow. I notice for the first time that she's not wearing her glasses. I thought her eyes were large before, but without those thick black frames, she has anime eyes.

I offer her an arm, and she tucks her hand in the crook of my elbow.

The tips of my ears burn. "You look amazing."

"Your text said to wear a costume, I assumed that you would be dressed as Roman too."

I check my Converse and jeans. Definitely not something a rogue would wear. Darcy, or rather Poppy's plague mask, bumps against my thigh. An idea strikes me like Inspiration.

"Give me a minute." I run back to my truck.

I rip through the cab and pull out my Hellfire Club T-shirt, the one Darcy bought me at Fantasyland Comics.

A couple years ago, Alex and I went through a whole ninja phase. I emerge from the truck with my face completely covered. I shove makeshift paper horns into the folds of a makeshift fukumen mask.

I return to her. "We're in this together."

She smiles, and I am suddenly very grateful for all the time I spent watching *Naruto* with Alex.

"So, how are we doing this?" she asks.

I reach into my pocket and my fingers close around a rolled-up piece of paper. I pull it out and read.

"Hark! Below lurks a villainous creature. Enter only those who dare to hunt it down!"

I read the scroll so fast that I have to gulp for air before I continue. "Fair Maiden, do you dare fight the repulsive, hideous, extremely annoying troll lurking beneath?"

"Hey!" Alex yells.

Darcy giggles. I look up from the parchment. She's staring at me.

Suddenly, everything feels too hot under my mask. I lose my spot and fumble with the script.

"Step aside, sir." Darcy raises her staff. "I have a troll to slay, a town to save and this cute rogue to woo."

Thank god the mask covers my cheeks. My face is so warm you could forge weapons with the heat. I step aside with a bow.

"Fee, fi, foe, fum!" Alex bellows.

Darcy slides down the small ravine and laughs. "I thought you were a troll, not a giant!"

"Screw it!" Alex lunges at her. She dodges him with ease, and he stumbles past.

"I shall slay you, fowl troll!" Darcy points her staff at him. She waves her fingers and speaks an incoherent incantation.

I hand her an oversized foam d20 that Michelle let me borrow. Darcy tosses it high in the air and rolls an eighteen.

Alex fakes his demise and crumbles to the ground. After a dramatic pause he opens one eye and peers at Darcy.

"I concede." He stands and brushes grass off his jeans. "By the way, you two need to stop troll-shaming. We're just misunderstood!"

This has Darcy laughing so hard that she has to plop herself down in the grass.

"I'm filing a complaint with my union," Alex adds, before he climbs up the slope. At the top he waves down to Darcy. "See you later, Poppy!"

Then, before he walks past to his bike, he winks at me. That's when I realize my mistake. I'm never going to hear the end of this. We'll be playing the twelfth edition of *D&D* in our senior home someday, and Alex will still be bragging about how he was the star of my first date.

Darcy's voice brings me back into the present. "Hello? Mr. NPC Quest-Giver Person?"

I lean over the side of the ravine. "You vanquished the troll, mighty hero! If you scale the side of this steep cliff, the town will reward you handsomely."

I offer her my hand, and she takes it. We engage in a little tug-of-war as I pull her up. She reaches the top and I yank too much. We stumble back as she collides into me.

Right. Physics. That's how reality works.

"Sorry, Art. I wasn't expecting the extra leverage."

"No worries." I let go of her. "I shouldn't have been so rough."

Her wig sits crooked now; her eyes bright. "This was the best first date ever."

I rub the back of my neck. "Yeah?"

"I mean —" She sweeps into a curtsy, her voice turning to Poppy's voice. "I've dispensed with the evil troll, good sir. I shall claim my reward now."

"Yeah, that's right. Your reward." I reach into my back pocket and pull out a sketch. "A portrait for the lady."

Darcy hesitates, then reaches out. I think she's reaching for my drawing — a sketch of Poppy — but instead, she pulls down the bottom of my mask. "I had something else in mind."

She leans in on her tiptoes and kisses me. Lightly.

At first I'm so shocked that I just stare at her dark eyelashes against her cheeks. Her lips brush mine like she's asking me to kiss her back.

Darcy pulls away. "I'm sorry! I shouldn't have done that!"

My arm shoots out and I circle her waist. I say the first thing that comes to mind, my voice quiet and hopeful, "Let me reroll that kiss. Please."

She squeezes her eyes shut. Her nose scrunches up in embarrassment. Then, she peeks an eye open and smiles up at me. The only reference material I have is from that one kiss at camp. So I try to remember every kiss I've ever seen in movies, television and video games. I think about all the comic-book kisses. Then, I go for it.

My free hand reaches up and I touch her cheek with my thumb. Her skin is soft, and she has a single freckle beside her right eye. I swallow and glance at her lips before I lean down.

The kiss is a Peter Parker, Mary Jane moment; a Han Solo, Princess Leia tribute; not even Aragorn and Arwen can do better. It's the most perfect kiss in the history of nerdy geek kisses ever.

I'm not hanging upside down, so I keep things simple.

That's when Darcy leans into me with her hands on my chest. I cradle her face between my palms and kiss her harder.

A rush swells through me. I feel light-headed. I stare down at her and I'm embarrassed by how much more I want.

"Wow," she says.

"That was —"

Her arms drape around my neck and she pulls me in for another kiss.

The Path

Roman didn't realize he'd passed the clinic until Poppy's hand shot forward and tugged on his sleeve. Her fingers grazed his wrist for the briefest moment and Roman's entire body seized. He halted.

On the walk into the city, Poppy had explained what she could about the Path and how she'd become involved with the secret organization.

"Penn found me," she had whispered to Roman as they walked. "He was badly injured after a run-in with some noble's guards and stumbled into my clinic. He could barely breathe, but he had this young woman with him. She was pregnant and about to give birth. Penn insisted I deliver the baby before even allowing me to look at his wounds.

"After that, he just kept showing up, and every time he came to the clinic, he brought someone sick or scared or malnourished. Some were branded as heretics, some weren't. I'd treat them and I'd never see them again. It wasn't until much later that he brought Beckett with him. They asked if

I would join them and offer sanctuary to those fleeing the Baron's holy war. I agreed."

"Amazing," Roman had said, hanging on her every word.

"Penn sent word yesterday. He insisted that I hire additional protection for the clinic and told me where I might find you. It wasn't easy, I've searched every tavern in the Ditch for the last two days."

Roman couldn't bring himself to admit that he'd spent the days following Beckett's execution in hiding. The drinking had only begun when he'd realized he couldn't outrun his guilt. Now, with each step, shame sobered him.

"We're here," Poppy said. Her breath tickled his lips, and he realized just how close they were standing, his head bent down toward her upturned face. When had he moved?

Moira cleared her throat, and Roman's gaze shot to her. She hid her smile by pointing to the clinic door. "It's unusual to see marks belonging to the Old Gods on display. Deyja, if I'm not mistaken, right? And her lover, the Twisting One? What's his name again?"

The clinic door looked like all the doors in this part of the city. This district was full of doors with chipped paint and splintered wood, except this door had a small moth — the symbol of Deyja, the goddess of death, life and renewal — carved into the worn wood. A snake wrapped around the moth, chasing its own serpentine tail. The symbols were so small, so faded, that a random passerby would miss them altogether.

Poppy stepped back, then fished a set of keys from her skirt. When she turned away from Roman, he felt the absence of her attention keenly. He wanted to fold Poppy up in his arms and inhale her. What was happening to him?

"Aader, the King of the Underworld, ruler of rivers and roads," Poppy said. The lock slid open with a soft click.

"Deyja's Path," Roman said.

"The Path leads to death?" Moira leaned closer to examine the carving. "Or to freedom?"

"Sometimes to both," Poppy said, nodding. "You will soon learn, this is no ordinary clinic. Come."

Except, on the inside, the room looked exactly like an ordinary clinic. Empty cots crowded the edges of the small room, some with unmade linens, but most sat untouched. An armoire rested along the farthest wall, stocked with healing herbs, poultices and medicines. When Roman stepped over the threshold, his nose twitched with the heavy scent of iron and salt. *Blood and sweat*, he thought.

"This way." Poppy ushered them into a back room.

Roman's first instinct told him to assess the situation. He glanced around the room, his eyes drawn to a large rug that covered most of the floor. With confident strides, he walked over and flipped up a corner of the rug. Nothing. No trap door, no secret passage.

Poppy pressed a hand to her mouth but not before an amused laugh escaped her bowed lips. Aware of everyone's eyes on him, especially Poppy's, Roman rubbed the back of his neck as heat flickered across his skin. He dared a glance at the hedgewitch, but she was all good humor and kindness. Soon, he couldn't help but laugh too.

"Over here," she said between giggles, and motioned to a small altar tucked into the corner.

Candles burned around a basin of water. Poppy fished a coin from the purse tied to her waist, kissed the metal, then flicked it into the water. As soon as the silver piece sank to the bottom of the small pool, stones began to shift. The altar descended to reveal a secret set of stairs twisting down into the ground.

Poppy lifted her skirt with one hand, and with the other, she found Roman and guided him down the spiral staircase.

As they reached the bottom, his breath hitched in his chest. It was as though she had transported him between worlds.

Braziers, torches, tapered candles and all manner of light sources extended down the long hallway before them. People hurried from one room to the next, carrying blankets and bowls of food. From down the corridor, Roman heard rowdy laughter.

Poppy dropped his hand, and he felt the loss of her touch in his bones. She took Roman and his friends on a tour through the labyrinth of chambers that extended much farther than he would have expected. There was a mess hall, an infirmary and finally, Poppy's own workshop.

Roman went to find a warm meal, before his boots carried him back toward the hedgewitch.

From his vantage point by the open door, he leaned against the doorframe and watched her work. She was either very good at pretending he wasn't there, or completely oblivious to his presence, and Roman wasn't sure he liked either option.

On one hand, he didn't want to be invisible to her; quite the opposite, actually. If she'd listen, if she'd ask him, he was certain he'd crack himself open and share all he was with her.

On the other hand, the idea of her being unaware enough for someone to sneak up on her sent a chilly tingle down his spine. In that moment, he knew that he'd do anything to protect her. Anything.

Absorbed by her work, Poppy hummed a familiar drinking

song and picked up a bowl. She began to turn around. Not wanting to frighten her, he knocked against the doorframe by way of announcing his presence.

It was no use.

Poppy shrieked. The mortar and pestle she'd been using fell to the earthen floor with a dull thud. Pink flower petals spilled across the ground. She glanced at Roman, color high in her cheeks, then crouched to her knees without a word.

In two long strides, Roman crossed the room and knelt beside her. He scooped up a handful of petals and deposited them into Poppy's bowl.

She stood. "Thank you."

As Roman followed her to standing, he noticed something over her shoulder: the familiar, dangerous Hebenon plants littered across her worktable.

"What are you doing with those?"

Poppy bit her lip. "I study them," she said.

Intrigued, Roman stepped around her and leaned down to examine the flowers. Most were dried in bundles, but some were fresh. He wanted to ask how she'd gotten them but was afraid she'd say that she went to forage them herself. Roman knew how dangerous the forests were. Then again, he suspected she knew that as well.

Poppy set down the bowl of petals on the table, her arm close enough to brush against him.

"Did you know that Hebenon seeds are mind-altering? They have a hypnotic effect when crushed into a powder. And did you know that the petals can be used as an antidote, instead of a poison? In the right dosage, of course."

Her words tripped over themselves as she became excited. Roman smiled, lifting a blossom from the table. "Is that so?"

"Yes." She twisted the stone pestle in her hand, and the petals turned to dust. "Imagine all the good we could do, all the people we could help, if we didn't fear the river?"

Roman continued to study the Hebenon flower in his hand. "What if there's no good in the plant? What if all the flower does is hurt?"

The pestle stopped grinding. "I know that's not true."

"You're an idealist," he said, his voice sad. Poppy looked up at him with wide, curious eyes. Roman leaned closer. Dragging his blackened nails behind her ear, he tucked the Hebenon blossom there. The pink matched her hair, just as he knew it would, and created the impression of flowers sprouting from her braids. "That's beautiful."

Poppy leaned forward, her eyelids drooping closed, her mouth turned toward his. He snaked his arms around her waist and pulled her even closer.

Then a shadow darkened the door.

DARCY IRL

My eyes fly open, as I realize how close Art and I have leaned toward one another. His arm rests around the back of my chair, his face only inches from mine. Were we about to kiss? In front of the entire table?

No one says anything. I ease back into my chair, the shifting of my body setting Art free from the fantasy. Once we pull away, the entire group descends on us like a flock of hungry harpies.

"Are you two a couple now?"

"That was the best role-playing I've ever seen."

"They weren't role-playing."

"What was that?"

"Oh, to be young!"

The voices blur together. I try to follow who says what, but the onslaught happens so fierce and fast, I have no reaction time. Overwhelmed by the chaos we've unleashed, I look to Art. He offers me a tentative, half-smile, but then a wolf whistle cuts through the flurry of curiosity, and Art jumps so much that he hits his knee on the table. I wince.

He bends forward and covers his face. "Is it that obvious?"

Michelle reaches across her GM screen to pat his elbow. "It was obvious even before Darcy came to Game."

That grabs my attention. "He mentioned me?"

Alex and Robert snicker. Michelle gives them a withering look. "He was encouraged to tell us about the girl he was spending so much time with, but we're not going to say more than that."

"What? You have to tell me now! What did he say?"

"You'll have to ask your boyfriend that," Alex pipes up.

I stare at Art. He lifts a shoulder in the smallest of ways, his face full of hope. I like the way he's looking at me, but the word *boyfriend* echoes an alarm.

What do I do about James?

We all agree to finish up for the night. Art ushers me to the truck before anyone else can ask embarrassing questions. Robert will take Alex home. But when we're alone, we don't breathe a word to one another.

Am I the type of person who can flirt with Art while still technically being in a relationship?

I don't even want to be in that relationship, but every time I think about trying to break up with James again, I panic.

I feel as though there's a rule lawyer sitting on my shoulder or something, and they constantly remind me that James is still technically my boyfriend. Even so, I've been flirting with Art this entire time.

Normal people get little angels and devils; I get *D&D* player types?

Art holds my hand as we walk to my front door. I can't remember the last time James did anything that sweet. Out of nowhere, he asks, "Do you think we're moving too fast?"

Probably, I think. But instead I deflect with a question of my own. "Do you?"

"No," he says right away, then pauses. "Maybe? I don't know. I've never done this sort of thing before.

"I mean —" He motions between us. "We've only known each other for a month. Is it normal to feel this way about someone I just met?"

I lean in. "And how do you feel about me?"

He rests his forehead against mine. "Isn't it obvious?"

My heart races and I move closer to kiss him, but I miss because he pulls back.

"I know what I feel," Art says, "but what if you find out how boring I am? Or there's something about me that you don't like once we've known each other longer? What if —"

"What if there's something you don't like about me?"

"What? No! That's just, that's not what I mean."

The night feels quiet but with a high enough Perception, I hear vehicles on the highway in the distance.

"Okay," I say. "So, ask me anything."

"What?"

"Ask me any question you want, and I promise to answer honestly."

"I don't know what to ask."

"Anything, don't overthink it, just ask. Ask me about my favorite color."

He exhales. "Okay. Who is your favorite superhero?"

"Starfire, from the old *Teen Titans.* You?"

"Aquaman, from the comics."

I snort. "That's no one's favorite, Art."

"See, this is what I mean. What if the fact that I like Aquaman drives you away?"

"Not possible." I shake my head with a smile and take his hand in mine. "All right, my turn. What do you like about me?"

"Everything?"

I fold my arms. "That's not a real answer."

His entire face turns pink, and his eyes slide to the side. "You have a pretty nose," he whispers in the direction of Mr. Watkins's lawn.

"My nose?" I blink, wondering if I heard him. His ears turn red in confirmation, and I snicker. "You think I have a pretty nose?"

Art wipes a hand down his face, then rubs the back of his neck. Still unable to look at me, he groans as if answering my question is a new form of medieval torture. "It sounds so dumb when I say it out loud."

I slide my hands up his chest, and that gets his attention. He looks back at me with a sheepish smile, then I lace my fingers together around the back of his neck.

"No," I say. "Tell me more. I like hearing you confess."

"I think —" He shakes his head with a self-deprecating chuckle. "I think you terrified me when we first met."

I raise an eyebrow. "For real?"

"I mean, I was a nervous mess, and you were this edgy city girl. Then you started talking about *D&D*, and I knew you were a huge dork, like me."

"Hey!" I smack his shoulder.

He loops his arms around my waist. "I like the way you talk nerdy to me."

Now it's my turn to groan. "Is that a line? That better not be a line."

"But mostly, I admire your courage. You're brave in ways that I could never be. Moving here, making new friends,

joining our game, the QSA, and you make it all look easy."
He lets that sink in, then kisses my temple. My stomach flips,
and I tighten my grip behind his neck to pull him closer. He
leans in, and I hold my breath. Mouth hovering over mine,
he whispers, "Your turn."

Art pulls away. My pulse roars in my ears. I shoot a withering glare up at him. He beams back, his crooked smile looking
almost smug. Fair is fair, I guess.

A million things come to mind. How tall he is, the way his
hair defies gravity, his writing and drawing, our mutual love
of Game. But one thing stands out more than anything else.

"I like how gentle you are."

"Gentle," he echoes.

"You're kind," I say, forcing myself to hold his gaze. He
needs to hear this; I need him to hear me. "And you make
me feel safe."

That teasing expression melts from his face. He smiles
with his whole body and pulls me so close that I lift onto my
tiptoes.

"Would you be my girlfriend, Darcy?"

ART IRL

The way Darcy smiled at me felt like the start of an adventure —
tentative, almost unsure at first, then quickly eager and excited.
She kissed me, her mouth mischievous on mine.

"Yes," she said.

We only got five more minutes before someone inside
Darcy's house turned on the porch light.

Now, I'm at home and in bed, but I can't sleep like this.
I stare at the ceiling.

"Girlfriend." I test the word in the dark. *Girlfriend* feels
unreal, made-up; a fake word from some fantasy language
that I've never learned.

"She likes how gentle I am." I laugh to myself. "I have a
girlfriend."

Real life strikes, and I sit up. A stack of character sheets
and notebooks topple from the edge of my bed. They slide off
in slow motion, then land with a distant thud.

I'm going to have to tell Dad.

...

"I don't understand," Darcy says. She laces her fingers through mine. "Why do you have to tell him?"

We're parked outside her house after school. Most of the trees on this street have already lost their leaves and the weather is cold enough to want the truck heater. We could go talk inside, but Monica is home. Besides, the privacy of the truck is nice.

"I just have to. It would be so much worse if he found out from someone in town."

Darcy makes a face. "So just tell him."

"Things aren't that easy, Darcy. He's — well, we've never been that close."

"And?"

"I don't even know how to talk to him about something like this."

Darcy smiles, and suddenly I'm distracted. I've kissed that mouth.

"Just keep it simple," she says. "Tell him, 'Dad, I'm running away with the girl of my dreams! We're having a baby and joining the circus!'"

I snort. "You obviously haven't met my father."

Darcy twirls her finger around a red curl in the middle of my forehead. She styles the hair like I'm Clark Kent. "Just tell him you have a girlfriend, babe."

I'm about to tell her that nothing with my Dad is that simple, but I come to an abrupt halt. "Babe?"

Darcy's eyes flick to the side. She looks out the front window, her expression distant, almost stony. "Let's pretend I didn't say that."

"Wait, are you embarrassed?" I ask. "Because of a nickname?"

She crinkles her nose, and her glasses slide down. "Let me out here, I can't look at you anymore."

I laugh until my sides ache. Embarrassed Darcy might be my favorite. When I've regained control of myself, I reach out and take her hand. "I don't hate it, my most radiant goddess."

She buries her face in her hands.

"Too much? What about sweetums?"

"Art, focus! What are you going to say to your dad? About us?"

"He'll be home tomorrow morning," I say with a shrug. "Maybe I can just text him? Or leave him a note on the kitchen counter?"

The sound of the garage door wakes me up the next morning. My eyes are barely open, but my pulse is already hammering away in my chest. I jump out of bed, race downstairs and into the garage, forgetting that I'm wearing my crumpled Hellfire Club T-shirt.

Dad doesn't see me right away. Half his face is obscured by his hand, as he talks on his cell phone. He says something about "Obviously you need to do a corporate search before registering the judgment."

Whatever that means.

"Look, I just got home, McCoy. I'll speak with you later." He hangs up on one of his many associates. I think McCoy works from the Toronto office? Maybe a junior lawyer?

Dad stuffs his cell into the pocket of his suit jacket

before he swings a briefcase over his shoulder. The bag is black leather and embossed with his initials, *M. A. B.* Marcus Arthur Bailey. I think I prefer Darcy's messenger bag. I smile, as I try to imagine her buttons and pins on Dad's briefcase.

"You're up early." He starts walking over to me but halts on the other side of the doorframe. "What are you wearing?"

I look down and curse myself, but before I answer, he passes by me.

"It's from a TV show," I say, following him inside.

He leaves his briefcase in the foyer, then marches into the kitchen, looking around at the immaculate countertops.

Heaven help us if Dad came home and the house was messy.

"Where is your sister?"

"She went to a friend's house last night for a sleepover," I explain. "It wasn't a school night so I thought it was fine."

He unfastens a cuff link. "Did she finish her homework?"

I don't really have time to respond because he keeps going.

"She's not supposed to go over to her friends' houses unless all her homework is done, Arthur. You know that."

Dad has this special talent of talking at me, not to me. He's already going through the cupboards and pulling out coffee supplies — beans, grinder, French press — all while talking at me like I'm some low-level NPC in my own kitchen.

I mean, I understand, sort of. I've always been aware of how much Dawn and I look like our mother. I think maybe Dad's always been aware of that too. We're tall like him, but that's where the resemblance stops. The hair, the freckles, especially my blue eyes, all look like the folded-up picture of Mom tucked between the pages of Dad's Bible.

"Do you want some coffee?"

I hesitate. Coffee is good. Coffee is a start.

I sit down at the breakfast table. "Yeah, thanks."

The buzz of the coffee grinder stops and is immediately followed by the warm, wafting scent of Colombian dark roast. I inhale.

"So, Dad," I begin. "There's this girl —"

The door swings to the side, and I suck in a sharp breath.

Darcy's standing on our front step. Her dark hair cascades around her face in gentle waves, and her nose is tucked into a giant plaid scarf.

She peeks up. "Hi."

"Hi."

She steps through the doorway and takes in her surroundings: the glass chandelier in our vaulted entrance with the sterile walls painted a soft gray. I shift my weight, unsure what to say.

I take her coat. "So, welcome to my house."

"This is —"

"Expensive?" I hang her jacket in the closet alongside a row of my dad's black wool outerwear.

Darcy arches an eyebrow. "I was going to say, 'not what I imagined,' actually. It looks like a show home!"

The house didn't always look this way. I remember crayon artwork on the fridge and family pictures, but after Mom died, everything changed. Now, we have a cleaner who comes twice a week and a dad who can't stand being here but is too scared to move on.

Dawn walks straight into Darcy and wraps her in a warm

hug. "I'm so glad you're here! After supper, I'll show you photos of Art as a baby."

"Don't even think about it or I'll tell Dad about your last math test."

Dawn's face sours as she releases Darcy.

"Arthur," Dad calls from the kitchen. "Don't be rude. Bring Darcy inside."

I don't point out that we're already inside because he really means bring her into the kitchen. I glance at Darcy one more time before leading her toward my father.

Dad straightens his tie, then holds out his hand like he's meeting a new client, rather than my girlfriend. "You must be Darcy."

"That's me."

It's as if she's changed all of her character stats and given herself a plus-ten to Charisma. She's not standoffish or thorny; she's engaging and charming. As Dad serves steak, regaling us with his latest contract exploits, Darcy laughs at all of his jokes.

If life were an RPG, she'd be killing this side quest. Succeeding on every roll of the dice.

But right now, real life is better. Better than any book, or movie, or video game. Better than playing in an RPG. Everything is perfect; the four of us sitting around a dining room table, eating supper, and laughing about Dad's travel stories and talking about school. We almost seem, well, normal.

I nudge Darcy's foot with my own. She glances down, then smiles back up at me.

"So, Darcy, what do your parents do for a living?" Dad asks.

"Well, one is a hair stylist-slash-stay-at-home mom, and the other is a doctor." Darcy spears a few pieces of asparagus with her fork.

"Did your father just start at the clinic? I thought they gave that job to a female doctor."

"They did." Darcy's voice is honest and sincere.

That's when I realize I never told Dad about Darcy's moms. The room tilts. I see the cracks in my perfect little fantasy.

Dad's dark eyebrows, brushed with several strands of gray and white, scrunch together. "You just said your mother was a stay-at-home hairdresser?"

"That's right." Darcy's eyes shift to me. I focus on my plate. Darcy looks back to Dad, and an uneasy silence settles in around us.

"I feel like I missed something," he says, his voice clipped.

"Art? He doesn't know?" Darcy's eyes grow wide behind her glasses, as if she's begging me to explain. "You didn't tell him?"

I should have. But she's right. I didn't.

"Tell me what?"

I open my mouth to explain when Dawn cuts me off.

"Dad, did you see my last math test? I think I'm going to need a tutor."

Dad dismisses my sister with one glance. Dawn's mouth snaps shut.

"What do you need to tell me, Arthur?"

My body tenses. I want to be brave enough to tell him, but with my fantasies crumbling around me, I can't. I freeze.

Darcy presses her foot against mine, when I look up, she's smiling at me as if to tell me that everything's okay. She doesn't know Dad like I do, but before I can stop her, she charges forward. "Nothing bad, Mr. Bailey. Just that I have two mothers, and you're correct, one of my moms is the new doctor."

"Really?"

"They've been together for nineteen y —" Darcy begins.

Dad ignores her and stares at me in disbelief. "And you're all right with that?"

Darcy's mouth snaps shut.

"I don't see what the big deal is," Dawn answers for me again.

"Big deal?" Dad struggles to keep his voice diplomatic. "Have you completely forgotten how we raised you?"

"Dad!" Dawn begs. "You can't say that."

I set down my utensils. "What?"

"I think I should leave. This is —" Darcy's voice catches on a shaky exhale, uncertain in a way that isn't like her. She tilts her chin toward me, her expression carefully neutral, but beneath the table I see the way her hands tighten in her lap. That's when I realize how much she's holding back. For my sake.

If she were angry, if she rolled for Initiative and entered into combat ready to defend herself, that would be something I could handle, but seeing her tiptoe around my Dad to protect me feels wrong.

The guilt stops me from interrupting her, and she moves to stand. "This is obviously a family matter. I should go."

"Art," Dawn says under her breath. "Do something."

I collect myself and reach for Darcy's hand. "You don't have to leave," I say, then turn to Dad. "You should at least meet Darcy's moms. Please, Dad? For me."

His chair scrapes across the hardwood floor. He shakes his head. "This would have never happened if your mother was still alive. Arthur, I can't believe you thought I would allow this."

I don't fully realize what he's said until Dawn sniffles beside me. Stunned, I look from my little sister to my new girlfriend, then back at Dad. "What did you just say?"

His eyes narrow at Darcy. "You were right. It's time for you to leave."

I offer to drive Darcy home, but she says nothing to me the entire rest of the time we're inside the house.

Outside, she explodes.

"Your dad is a homophobe!" Her feet pound against the sidewalk as she rushes away from our home. "Oh, my god, he hates me! Did you hear him? He sounds like a cartoon supervillain!"

I follow her. Cold stings my bare arms; tears prick my eyes. She's not wrong. The worry lines in Darcy's forehead crease even more.

"Art, are you okay?"

"I'm sorry." I wipe my eyes with a wrist. "I'll talk to him and explain. He'll understand. Everything will be fine, I promise. Text me when you get home?"

Everything isn't fine though.

She leaves. I go back inside and before the door closes behind me, Dad's voice rings out like a royal proclamation. Or a supervillain.

"You are never to see that girl again!"

The Baron

An open letter lay on the table where Poppy sat reading. Roman knew from the expensive parchment, embossed with the Sangray crest, who had inked the words.

He leaned over her shoulder and read, while the rest of his friends waited across the table. Bile coated the inside of Roman's throat, as he glanced over his father's neat, controlled handwriting. His eyes tripped over fragments of the letter.

The Most Honorable Baron Sangray Blackwood. To Poppy le Fey ... hereby summoned ... present yourself at Sangray Castle by midday, three days hence ... Do not disappoint your lord ...

"It's a summons." Roman's voice cracked. This was bad. Very bad.

"How —" Poppy's question faded from her lips as she stared out at the refugees and runaways crowding the mess hall. "He knows where I am. Oh, gods, what if he knows about the Path? What if we led him here?"

Roman flinched. The desperation in her voice scared him; or rather, the idea of her being held prisoner by his father

VICTORIA KOOPS

scared him. He seized the letter from the table and crushed it in his fist, resolve hardening in his chest. He pushed the letter into his pocket and sank to a knee. He'd give anything, anything at all, to keep Poppy from his father.

Roman gripped her hands. He begged her with his eyes, then with words. "Please don't go. This is a trap, it must be."

Poppy leaned forward, pressing her forehead to his. Her voice was low. "I have to. If I don't, he'll come here."

"Then run. Take everyone and leave the city."

Roman hadn't expected the kiss. The soft press of her lips on his completely disarmed him. Poppy pulled back, melancholy etched into her sweetheart face. He wanted to reach forward and smooth the lines of worry between her eyebrows, but the determination in her gaze pinned him in his place.

"I won't. Not when I can buy them time to escape."

"It may be that he's summoning you for another purpose," Moira said. She meant it as kindness, but her optimism curdled Roman's insides.

Roman's head snapped toward his friends. They didn't know his father, not like Roman did. "And what if he kills her on the spot? Or worse, forces her to reveal everything she knows about the Path?"

Moira's expression was soft, understanding. "Then we'll need a plan."

"Preferably one that doesn't involve torture," Kastor added, undoing any sense of comfort Moira had given Roman. "Nasty business."

Roman looked at Poppy and found that she was nodding so vigorously that the Hebenon flower he'd tucked behind her ear had slipped to the ground. She bent her head toward his friends, and they began the preparations.

Roman barely heard the planning, his thoughts far away. By the time they agreed on a course of action — a plan involving disguises and infiltration — he'd already made up his mind. He was the only one who could protect the Path, his friends and Poppy. He was going home.

A strange nostalgia tightened Roman's chest, as he snuck down the hallways of Sangray Castle. This place — the beating of patrol boots on the battlements, the heavy tapestries along the walls and the smell of damp rocks — this was all he'd known growing up. Once, this was all he had wanted — a seat beside his father. A chance to prove himself.

Then he'd met Matilda. She was the eldest daughter of the wealthiest merchant in the city. Fair and graceful, she had all the makings of a future baroness. And she'd wept when her father introduced Roman as her future husband. Where he'd stood, she'd only seen a monster, and when his father had told Roman to ignore her — that her desire was inconsequential to their goals — something had broken inside him. Not his heart — he hadn't loved poor Matilda — but his blind obedience.

By that point, he'd witnessed so much cruelty. His forced betrothal had only been the final straw. He'd left that night.

Now, the door to his father's personal study opened without protest. Roman rolled his shoulders back. He could sneak in, slip a knife between his father's ribs and be done with it, but he wouldn't. Secretly, a small piece of him wanted to see the look of surprise on his father's face.

The Most Honorable Lord Dietrich Sangray of Blackwood

stood beside the large stone fireplace, his back to Roman. His broad shoulders curled toward the flames, head bent low, as though he could see something in the embers. Not a thread or hair stood out of place. His clothes, a deep green over-tunic and fur-lined robe, looked new. Even with his back turned to Roman, his father commanded the space.

"Well —" his father said into the fire. "Have you come back to your senses, then, boy?"

Roman closed the door behind him wordlessly. His father rounded on him. Instinct forced Roman to take the smallest step backward, but nothing escaped his father's careful scrutiny.

An oily smile slid across the man's mouth. "Still twitchy, I see."

Heat burned through Roman's face. He tried to sound confident as he lifted his chin and spoke. "I'm not the same as when we last met, my lord father. Don't make the mistake of underestimating me."

His father tilted his head to the side, critical gaze assessing Roman. "I can see that. You've the look of someone capable now."

And by capable, he meant deadly, Roman knew. His father motioned toward an armchair, one of a pair resting by the fireplace, his gesture a wordless command.

Without thinking, Roman marched across the room. He waited until his father eased into a chair first, before planting himself in the matching upholstered fabric.

His father uncorked a glass decanter and poured himself a healthy measure of clear spirits. He knocked the alcohol back, poured two more, then handed one of the glasses across to Roman.

Roman wouldn't lose himself in the drink. If he was going to survive this evening, he'd need all his faculties, but still, he took the offering and swirled the spirit in the glass.

When his father's eyes rested on him without remark, Roman spoke as if compelled. "Father, I've come with a bargain," he said. Still his father remained silent. "I will return and do as you wish. I'll fulfill my duty, marry whichever lady you put in front of me — and I vow that you will not die by my hand."

A bark of laughter erupted from his father, as he tossed his head back. "How generous!"

Roman's black fingers gripped the polished wooden armrest. He pressed his lips together and waited for his father to stop laughing.

Finally, his father set down his drink and leaned forward. "What do you want in return? Why are you really here?"

Roman had practiced this on his way here. With a steadiness he didn't feel, he produced the crumpled letter. "Poppy le Fey, the healer. She and her work are under my protection. I want your word that no harm will come to her or her patients."

"Patients," his father scoffed.

Roman's jaw tightened. He hadn't even made the worst of his demands.

His father sobered. "Fine. I will leave your playthings alone, son. You return, do as I command, and I will allow the Path, and your Lady le Fey, to continue operations. Do we have an agreement?"

Roman stared at his father's outstretched hand, then braced himself as he looked up at the intense blue eyes fixed on him. "There's one more thing. You will leave Durgeon's

Keep, and your holdings, to me. I want you to leave the Barony and never return."

True shock, an expression Roman had never seen his father wear, widened his familiar eyes and dropped his jaw.

Swallowing, Roman pressed on before his father could collect his wits. "Return to the capital, to the High Court, take all the earthly possessions you desire, and dazzle the nobles with epic tales of your adventures. Petition the king for more titles, land on the other side of the mountains, steal and swindle your way to a dukedom for all I care, but never return to the Barony of Blackwood or the Durgeon Forest again."

Glass shattered against the fireplace mantel. Shards exploded toward them both. Roman turned his head, but not fast enough. A cut stung across his cheekbone.

When he opened his eyes, his father's shoulders heaved. "You dare! You treasonous bastard. Guards! Guards!"

DARCY IRL

I tuck my toes under Art's thigh, as I draw a heart on the side of a manila folder. The file contains all of our storytelling project notes. Art's drawings are more skillful than mine, but my heart has our initials inside, so that's something. The smell of fresh paint is thick in the air despite the open window. Without our family photos hanging on the bare walls, the house still feels naked, but slowly, everything is coming together.

Behind us, Monica's home studio is taking shape too. There's a new sink with a shelf of assorted hair products. Right now, that little room is open to the rest of the basement, but a pair of French doors leans against the wall. Once those doors go up, Monica will be ready to take on new clients.

Remembering what happened with Carrie's patients at the clinic, I wonder how long it will take for Monica to book clients. Or if anyone will call to book an appointment at all.

My flash of anger turns into a shiver, as cool fall air sneaks in through the open window. I abandon the file folder on the couch and snuggle into the length of Art's torso.

"It's kinda fun being forbidden lovers." I circle my arms around his neck and rest my chin on his shoulder.

"You're not taking this seriously."

I sigh and sit up. "Are you talking about our homework?" My eyes flick to the cue cards we've been working on for our presentation. "Or your dad?"

Art runs a hand through his hair. "Both? I don't know."

I grab my laptop. A stack of loose-leaf pages shifts: our presentation. I have a digital copy but Art likes to work with the physical. He doodles on the papers too. Beside his notes are elaborate scenes of towers and war banners. On one page he's drawn a dragon's tail.

"Does he know where you are now?"

Art braces his elbows on his own knees. "I told him I was doing homework with a friend."

"Well, you're not lying. Not really. I mean, you are doing homework with a friend. Besides, didn't you say he was leaving for Vancouver in a few days?"

"That's not the point. He probably thinks I'm over at Alex's place."

He flops backwards into the soft cushions and stares at the stucco ceiling.

I consider the slope of his neck at this angle. His Adam's apple bobs up and down as he swallows his anxiety. I push my computer away and lean back with him. Looking up, I wonder why anyone would want their ceiling to have little white pimples. I take a deep breath. "Everything's okay. We'll be okay."

Art squeezes my hand. My insides melt.

"At least I have you," he whispers.

I don't mean to, but I think about James. He pops into

my head and the familiar guilt follows. I've been ignoring his texts and phone calls, but he's not taking the hint.

"Hey!" I cast out the thought of James with every spell slot I have available. "The others should be here soon!"

"My dad would kill me if he knew I was helping you with the QSA," he says, as he picks at imaginary fuzz on his jeans. "Maybe I should go. I mean, what can I really do to help?"

My entire body stills, disappointment tightening my muscles. Until now, I'd been willing to give Art the benefit of the doubt. Despite his father. But this? How am I supposed to ignore the homophobic undertones? The fantasy of us — star-crossed lovers and all — fractures, as my heart wilts.

"Are you kidding me?" I ask. I stand, unable to hold myself back. Anger starts to replace the disappointment, and venom creeps into my voice, potent enough to do poison damage. "You're going to bail? Because of your dad? Art, silence is still a stance."

He doesn't respond.

"Look," I exhale, teeth clenched. "It's about showing support, being an ally. I'm not sure I can be with someone who isn't willing to fight for what's right."

My mind wanders to James. That's different. We're talking about social justice, not teenage drama, after all.

Silence fills the void. I don't point out that Dawn is going to be here too, and she doesn't seem to mind their father finding out about our planning meeting.

Art stands and he might be leaving. Fine, I don't need him. I stare at Monica's new studio and my eyes sting.

Then, with a measured grace that would do any rogue proud, he pulls me close. I try to stop the tears, but he rests his head on top of mine and I cry into his T-shirt.

"Roman's the type of person who would stick his neck out to help you," he says. The tiniest hint of resentment colors his voice. "You're right. I'm sorry, I want to be an ally."

I cry, then laugh. Soon our foreheads are pressed together, his arms are around me, and my hands are on his chest.

"Are you kidding me? You are Roman. He wouldn't be anything without you."

Someone rings the doorbell. Grateful for the excuse, I bolt to my feet and cross to the staircase just in time to watch Monica answer the door.

"Hi, everyone!" Monica says, and I can tell just by the sound of her voice that she's smiling like an idiot. "Darcy and Art are downstairs. Come this way, don't worry about your shoes, we're painting so you can keep them on."

My mother leads Mack, Dawn and Wyatt downstairs.

I step aside to make space for everyone, and after a big hug from Dawn, everyone settles into a spot around our coffee table. Mack shrugs off a backpack and pulls out their laptop. Dawn flounces over to sit beside her brother, depositing a huge grocery bag full of snacks on the table.

"Rainbow couldn't come — she's working — but she gave me snacks to bring."

Wyatt reaches into the bag and pulls out a granola bar. "Nut free, vegan and organic. Where did you find these?" he asks with one dark eyebrow lifted in disbelief.

"Rainbow packed those for me." Dawn snatches the granola bar back. "There's chocolate and chips for you."

"And homemade dumplings," Mack says. They produce a glass container and press it to their chest. "Bless you, Mrs. Yee."

Once we're settled in, we start our research. Wyatt and Mack take turns explaining what happened the other times they attempted to start a QSA at the school.

At first, Mack was the only openly queer student, but it was only a few weeks into their grade-nine year before Wyatt approached Mack and came out. When the two of them asked the school about starting a QSA, they were told that there wasn't enough student interest. Apparently, the student handbook says that there needs to be at least four students signed up to run a club. It wasn't until this fall, when Rainbow and Dawn started high school, that they had four people, but when they asked again, they were told that they needed a staff supervisor.

"Who have you asked?" Art's cheeks are bright red, his eyes downcast. I blink at him, a wave of pride ballooning in my chest. He might not totally understand why the Queer-Straight Alliance is so important to me, but he's here and he's trying. Maybe we're not doomed star-crossed lovers after all.

"Madame Cosette, Mrs. Wilson and Mr. McLean."

Art looks up, smiling. "I think I know who we can ask."

We don't hold hands in school. Art is convinced that his father has spies, which is just too Evil Overlord for me. His dad might be a supervillain but is he the all-seeing-eye kind of evil? Really?

Lucky for us, we still have first-period English and the storytelling project as an excuse to be around each other without raising too much suspicion.

After class, Art and I pack away our papers and books with slow movements. We linger in an attempt to speak with Ms. Stacey alone.

Annoyingly, Hannah remains after class, and clutches a thick volume of paper, tied together with a yellow ribbon, to her chest. "I just want to make sure I'm meeting all the criteria."

Ms. Stacey eyes the short novel with a mixture of exasperation and amusement on her face. Hannah, oblivious, stares at Ms. Stacey with fervor.

"Hannah, I'm absolutely positive that you've met — nay, surpassed — the criteria for this assignment." Ms. Stacey chuckles. "Now, you better hurry, or you might be late for next period."

Hannah's eyes grow wide, and she grabs her things in seconds. Her, late to class? Never.

I smile at Hannah as she passes us. I'm trying this new thing. It's called being nice. "Hey, Hannah."

She stops. "Hi, Darcy?"

Hannah glances at Art, and her skeptical look melts into a sunny smile. Before sashaying away, she adds a perky, "Hi, Art!"

I glower at her back as she disappears from the room. So much for being nice.

Today, Ms. Stacey is wearing dinosaur earrings. Two mini triceratops swing around her neck as she looks from me to Art. It might be my imagination, but there's something conspiratorial in the way she looks between us. We're standing a perfectly respectable and inconspicuous distance from each other.

She smiles. "To what do I owe the pleasure?"

We drift closer to her desk.

"Is this about your group project? Because, unfortunately I am unable to assign new partners this close to the deadline. I already explained this to your father over the phone, Art. He seemed very put out."

This time I don't imagine anything, because she winks at Art, and I know that she knows. My face gets warm, and I'm surprised when Art doesn't even bat an eye. Instead, he lifts a hand and high-fives our teacher. High-fives!

"You're the best, Ms. Stacey."

"What can I say? I'm a sucker for a good star-crossed love story." She considers for a moment, then adds, "So long as this one ends better than Shakespeare."

Now Art is blushing too. He laughs and runs one hand through his hair.

"It, it's not about the project, Ms. Stacey."

"Then I repeat my previous question, to what do I owe the pleasure?"

Is the classroom smaller? Laminate tables and blue plastic chairs feel as though they're piling in around me.

"We wanted to talk to you about starting a school club."

"Go on."

Art squeezes my hand.

"Well —" I suck in too much air at once. "Our group of friends has been trying to start a Queer-Straight Alliance, and they've been given these excuses every time they try to organize something. And I'm sure you've heard that I have two mothers, but I'm also bisexual."

Ms. Stacey nods, no hesitation.

"And the other day I was called a dyke, so I thought —"

Ms. Stacey puts her hands on her hips. "That is unacceptable. Darcy, did you report that?"

I shake my head. At the time, reporting didn't seem like an option. I mean, what would I have said? That a stranger I didn't see and couldn't identify was bullying me?

"No," I say. "But I think my mom might have. Besides,

that's not the point. Obviously, this school needs a QSA. Thing is, we need a teacher supervisor to support the club."

She stills, considering me, and I'm worried she's going to say no. I prepare myself for the disappointment. Ms. Stacey sighs. "I'm so sorry, Darcy."

Here it comes: the rejection.

"I'm sorry that happened to you here." Her voice becomes more forceful as she continues to talk. "What an excellent idea. A Queer-Straight Alliance. I'm embarrassed that I never thought of starting one. I would love to help!"

Ms. Stacey's dinosaur earrings shiver with excitement.

We just won our first boss fight. I don't stop myself from the celebratory happy dance, as I jump up and down.

"You'll need to explain your plan to Principal Elliot too. I'll shoot him an email and tell him to expect you," Ms. Stacey says.

Art swings me around with a hug that would make Bearpuncher proud. When he sets me down, I'm almost breathless from laughing. "Thank you, Ms. Stacey."

"No, please don't thank me," she says. "I'm honored you trusted me enough to ask. Thank you. Both of you."

ART IRL

Darcy tosses her messenger bag onto the seat of my truck and bounces in after it with a huge smile slapped across her face.

"I've figured it out," she announces, her eyes wide and eager. I lean over to kiss her. Dad left for work this morning, and a weight has been lifted, if only for a couple days.

Darcy leans her rosy cheek into my lips, as she fumbles with her seat belt.

"What did you figure out?" I start the truck.

"Your Dad's ability scores. He's smart and intimidating, so that means higher than average Intelligence and Charisma. Maybe twenty in Charisma, eighteen Intelligence, and I think his Wisdom score is his lowest. I just can't decide if he's Lawful Evil or Lawful Neutral."

"He's not evil." I defend him as if compelled by birthright. I mean, I know my dad's a jerk, but evil seems a bit extreme.

Staring over her glasses, Darcy is unconvinced. I bump her shoulder with mine. I have to lean way down. "You do that for everyone you meet? Or just the people who toss you out before you've finished your supper?"

"Very funny. Just for that, I'm not going to share your ability scores."

"Hey, no fair!" I reach over and grab her hand in mine.

We're already halfway to her house when I remember to ask about the QSA meeting with Mr. Elliot. I would have offered to come but couldn't risk Dad finding out, so she went with Wyatt instead.

"So, how did it go?"

"Good! He said that we are welcome to host a QSA at school!"

"Really? That's great!"

"Well, provided we get approval from the School Community Council. According to Mr. Elliot, the SCC, which is organized by the 'fine, upstanding parents of our school,' controls everything from school fundraisers to extra-curricular clubs."

"The SCC?" I ask, my question distant and slow as if said by someone else. This is bad. Really bad.

"Yeah, that's what he said. We're going to prepare the presentation at my place. I'd really love if you came to help," she says. "Wyatt suggested we co-present — him and me. Honestly, I think it would be better for Mack to join him, but Mack flat-out refused." She continues to ramble about potential talking points, but I hardly hear her.

Darcy reaches over and touches my hand. My foot pops off the clutch, and we grind to a halt. "Art? You okay? The truck stopped."

For once, my face doesn't get hot. I feel the blood drain away, replaced with icy fear. "Dad is on the School Community Council."

DARCY IRL

Art squeezes my hand one last time, then slips into the throngs of people entering the gymnasium. For an aching moment, I'm alone. The farthest wall is decorated with school banners that remind me of heraldry flags. Small talk rings in my ears like the clanking of armor.

It's the night of the School Community Council meeting, and despite countless hours of preparation, my heart races and my palms sweat. Our unsanctioned club met at lunch and after school every day this week. We've done all our research, practiced until Wyatt and I had our speech memorized, but I still feel like I'm going to be sick. On the drive here, Carrie and Monica couldn't stop giving me advice.

"Your anxiety response means this is important to you, love. That's a good thing," Carrie said.

"Use that nervous energy to fuel your resolve," Monica added. "You can do this."

While they tried to do the supportive parent thing, I couldn't stop thinking about how if this doesn't work, if our QSA doesn't get SCC approval, then I'll have failed my friends. Even worse, I'll have failed my moms.

The room spins and I remind myself to breathe. A distraction, I need a distraction. Imagining a great army marching into battle, I fidget with my cue cards, fanning myself, smacking them against my thigh, now and then thumbing the edges of the little stack. I scan the gathering crowd. Where's the rest of the QSA?

Ms. Stacey waves. Her bright yellow dress catches my eye, then I notice Wyatt, Mackenzie, Rainbow and even Dawn following in her wake. Relieved tears prickle at the corners of my eyes. I swipe under my glasses and wave back.

They're all smiles and finger guns. Ms. Stacey ushers them into the front row, and Wyatt marches across the gymnasium to join me at the stairs to the stage. He looks more drab than usual in a gray blazer and black tie. He reaches for my cue cards, and I smile. His nails are painted in rainbow colors.

I hand over our speech. Eight cards total. Introduction. Personal experience. Statistics. School motto. Safe spaces. QSA overview. Conclusion. Questions.

Wyatt flips to the conclusion one more time, just as Principal Elliot passes us and climbs the stairs to the stage. That's when Wyatt holds a card under my nose.

I'd recognize that precise writing anywhere. *You've got this.*

I strain to see Art. His six-foot frame and red hair shouldn't be difficult to spot, but I fail my Perception. Where did he go?

Mr. Elliot taps the mic. "Hello, everyone. Welcome."

I catch a flash of red hair from the corner of my eye. Then I notice Art's father and sister sitting next to him.

Marcus sits tall in his seat, but Dawn's arms are folded across her chest, and she's hunched low. I thought she was sitting with Ms. Stacey. My hands tremble as I wonder what happened. Why did they have to sit in the front row?

I look for my own parents. I spot them standing at the back of the room, holding hands, their chins lifted just enough to look purposeful. Their anxiety is my anxiety. They weren't exactly thrilled about this meeting. Not that they weren't supportive, because obviously they are, but they worry. I get that now. I worry about them too.

I look back toward Art and instead make eye contact with his dad, who's looking right at me. Art stares ahead in a noble attempt to ignore his father. He fails when Marcus leans in and whispers to him. His entire face goes an angry red, and he sinks down in his chair until the woman behind him can see over his head. Suddenly, Art's dad looks like a giant beside his hunched-over son.

If my mom is a dragon, Art's dad is something infinitely worse. He's the type of villain with an agenda, one who will smile at you before he burns down your village. I look away.

Wyatt takes a deep breath beside me, then exhales slowly.

We're not the first on the program, but I can't seem to pay any attention to the meeting proceedings at all. I'm almost surprised when Mr. Elliot says, "And now, we'll hear a student proposal from Mr. Wyatt Cyr and Ms. Darcy Larocque-Evans."

My limbs are mechanical as I follow Wyatt onto the stage.

I might faint. Empty faces stare back at us, and I'm fully aware of my moms, Art, Dawn, the entire QSA and Marcus out there in the crowd. Like, who even faints in real life anyway?

I breathe in. Not me. Not today.

Wyatt sets the cue cards on the podium. He's split the

cards into two smaller stacks; one for him and one for me, just like we practiced. His chin dips in the smallest of nods, I respond with a thin smile. When Wyatt addresses the audience, he's all charm. In game, Charisma would be his highest stat for sure.

"Good evening, everyone," Wyatt says, his clear voice carried to the back of the gym by the microphone in front of us. "My name is Wyatt Cyr and this is Darcy Larocque-Evans. We're here today to present on and advocate for a Queer-Straight Alliance at Unity Creek High. In our presentation, we hope to share our stories with you and demonstrate the need for a QSA here."

My eyes flick to Art in the front row. He straightens in his seat and gives me two thumbs up, even though his dad is right there. Instantly, I'm braver, more like a heroine than a nervous student.

I avoid clearing my throat, as I continue with my part of our prepared speech. "As some of you know, my mother is Dr. Carissa Evans, the new general practitioner in town. We moved to Unity Creek at the end of September.

"You may also know that I have two mothers." My voice is steady. I brace myself for a ripple of whispers, but instead there's just this uneasy silence.

At the back of the audience, Monica holds her hands to her chest and Carrie has a tender arm around her shoulder. They don't look as if they're putting on a brave face anymore; they're proud. Monica wipes her eyes with a palm of her hand.

"And I'm so thankful to be their daughter," I add. "I come from a diverse family, and I fully believe in celebrating our differences. I believe in equality for all."

Monica blows her nose with a tissue.

"My family's personal experiences moving to this community have been largely welcoming and positive, but even in our short time here, we've witnessed, firsthand, acts of prejudice and violence toward us because of who we are.

"There are those in the community who refuse to be treated by my mother at the clinic. A brick was thrown through our living room window. And I can think of more personal examples." I glance at Art's dad. His expression remains neutral, unaffected. I stumble over my words. Shuffling my cue cards, I try to find my spot.

Wyatt lays a hand over mine to stop me. He looks out at the crowd as he takes over. "School is supposed to be a safe place for everyone, and we would like to encourage safety in our school by proposing the formation of a QSA. We've already obtained student interest, without being permitted to advertise in the school yet, and are pleased to welcome our initial members."

He doesn't mention that there are only six members, Mack/enzie, Rainbow, Dawn, Art, plus Wyatt and me. He points to the bottom of my cue card.

I continue from there. "This interest, along with the challenges my family has experienced being the first openly queer family in town, demonstrates the necessity for a high school QSA in our community."

Wyatt resumes his part of our presentation. He shares statistics that make my toes curl; numbers about queer students with anxiety and depression, about the likelihood of suicidal ideation, all because of bullying, prejudice and homophobic ideas.

"If we are able to come to a consensus here tonight, we'll have the opportunity to prevent further harm and create a positive impact in the lives of 2SLGBTQIA+ students, families and beyond," I say. "The next step will be to formally register as a Queer-Straight Alliance with our local chapter organizers. Through the year, the QSA will hold regular meetings and organize Pride events in our school and community."

"Finally," Wyatt adds, "our school motto is 'Working together for a better tomorrow.' With the support of the School Community Council, Darcy and I, along with our first members, believe that the QSA will embody the truest meaning of those words."

I conclude, "At this time, we'll try to answer any questions you have."

The sound of a chair scraping across the gym floor makes my stomach drop. Out there, in the front row, Marcus Bailey stands.

He casts a long shadow across Art's panicked face, as I look frantically back at The Moms. Carrie takes one step forward.

Then he smiles. I wish he looked more monstrous, but he's friendly and warm. Even his baritone voice is charming. "I think Mr. Cyr and Ms. Evans deserve a round of applause. Don't you?"

He starts clapping and soon the entire auditorium is applauding us.

I'm not sure what to do. From Art's expression, he's not either.

When the audience quiets, Art's dad continues. "I just have one question. Exactly how would your little club improve student safety?"

Mr. Bailey stares up at the stage, earnestly waiting for my response. I have some experience with cult leaders, fictional ones of course, and they're total jerks. The problem with a cult leader is that he looks nice, sounds nice and says everything right. How am I supposed to respond?

Fine. I can play his game. "We would be providing both queer students and straight allies a safe space with the QSA."

Another woman, with an I-Want-to-Speak-with-Your-Manager haircut raises her hand. "Are you saying that our school isn't safe?"

The implication hangs in the air. The audience stirs. I'm losing them.

"No, no," Mr. Bailey says. "I'm certain that's not what she means. Is it, Ms. Evans?"

I mean — the school isn't safe — but I can't say that. Can I?

I glance toward Wyatt, and he gives me the tiniest shrug, as if he knows what I'm working up the courage to admit. And maybe he does, he's been navigating this school a lot longer than I have, after all. I take a deep breath in, just like he did at the start of all this, then exhale.

"Actually, Mr. Bailey —"

"Regardless," he interrupts. "If this is about school safety, perhaps the name of your little club should reflect that? Queer-Straight Alliance might send the wrong message."

"We could brainstorm different names for the club," suggests a parent.

"What if we had Safe School signs instead?" says a man.

The gym devolves into heated discussion on the most politically correct way to demonstrate school safety. No one is discussing the QSA anymore.

My stomach twists into a knot, and hot tears prick at my eyes as realization dawns.

I never stood a chance. Mr. Bailey was always going to win

this fight. He knew that, Mr. Elliot, my moms, even my friends knew that. And I think maybe Art knew I would lose, too.

I'm about to collect our notes and leave the stage when Wyatt stops me by pointing to the back of the gym. "Yes, Ms. Larocque-Evans?"

"Thank you, Wyatt!" Monica shouts from the back of the gym. She surprises herself, Carrie and most of all, me. After the initial shock, she marches down the aisle like fucking Wonder Woman. "You still haven't answered my daughter's proposal."

Art's dad sits. "Of course student safety is important. It is the SCC's responsibility to make sure that all students feel safe, not only the ones with alternative lifestyle choices."

People clap some more.

Suddenly, I see Mr. Bailey wearing a deep green over-tunic and fur-lined robe. He transforms into Baron Sangray himself and stands before me with an oily smile. He's the perfect storybook villain. But this isn't how this is supposed to work. The bad guys don't win at the RPG table.

Mr. Bailey turns to the other parents in the front row. "Now, I'm in favor of such a progressive initiative, but I'm worried we haven't considered all the impacts of starting a club such as this in our school. We should be careful with our next steps. We wouldn't want to offend anyone by voting in a QSA tonight."

There's lots of nodding and murmuring in the crowd. Art's dad has won.

I freeze at the podium, unable to stop the tears. Wyatt touches my shoulder and directs me to the stairs, while Principal Elliot reclaims the mic.

"We will table the subject of a Queer-Straight Alliance

at the school until further notice. I invite concerned parents to contact me directly, so I can answer any remaining questions. Thank you for your presentation, Mr. Cyr, Ms. Larocque-Evans."

I can't really hear him. I walk, chin up, tears wetting my cheeks, past the front row where Art is sitting with his despicable father and where Dawn shoots to her feet; past Ms. Stacey, who is trying to catch my attention with a sympathetic shake of her head; and even past both of my mothers, who are standing beside the exit door, ready to blow this popsicle stand.

Monica opens her arms to me for a hug. The full reality of what just happened crashes in on me when I see the concern in her expression. She's worried about me.

I'm crying, and people are staring. Mack puts an arm around Wyatt, Rainbow beside them. All three turn around to meet my gaze. I look away, then notice the open door.

I burst through the exit, dash down the hall and out of the school into the night. I take a deep breath. The cold air hurts my lungs. Then I run.

I run as fast and as far as my legs will carry me. Tears stream down my cheeks, and I gasp for air, my nose dripping. I wipe a sleeve across my face.

When I can't run anymore, I walk forward with no destination. Before I know where I am, I recognize an old wooden bridge, red swing set and the Fairytree.

Our park.

I plop myself on a swing and kick off my ballet flats. The sand is cold against my feet, and I sigh as the tiny grains squish between my toes.

My phone vibrates. I check the message — a text from Monica — and notice that James has spammed me again.

I don't have the energy. I lock the phone.

Bitter tears burn my eyes. By myself on the lonely swing, I don't have to hold back for anyone anymore. I'm crying — although crying might be too nice a word for the body-shaking sobs.

I go through several waves of bawling and realize just how tired I am, when the crunch of tires on gravel interrupts me. I spin, the swing chain twists, as I look toward the parking lot. Two sets of headlights point directly at my face, and I'm blinded.

I'm still seeing spots when I hear the slam of car doors.

"Darcy?" Carrie runs over. She's kneeling beside me, both arms around my shoulders, before I have time to respond.

"Mum," I whisper, "I'm so sorry."

Carrie pulls away. Her fingers are firm as she holds my shoulders. She looks deep into my eyes. "You have nothing to apologize for. We are so proud of you, love."

"But we didn't get permission to start the QSA."

"Not important. You did the right thing, and you know what, we'll figure it out together. Hell, we'll go public if you want.

"Darcy, your mother and I love you more than anything. More than a club and definitely more than this stupid town."

I smile and hug her back. Over her shoulder I notice everyone else.

Wyatt's loosened his tie. Mack stands next to him. Rainbow shifts her weight from one foot to another, and finally, Dawn. She wraps her arms around her narrow waist and avoids looking at me.

I disengage from Carrie and stand up. "Hey."

Mack looks from Wyatt to me, then to Rainbow and

Dawn, and I notice the red in Mack's eyes. They've been crying too. Without a word, Mack folds me into a hug. Soon, everyone follows. Our foreheads press together and warm arms squeeze into me from every direction. Everyone, except Dawn. I look around.

She stands off to the side and wipes tears away from her eyes with angry, jerky swipes of her hand.

"Dawn?" I ask.

The hug splits open and Rainbow motions for her to join us.

Dawn shakes her head. "I'm so sorry," she sobs. "My dad — I can't — I hate him!"

Tears rise in the back of my throat. I can't speak without crying, so I walk over and pull Dawn into a tight embrace. I shush her softly as she cries into my hair. Soon, the rest of the unofficial QSA joins us. When my own emotions have settled, after Dawn's tears have dried, I pull back enough to look her in the eye. "It's not your fault. Okay?"

The Moms step closer. "It's none of your faults," Carrie says, her voice final. "And this isn't over."

I look around at my friends. We've been dragged through a hellish battle, but Carrie's right. This is far from over. Then, I realize that Art is nowhere to be found. I turn to Dawn. "Where's your brother?"

Dawn's voice is still small, unsure. "He went home with Dad."

I try to ignore the sting of his absence. He's probably covering for Dawn or trying to talk to his father, I tell myself.

Monica puts a hand on my shoulder. "Let's go home."

I smile and look at my friends, at my moms. Aside from Art's absence, home feels right.

ART IRL

I stick close to the house for the rest of the weekend, and I only see Darcy once at the library. I hug her, and she tells me she doesn't want to talk about the SCC meeting yet, so we don't. Instead we put the final touches on our storytelling presentation.

Dad and I have an uneasy truce. We don't talk about the SCC meeting either, and I try my best to avoid him at the house. When he announces on Sunday after church that he'll be going to Montreal this week, I have to stop myself from breathing an audible sigh of relief.

Against my better judgment I invite Darcy to our place after Dad leaves.

We park in the driveway and even though this was my idea, I still rush her inside. I know she thinks I'm being paranoid, but if I were prepping this game, I'd hide spies in the neatly trimmed privacy hedges.

I show her all the public spaces. We walk through the entrance, kitchen and dining room again, then I show her our basement, complete with a sixty-five-inch flat-screen, in-house surround sound and vintage theater seats.

She eyes the popcorn maker in the corner. "Why don't we ever do homework at your place?"

Upstairs, I skip showing her Dawn's room and Dad's office, and instead rush her into my bedroom.

"Your room's cleaner than I thought it would be." Darcy eyes the perfectly made bed.

A few personal effects, like a framed Captain Marvel edition, signed by Sam Maggs, my computer and an alphabetical row of *D&D* sourcebooks sit on a metal desk in the corner. Other than that, my decorating skills could be described as nonexistent. The only indication that this isn't the set of some movie, like the rest of our house, are the stacks of paper around the room. There's a mountain of homework on my desk, some character sheets on the nightstand and a pile of old sketchbooks in a laundry basket at the end of my bed. She's right, my room isn't messy, there's just lots of paper — everywhere.

"Not all guys are slobs."

"Clearly." She sits cross-legged on my bed, then pulls the character sheets from the nightstand. She looks at Roman's sheet and smiles before flipping to the next page. It's the unfinished game recap I was writing. I squirm instead of jumping across the room to rip it from her hands.

"'A letter sits on the table,'" she reads.

"No," I whine, flopping down beside her. "Don't do that."

"Why not?"

"It's not ready."

"Please?"

She promises to stop reading the pages out loud, and I'm torn between watching her read and leaving the room altogether. In the end, I decide to lean back on the pillows beside her and stare at the ceiling until she's done.

There's no house rule against having girls in my room, but it probably goes without saying that I shouldn't have Darcy here, let alone spread out on my bed.

Maybe that's why I jump like we've been caught doing something we shouldn't be doing when Dawn opens the bedroom door. I didn't know she was home. I thought she was going to Rainbow's house this afternoon.

She walks in. "Knock, knock!"

I sit bolt up and move as far away from Darcy as possible without actually throwing myself off the bed. Darcy raises an eyebrow at me.

"Hi, Darcy!" Dawn plunks herself down on the corner of my bed, oblivious to my discomfort and racing heart. "How are things?"

Small talk ensues, and I sit in my corner. How can Darcy be so calm when all I feel is a dark hatred for my little sister? I'm thinking of the quickest ways to evict her from my room.

"What do you want?" I interrupt whatever story Dawn is expressing with animated hands.

"Rude." Dawn's glare isn't playing any games. Darcy offers my sister a small smile, as if to apologize for me.

I stand. "Well?"

"I was just wondering if I could spend the night at Rainbow's place?"

I'm about to say yes when Dad's voice echoes back in my memory. "Did you finish your homework?"

Dawn's nose scrunches up and she makes a little "blech" noise.

"Come on, it's just a sleepover." Darcy winks at Dawn,

then moves across to stand beside me. She bumps my arm with her shoulder. "You sound like your dad."

I stare at her in disbelief. How can she say that? Even as a joke.

The sound of Dawn's easy laughter feels like a sucker punch.

"Did. You. Finish. Your. Homework?"

Darcy and Dawn stop laughing.

Dawn throws herself back on the bed with dramatic flair. "But I hate it!"

My teeth clench together. "I don't care. Homework. Now."

She whines. I'm about to tell her to get off my bed and get out of my room, but Darcy starts talking first. "What's giving you trouble?"

"Math. Always math."

"I'm pretty good at math."

I try not to resent my sister even more when Darcy goes downstairs with Dawn to help her with her homework.

Five minutes pass, then ten. After twenty minutes, laughter bursts up from downstairs, and I can't stand it anymore. I'm about to go see if they're actually doing homework, when a muffled buzzing sends a random vibration up my leg. I almost crawl out of my skin until I realize it's Darcy's phone. I grab the cell and start to head downstairs.

I don't mean to look, but the screen automatically lights up when I turn over the cell. A text from James. As in, James, Darcy's ex-boyfriend.

And it's not just a text.

There's an attachment: a dick pic.

DARCY IRL

I leave the living room, where Dawn has a selection of old photo albums spread out for my viewing pleasure on top of her math homework. My sides ache from laughing. Two words: baby photos.

I'm still giggling when I push open Art's door. "You were surprisingly pudgy as a baby!"

The deep crease between his eyebrows catches me off guard. My laughter tapers away.

"What is it?" I close the door behind me and take a step closer. I bet his dad said something. What would Mr. Bailey do if he knew Art and I were still dating?

But it's not Art's dad.

It's James.

Art shoves my cell phone toward me. "I don't know. You tell me."

I see the name at the top of the screen. This is bad. Then I notice the picture.

"I thought you broke up with him, Darcy?"

I look up into Art's slate-blue eyes, and even though he's angry right now, I know I have to tell him the truth. I'll explain everything: how I tried to break up with James and how I was scared. Art and I can figure out what to do together.

I roll for Willpower.

And I fail. "I did, Art! I swear!"

"Then do you mind explaining why he's sending you this?"

I wince, but instead of the truth, a half lie rolls off my tongue as if I've rehearsed this role-play. "He's been harassing me. I broke up with him, and now he won't leave me alone. I don't want these messages! I never asked for them!"

I mean, that part is true. I don't want any sexts from James.

"Here, I'll delete his number right now, in front of you. I should have done that a long time ago."

Art's whole body relaxes, and his eyes soften. He holds the phone out for me, just long enough for the phone to scan my face and unlock. I reach out, but of course the cell buzzes in his outstretched hand. Another picture. Just. Perfect.

Art's fingers tighten and he snaps the phone back up. He starts to text back.

"Art?" My voice is shaky.

"I'm just making sure he leaves you alone. I'm not going to let some asshole harass my girlfriend." He sends the message. "Especially like this."

I freeze. I think about the last time I tried to talk to James. Maybe Art isn't the jealous type, but James is, and in his head, we're still together.

"What are you saying to him?" I try to sound as if I'm okay and not totally freaking out.

"I just told him to leave you alone, that's all." Art hands me back my phone and kisses me on the cheek. "Let me know if he keeps bothering you, okay?"

"Sure." My hands are sweaty when I shove my phone in my pocket.

"We need to go, otherwise we'll be late for Game."

Art's sent text glares at me from the back-lit screen as we drive to the Anderson house.

> Hey asshole! This is Darcy's boyfriend.

> Take a hint and leave her alone or we're going to the police.

Read at 6:46.

The Nixwyrm

Dried blood sealed Roman's left eye and his head rang, flashes of the fight returning to him as he awoke. At least he'd managed to take down three of his father's personal guards before being captured.

He pushed himself to sit up and survey his surroundings. He was underground. Somewhere in the darkness, water lapped against a shoreline. The air smelled heavily of wet things. Roman blinked to adjust his eyes, the crusted blood flaking away, until he could make out the shapes of jagged teeth — no, rocks — protruding from a cavernous ceiling. Not ten paces away, fathoms of inky-green water pooled in a giant underground lake.

Stones scattered behind him. Roman swiveled his head around and narrowed his eyes, desperate to locate the source of the sound. A staircase carved into the cavern wall lay empty. More rocks fell, and Roman swore. He couldn't see clearly enough.

What sort of horror had his father planned for him? Nothing good for a treacherous son. He struggled against his binds, but the ropes held fast. He could hear footsteps now; the unmistakable tread of boots approached.

Roman closed his eyes tight.

Then, the cool bite of metal slid between his bound wrists.

In front of him, someone's breath kissed his cheek. "Did you miss me?"

His pulse jumped to his throat, and his eyes flew open. Poppy. At once, relief and fear flooded through him. She was here; she couldn't be here. Head whipping around, he found them all: Kastor, who held a witch light between himself and Bearpuncher; Moira, who knelt behind Roman and sawed at his tied wrists; then Poppy, who smiled in front of him.

Roman's wrists broke free, and Moira handed him the knife. "Your feet," she said. "Now. We don't have much time."

Roman was lightning. His attention zeroed in on one goal, and one goal only: get everyone away from him. This wasn't his tomb, it was a trap.

He jumped to his feet and dragged Poppy up with him. "How — no. No time for questions. You need to leave. Now." He looked at each of his friends. "All of you."

Poppy gripped his forearm. "It's too late to run away," she said, her voice low. He was about to ask her what she meant, when the stones began to rumble and the water began to ripple. "She's here."

"She?" Roman asked.

A powerful serpent erupted from the underground lake. It rose from the depths, frothy green water dripping from horns fanning around the monster's face, with a long body that stretched as tall as St. Oswin's Tower.

Poppy's eyes were wide with wonder. She breathed a reverent sigh. "The Nixwyrm."

"I — I thought she was a fairy tale," Kastor said.

Roman wheeled to face the wizard. "That doesn't look like any fairy tale I've heard before, old man."

"She won't hurt us." Poppy stepped forward, arms outstretched as if to pacify the monster. "She's only a woman, a daughter of Deyja like me. Hush now, dear thing. Easy."

The Nixwyrm seemed to still, its clouded pink eyes transfixed on Poppy. Roman watched in horrified fascination as she took a step, then another. The closer she crept, the louder his heart thumped in his chest. When the water pooled around her ankles, Roman couldn't hold himself back any longer. He went to follow her but was stopped by a firm hand on his shoulder.

Bearpuncher nodded toward the serpent with a jut of his bearded chin.

Instead of swallowing Poppy whole, or knocking her into the cavern wall with its mighty tail, the Nixwyrm lowered its horned head. Poppy reached her hand out. Her fingers caressed the snake's scaled head.

Cloven air whistled over Roman's shoulder. An arrow pierced Poppy's back, then another and another. The first in her shoulder, the second to her side and the third — the last arrow — sank clean through her heart.

Several things happened in that next moment: Poppy gasped a ragged suck of desperate air, the Nixwyrm tossed its head back in the air and shrieked, and Roman sagged forward. The sound of the giant serpent's keening split his ears, but he hardly noticed as he scrambled to Poppy's crumpled body. She lay half-submerged, her boots still on the shore.

She wasn't moving.

Roman pulled her into his lap. Her wounds were weeping blood. Dimly, he tried to apply pressure to the worst of the torn flesh, his hands splayed over her heart. She shuddered.

"No!" Roman's hands were slick with blood, his tears falling onto Poppy's agonized face. "Don't leave me. You can't die."

From somewhere that seemed very far away, Roman heard the Nixwyrm fall into the water with a mighty splash.

Then orders hollered from behind him. Head dizzy with grief, he looked toward the restless water. In moments, giant cascading waves would sweep them both away. He wanted the lake to claim them. As he braced himself with Poppy's body limp in his arms, he recognized the voice barking orders. Roman's head whipped around. On the cavern stairs, his father and twenty-odd guards filed toward the lake. A bow rested in the Baron's grip, the bowstring relaxed in his hands but still nocked with another arrow.

Rage tore through Roman's grief. He pulled Poppy farther onto shore just as the wave crashed against the cavern floor. He lowered his face to whisper a final promise, his mouth pressed to her cold temple. "Be patient with me, my heart. There's something I need to finish, but I'll return to you. I swear it."

Then he tried to stand. He'd kill his father. *The Baron*, he thought with lethal resolve. His father was already dead to him.

A second wave knocked into his knees, and Roman stumbled forward. To get to the Baron, he'd have to fight through the wall of Sangray guards. Roman would cut through every single one.

Suddenly, Moira and Bearpuncher caught him by the elbows. They dragged him toward a ring drawn with magic on the cavern floor. Kastor finished the spell, and the Teleportation Circle glowed to life.

"We must go," Moira said with effort, as Roman pulled against her hold. "We cannot match his guards. It would be the death of us all."

Roman was about to tell her that he didn't care, that he'd buy the rest of them time to escape, but the words died on his tongue.

From the dark waters, where the Nixwyrm had fallen, a woman emerged. Though *woman* may have been too kind a description. She was robed in clinging seaweed and slimy algae; her long, dark hair was plastered to her sides, down her shoulders and back. Her skin, though wet, was not the rosy color of the living, but a familiar ashen tone — the sick gray of a corpse — and her fingers were blackened and pointed like his own. She hovered above the surface of the water, then stepped onto the lake and walked toward shore as if she were floating.

Roman's vision doubled. He stumbled.

The Baron pushed through his line of guards. He ignored Roman, ignored Poppy and ran into the water.

"Adele," Sangray's voice broke on the name, a name that inspired some sense of familiarity in Roman's addled mind.

"Dietrich, my darling. What have you done?"

Roman watched the Baron fall to his knees. "I couldn't let you leave."

"What have you done?"

"I kept you safe. I found a way to free you from her curse, Adele," Sangray pleaded.

Realization sobered Roman, temporarily stunning his warring anger and grief. Adele Sangray, the once Baroness.

Roman's mother. But she'd died, murdered when he was still in his small clothes, hadn't she?

The Baron continued to speak, "I made the necessary sacrifices so that we could be together again. I vowed it."

"You imprisoned me. Poisoned our waters. You burned Deyja's temples and killed my sisters, Dietrich. You've angered the goddess."

"She let you be murdered!" Sangray cried. "I will slay her and every other Old God to keep you."

Adele — Roman's mother — shook her head, slow and sad. "I told you, this was always my choice. How could you not trust me?"

The wet slap of flesh against stone drew Roman's attention toward where he had left Poppy. But she wasn't there. In her place lay a thrashing snake. With each violent shudder of its body, the snake grew larger. Soon, the new Nixwyrm was large enough that the rocks tremored beneath Roman's boots.

The ripples on the lake were small at first, then the entire surface became wild. Stalactites fell from the cavern ceiling. The Baron, Adele, the guards, Roman's friends; soon they would all be buried.

"We've got to leave. Now!" Moira and Bearpuncher resumed pulling on Roman's elbows. He fought against them until he broke free and dashed toward the water. Let the whole cursed House of Sangray die in this horrible place; let him die with Poppy.

Adele had different plans. As soon as Roman's boots hit the water, her attention snapped back to him. With unnatural speed and strength, she plowed into him. She pushed him back until his boots were within the Teleportation Circle. Before Kastor spoke the command, Adele folded something into Roman's hand, and pulled him into a fierce hug. "Your sweetheart will trap herself here. Come back for her, set her free, just like the old stories. Then seek out the goddess. She will bargain with you, son. Trade your life for the girl's."

Adele was already fading from this world when she held Roman back to look at him. She even had his black eyes. Roman gripped her forearms, as if he could hold on to her. Her smile turned sad.

"I'm so sorry, *elskling*. You deserved better from us," she said, pressing a cold kiss to his horned brow. "I love you."

Then she pushed him through the portal.

ART IRL

"Did you and Michelle plan that?" I ask, giddy. We drive toward Darcy's house. "That was epic. You were epic! The way you described the arrows. I can't believe Michelle killed your character. Are you okay?"

Darcy makes a noise of agreement. I glance at her from the corner of my eye. She's chewing her lip.

"Hey, what's wrong? If it's about Poppy's death scene, I'm sure Michelle will retcon it for you."

"No, it's not that. It's nothing."

"Darcy?"

"Nothing's wrong, Art," she says as we park outside her house. "I'm just thinking."

I put an arm around her. "Whatcha thinking about?"

Darcy looks out the window. "I have to tell you something."

I don't need a high Intelligence score to know that whatever she has to say is serious. What if she's breaking up with me?

Darcy shrugs off my arm, pulls the elastic out of her hair

and shakes her head. She rolls her shoulders back as if she's getting ready to fight. My stomach drops.

"What is it?"

She takes a deep breath and looks up at me. "You know I care about you, right?"

I do not like where this is headed. Numb, I echo her words back. "You care about me?"

She nods. "And I don't want to hurt you."

The words hang between us in my truck cab. I can't bring myself to ask what comes next. Nothing good can follow those words.

She wriggles in her seat beside me. "Art?"

"I love you," I blurt. As soon as the words leave my mouth, I realize my mistake. Darcy stares at me, her mouth open. Here I am thinking she's about to break up with me, and what? I go for emotional manipulation. I rush to add, "No! Darcy — I'm sorry, I shouldn't have said that. I don't!"

"Wait, so, you don't love me?" The hurt in her voice doesn't make sense.

"That's not what I mean." I lean my forehead against the truck wheel. "You obviously had something important to say and I panicked. I interrupted."

"Art?" she asks. "Do you love me?"

I open my mouth to answer her. Then, the passenger door swings open.

Crap. I expect Monica or Carrie and I brace myself for an earful, but neither of The Moms are there.

Before I even recognize the leather-clad, wild-eyed guy outside, he yanks Darcy from the vehicle.

Realization settles in too late.

"You little whore!" James hisses. He pulls Darcy so close

to him that she has to stretch up on her tiptoes. He grips her forearm at a painful angle. Tears are washing down her stricken face.

"James! You're hurting me!"

I scramble out of the truck.

"Let her go." My jaw is tight, teeth clenched. I close in on them.

Darcy's ex barely glances at me. His eyes flick over to me with the same amount of interest you pay a background character. "And you're putting out for this garbage?"

Darcy twists, hard, and tries to pull away.

James wraps his arms around her waist. He rubs his cheek against her. "Don't be like that, babe. Aren't you glad to see me?"

He nibbles her ear.

Darcy squirms. She tries to lean away. "Stop! Let go of me!"

I'm about to throw myself at him when she lifts the heel of her boot and stomps down on his toe. James squawks in pain. His arms spring apart. Darcy scrambles away. Swearing, he looks up just as she swings around. A sharp crack echoes down the dark street.

James holds his cheek. Darcy stands in front of him. Her dark hair flies around her face.

"Get lost." She bites out the words. Her hands are balled in tight fists. "I never want to see you again."

James takes a half step closer. I cut in instinctively and put my arm around Darcy. "You heard her. You need to go."

James wipes a furious hand over his eyes, his shoulders sagging. He sobs. Beside me, Darcy's body goes stiff. I tuck Darcy under my chin and turn her away. "Come on," I whisper to her. "Let's get you inside."

If I thought that James would give up, I was deluded. His eyes flick over to me. Whatever heartbreak he was experiencing is replaced with raw hate. "Is this the guy you've been cheating with?"

A lamplight flickers down the street, but otherwise the world stands still. I expect her to deny him right away. When she doesn't, well, her silence says enough.

"I'm her boyfriend." I stretch out the words until they sound more like a question than a statement.

"You're a sad fuck." James laughs. "Did she tell you we're still together? Did she tell you all the things we've done together?"

"What?" I stare at Darcy. Her cheeks turn red with anger or shame. Maybe both?

I don't have time to decipher her expression before James barrels into me. He catches me by the waist and pulls me to the ground. My breath is forced from my lungs. Little stars dance at the edges of my vision.

James pummels me. Blow after blow connects with my face. Pain shoots through my skull. My body curls inward, and I hold my arms around my head.

"She'll always be mine!" James' fist connects with my ribs.

Somewhere far away I hear Darcy. She appears over his shoulder. She is pulling him backwards. He elbows her square in the nose and she yelps in pain.

I'm going to kill him.

But she's made an opportunity for me. I see my window and seize the chance without a second thought. I throw my head forward and connect with his nose. He reels back. I punch him in the stomach. His body caves into the blow. As James swears, holding his belly, I scramble to my feet.

Blood is streaming down Darcy's face. I'm gasping for air. Fighting isn't fun in real life.

"What's going on here?" Monica screams. She's running across the lawn in bare feet.

"Mom!"

That's when Monica sees James. Her gaze is frigid as she takes in the scene, her eyes roaming from James to me, then to Darcy. Dark bruises are forming under Darcy's swollen eyes.

"We're calling the cops." Monica's voice is cold and sharp as ice. She points at James. "You're never going to see my daughter again."

He opens his mouth, then after a second's thought, presses his lips together.

On his way back to his car, James knocks into my shoulder and mumbles something about used goods. I grind my teeth so hard that I barely hear the slam of his car door.

As he throws his car in reverse, he flips us off, and launches straight into a car parked in Darcy's driveway. There is a crunch of metal on metal. Darcy steps forward, but Monica stops her. James doesn't get out of the vehicle. He drives off.

Inside, Monica dials 9-1-1 to report the assault, and the hit and run. While she's answering questions on the phone, I go into the bathroom to clean the blood off my face. I see Darcy hovering in the hallway. She has changed into a clean top and sweatpants.

In two long strides the distance between us closes, and I fold her into my arms.

Her whole body shakes.

"I'm so sorry," she gasps between stuttering breaths. "Art, I'm so, so sorry!"

I stare down at her. "You're sorry?"

When she avoids my gaze, I realize that James was telling the truth. The hallway is suddenly narrower and longer. I snatch my hands away and step back. "You were lying to me the entire time?"

"Art," she says, her voice raw. "I didn't mean to."

I don't wait around to hear anymore. I'm pulling on my runners and retreating out the door before the emotions can catch up to me. Betrayal. Hurt. Longing. Pain. Love. All my messy feelings are there, in one giant, bubbling pot, like a witch's potion. She cast a spell on me.

How could I be so blind? So stupid?

"Art!" Darcy's voice reaches across the lawn. "I'm sorry."

Her words are disjointed, staccato with hiccups, and her voice sends a bolt through my chest. *Christ.* I can't do this.

I crawl into my truck and slam the door behind me. A chivalrous knight would go to her and sweep her off her feet, comfort her and pat her beautifully messy hair.

Thing is, I'm a rogue, and rogues slip away without a trace. So that's what I do.

DARCY IRL

Thank god for moms who let you stay home from school when it really matters.

In fact, besides the preliminary line of questions — What happened? Are you hurt? Is Art all right? — and the answers — James and I broke up, I'm fine and it's probably over with Art forever — yeah, besides all that, The Moms leave me alone, giving me space.

I retreat until I'm out of the game and off the map.

I stay locked in my room most of the weekend. I rotate between reading sourcebooks, building new characters with tragic backstories, and sneaking between my room and the bathroom. Despite how chill my moms have been, I avoid being beckoned for an audience with the Lady and Lady of the House.

And I spend every other waking moment checking my phone for messages from Art. Which don't arrive.

On Sunday evening, there's a light knock on my bedroom door. I pause my ultimate comfort movie, *Shrek the Musical*.

"Come in!"

Carrie opens my door. Her blonde hair is getting long again. In a week she'll get frustrated enough for another trim. Free haircuts are one of the perks of being married to a stylist, I suppose. Her hair always looks immaculate.

She's holding a folder of papers in her hands. I'd recognize the file anywhere.

Both sides of the file are decorated in Art's handwriting and doodles.

I push myself up in bed. "Where did you get that?"

"He just stopped by."

I don't have time to worry about my messy curls. I swing my feet out of bed. I don't care that I'm wearing the same pj's I've been living in for the last two days, or that I haven't brushed my teeth.

Carrie hands me the storytelling project. "He didn't stay. He just said that you'd need these for your presentation on Monday."

"Oh." I crush a half-eaten bag of chips as I flop down onto the mattress.

Carrie sits beside me, her arms loop around my shoulders and she pulls me into a tight side hug.

"Chin up, love." Her voice is chipper and oh-so-British. "If the growing up thing doesn't work out for you, you can always live here. Imagine, you and your moms, hanging out night after night. We might even learn how to play that game you're obsessed with!"

I groan.

Carrie's laugh surprises me. Not because she's being unkind or mean-spirited, but because it's been weeks since she's laughed like that. I've missed that sound.

VICTORIA KOOPS

She kisses my cheek before she leaves. I stare down at the folder beside me.

I can't stop the soft smile as I look at Art's little doodles and flash fictions on the side of the manila paper. I pick up our project. There's a sticky note over the heart I drew.

Group Presentation. Monday morning. I finished it, you just have to show up.

I wake up early on Monday, my stomach churning as though today is the first day of school again. I stare at my stark reflection in the bathroom mirror. My hair is all done, curled with a hot iron into tame, Hannah Lawson-esque waves, but the blooming purple bruises under my eyes are alarming. I rub concealer viciously into the tender skin.

Turns out, when you get elbowed in the face, you get a black eye. Carrie said my nose wasn't broken. The bruising will stick around for a week or two. I think back to the time I punched Art with my keys. We would have matched.

The skin under my eyes is all chalky now. I give up and throw the tube of flesh-colored make-up into the garbage. Not like I have anyone to impress.

I don't want to change out of my pj's, but one look at the stained T-shirt and wrinkled shorts makes me reconsider.

Carrie pokes her head into my room.

"Hey, baby." She double-checks her watch. "You're not dressed yet? Hurry up, you're going to be late. I'll drive you."

I toss on a pair of jeans and wiggle into the first clean top — a green, knit turtleneck that belongs to Monica — that I find in a basket of folded laundry. Not my usual vibe, but at

230

least I don't look like a bridge troll anymore.

Carrie and I are out the door in five minutes. In another ten, I'm running into English class just as the bell rings. Even with one of The Moms driving, I'm barely on time.

I gravitate to my spot next to Art, who is already sitting beside the window. He's got a split lip. Before I can sit anywhere, class begins.

Ms. Stacey claps her hands. "Darcy and Art, you're first for presentations today. You can get set while I do attendance."

Art jumps up from his seat and sets out dice, pencils and character sheets. I edge my way through the rows of desks, avoiding his gaze, my trusty messenger bag on my hip.

Finally, everything is ready. Art looks out over the class. He stands up straighter, taking center stage, and I almost don't recognize him. Except that I do. He was this confident playing Roman. He looked just as brave when he confronted James.

"Our presentation is going to explore interactive storytelling." Art's voice rings out over the classroom, and he sounds just like a Game Master. "Through popular role-playing games."

He pauses for effect.

"Yeah, that kind of RPG. And more specifically, tabletop RPGs, which came before video games. Old school, with pencils and dice and little miniature figurines. Go ahead and laugh, but I promise, this is going to be the best English class of your life." He looks over his shoulder at our teacher. "No offense, Ms. Stacey."

Art's mouth turns up in a roguish smile. I love that smile. Sure enough, a few students laugh along.

"Now that we've got that out of your system, just trust me. As far as storytelling goes, there's nothing more fun than

VICTORIA KOOPS

playing a character in your own story. Besides, you might even get to slay a dragon or two."

Then, the whole class is off on an adventure. Art launches into a passionate explanation of *Dungeons & Dragons*, giving them just enough information to get the basics across. He peppers in a few pop culture references too, like, "And if you want to fight a Demogorgon, we can make that happen."

He wins the ability check, and the entire class is eating out of his hand.

I'm not sure how I'm supposed to follow that. When he turns the presentation over to me, I'm stunned.

I shuffle the index cards Art made me. "So, the first thing you need to do is think of a character idea."

I look up from my notes. A few classmates shift in their seats.

"Your character can be a one-dimensional archetype, like a fighter. Or a replication of your favorite fantasy character."

Art interrupts. "But ideally, character creation is more dynamic. We want to build three-dimensional characters, which will add flavor to our collective story."

I glance at him, but he looks away. He separates the class into groups of three or four. I hand out blank character sheets and a butt-load of dice. Once everyone has begun, we float around and help everyone build a character.

They're having a blast. Hannah even asks if we can try playing a quick game with their new characters — she built a halfling bard — but Ms. Stacey puts a pin in that idea because we're out of time.

People stop us after class to ask questions. We're both smiling like idiots as we accommodate our new fans. To my surprise, I overhear Art telling a few students that he would

232

run a one-shot for them at lunch. Finally, he meets my eye. I hand over the written component of our project, only half hearing Ms. Stacey's excited praise. She says something about embracing the spirit of the assignment, but Art's beaming at me. Who cares about an English mark?

I smile back, and for one fleeting, beautiful moment, it's as though The Incident never happened.

Then he turns away.

Thursday rolls around with no word from Art. I think about going to Game but fail my Saving Throw. Instead, I stay home and watch trash television.

My phone dings. I scramble to check the message; some delusional part of me is expecting a text from Art. I almost don't respond when I see Michelle's name.

> Are you coming to
> Game tonight?

> Sorry. Can't.

After texting her back, I pull the blankets over my head and start *Shrek the Musical* from the beginning.

This is rock bottom.

The Legend

The tip of Moira's sword pressed against the base of Roman's throat. "Give me one good reason to let you live, traitor!"

Roman didn't dare move a muscle.

"No traitor." Bearpuncher stayed Moira's hand. "Roman friend."

"Roman?" Moira shook out of Bearpuncher's grip. "Is that even your true name? He's been false with us since the beginning."

It had been the name his nurses called him growing up, but his full title had always been much longer and more pretentious. How could he explain that he had always been more Roman than he'd ever been his father's heir?

"How remarkable." Kastor leaned forward. "You look exactly like your mother."

Roman tensed. He hadn't known his mother, but he couldn't deny the physical similarities, just as he couldn't deny that the Baron was his father.

He hung his head in shame. "I never intended anyone any harm." His heart ached for Poppy, but he gritted his teeth. "How can I earn your forgiveness?"

He had almost worked up the courage to look up, when Bearpuncher clapped his back. "Nothing to forgive. You one of us. You Roman."

Roman's gaze shot to the Barbarian, then to Moira and Kastor.

Moira looked as though she was holding back about a hundred questions. She reached out a hand and braced Roman's forearm against her own to help him stand. "You can start by setting up camp. You've got the best eyes, and my backside aches from saving your stupid neck one too many times."

The low fire cast shadows and heat over Roman's tired face, and his eyes stung from holding back tears. He rested his forearms against bent knees and examined his mother's parting gift: a signet ring.

He knew without having to try it on that the band of gold, stamped with the crown and flowers of House Sangray, would fit his littlest finger. He was certain the ring would fit, in the same way he was certain that Sangray was dead. Why else would his mother have taken the time to press the ring into Roman's palm?

And if Sangray was dead, that made Roman the Baron of Blackwood and Lord of Durgeon's Keep.

He refused to slide the signet onto his finger. Not yet.

"We can't just —"

His friends stood together, just outside the warm circle of light cast by the fire, their heads bent in consultation. Kastor's portal had spit them out somewhere beyond the Ditch, on the edge of the Durgeon Forest.

If he strained his ears, he could catch every fifth word or so.

"The Baron."

"Nixwyrm."

"Cursed?"

"No. Blessed. The Priestess."

"So, the old legend —"

Despite the hollow feeling threatening to swallow him from the inside out, Roman lifted his head. His mother had mentioned an old story. "What legend?"

Moira, Bearpuncher and Kastor shifted collectively with discomfort. Moira avoided his gaze. Bearpuncher shuffled his feet. And Kastor twirled his mustache.

Roman repeated himself, his voice raw and sharp. "What legend are you talking about?"

Kastor was the first to come sit around the fire. When the others joined him, the old wizard leaned forward.

Deyja, the oldest of the Old Gods, roamed the world alone. She ruled over the darkness and explored her dominion astride a giant moth, but everywhere she traveled, she remained solitary. The only one of her kind, or so she thought.

One day, she met three siblings, young gods, new to mortal worship and their divine responsibilities. The eldest, a warrior woman called Elske; the youngest, a listless man named Myrkfure. Immediately, Deyja loved them both.

But the middle brother, a cunning, tricky man known as Aader, irked Deyja. He was arrogant, smart, and as the self-proclaimed King of the Underworld, he thought that he knew death better than she.

Deyja and Aader developed a rivalry. For centuries, they played games with each other, one always trying to outdo the other with marvelous creations, until the world was brought into life. When they stopped to admire their work, they realized that their feelings had changed. They had fallen desperately in love.

And as a result, they gave birth to a daughter — the Nixie — and gifted her the wilds.

The Nixie reveled in the mortal realm. She especially loved the rivers and would spend days on end playing and swimming with the currents.

When the Nixie was grown, many mortals sought her hand in marriage. Not only was she unnaturally beautiful — with black eyes and dark hair — but she was also a divine child, and therefore very powerful. The Nixie fell in love with a humble ferryman, someone who loved the rivers as much as she did. And to be with him, she refused all other suitors.

The Nixie was tending to the flowers along the riverbank when a spurned king snuck up behind her. In his hand he held a knife, coated in cursed hemlock, the only poison strong enough to kill a goddess. He plunged the knife into the Nixie's chest, piercing her heart and poisoning her blood. She fell into the river, her blood turning the flowers pink, the poison sickening the land.

The river was loyal to her and her parents, and so the waters carried the Nixie to her father's home in the underworld, the Aaderhall, where Deyja and Aader wept over her corpse. When the time arrived to lay her to rest, Deyja refused to accept the death.

The goddess used her divine powers to steal the Nixie from Aader and bring the dead girl back to earth. There, Deyja called a snake from the banks of the river. She begged the

VICTORIA KOOPS

snake to trade places with the Nixie, and the snake agreed, provided that Deyja swore to protect the snake's body. In her grief, Deyja vowed it would be so.

The snake traded places with the girl and took the Nixie's appointment in the underworld. With her husband satisfied, Deyja placed their daughter in the snake's body. She grew until she was as long as the river she had loved so well.

And since then, only poisoned flowers would grow along the banks of the Hebenon River.

"Or so it was told to me as a boy," Kastor finished.

"So, Poppy's — what?" Moira asks. "Dead? Transformed?"

"She's both," Roman said. Understanding slow. "Death and freedom, she said so herself. Sometimes the path leads to both. What if the Goddess transformed Poppy to stop her from dying?"

"Just like in the old story." Kastor nodded. "That has a lovely symmetry, doesn't it? And the Old Gods do love their tricks."

Roman stood, renewed determination coursing through his body. "And if she's not dead, then maybe we can set her free."

Moira pushed herself off the ground and crossed around to Roman's side of the fire. She laid a hand on Roman's shoulder. "I hate to be the voice of reason, but the cavern collapsed, Roman. How are we going to get down there to reach the Nixwyrm?"

A map of Durgeon's Keep sprawled before Roman's closed eyes. Sangray Castle, St. Oswin's Church, the fountain, all connected by the aqueduct system the Baron had built after his mother's death.

"I have a plan." Roman opened his eyes. Then he turned to his party. "How do we feel about blowing up a church?"

The Market

The Ditch market could barely be called a market. Pressed against the Outer Wall, the half-dozen tents clustered together were teeming with more pickpockets than vendors. Roman had never frequented the market, not in all his time roaming the underbelly of Durgeon's Keep, and definitely not as a lordling, but Kastor insisted that their quest to free the Nixwyrm — to bring Poppy back — required a visit to the boarded-up stalls.

"I know she's around here somewhere," said Kastor, more to himself than anyone else. His mustache shook as he twisted his neck around like an owl.

Roman blinked at the ramshackle display before him.

Then the wizard pointed a knobby finger right below Roman's nose. "There! That one."

There was nothing in that direction. No tent, no stall; the old man was pointing directly at the city's outer wall.

"Kastor —" Roman began.

"How do I look?" Kastor asked, as he tried to look at

himself in the reflection of Bearpuncher's armor. "Last time I came here, she was flirting with me. I swear it."

Over Roman's shoulder, Moira made a choking noise, halfway between a snort and laugh.

Oblivious, Kastor hobbled over to the wall. He knocked on the stone with his staff. At first, nothing happened. Then, the stones sank back and a round door appeared.

"Hurry now," Kastor called over his shoulder. "The entrance can be temperamental."

They hastened through and stepped into a room crowded with flora and fauna. Roman's horns grazed bundles of herbs hanging from the ceiling, while thick vines carpeted the walls. That someone could make anything grow in the barony amazed Roman.

"Kastor?" A woman with delicate lines framing her keen eyes set down a knife, halfway through chopping some sort of root. She stood behind a table that looked almost identical to the one in Poppy's workshop. Roman's mouth dried. "And you've brought friends. What can I help you with?"

"We need something powerful enough to bring down St. Oswin's Tower," Kastor said.

A wild smile broke across the woman's wide mouth, and Roman could see why Kastor fancied her. She had the same frenetic energy as he did.

"Well, you've come to the right place, dear things," she said with no protests or questions. "Welcome to Winona's Wonders and Wares!"

The Side Quest

"You have a problem, lady!" Moira called from the bottom of the cellar stairs. Across the cellar, a swarm of rats undulated at Roman's feet.

Winona's sing-song voice answered from the top of the stairs. "You simply need to destroy the vermin, then you may have as many components, potions and explosives as you can carry."

"This." Bearpuncher hacked his way through the hairy rodents, which shifted together with uncanny, synchronized movements, until he stood beside Roman.

"Was." Stab.

"A." Slash.

"Terrible." Stomp.

"Idea!" The Barbarian's axe ripped through the remainder of his targets, blood splattering upward and dotting the fur collar of his armor. Roman nodded his gratitude, then leaned against Bearpuncher, sides heaving with effort.

"Terrible? Yes," Kastor said. "Necessary? You know what,

probably not. We might have paid her instead."

Kastor tossed a flask of something aflame between Roman and Bearpuncher, nearly igniting Roman's cloak. Roman tore the garment from his shoulders and stomped on the singed hem, then wheeled around to glare at the old wizard. "Watch it!"

A bright smile illuminated Kastor's face. "But isn't this more fun?"

The largest rat Roman had ever seen, almost the size of a small horse, crawled out of the wall. He nearly spat his answer to Kastor. "No!"

The whole ordeal ended just as the sun crested the city wall. The morning glow pooled in through Winona's windows. Behind Roman, Bearpuncher heaved the rat corpse at Winona's feet.

As promised, she provided them with enough supplies to level a battlefield. Then, she waved and blew a kiss toward Kastor. Roman gritted his teeth.

The staircase that descended beneath St. Oswin's Tower lay in ruin. As expected. Roman paced the length of the center aisle inside the attached sanctuary. His footsteps on the flagstones and the gurgle of water from the sacred fountain were the only sounds in the empty building. He stared at his boots, as though he could see beneath the wood and stone, down into the underground lake below. Poppy lay there trapped and would remain so if they didn't move ahead with their plan.

Free the Nixwyrm. Summon the goddess. Bargain for Poppy's life.

ART IRL

"Art?" Michelle calls. "Got a minute?"

Alex's head pops up from tying his shoes and he raises an eyebrow at me. "I'll wait for you in the truck?"

I reach into my back pocket and pull out my keys; the familiar twenty-sided die triggers an anxious memory that I would rather push aside. Tossing the keychain to Alex is a relief. "Don't forget about the clutch."

He disappears through the door without acknowledging that he heard me.

Michelle invites me to sit.

I hesitate, but I can't say no. "Okay?"

I kick off my shoes and follow her to the living room. Upstairs is foreign, as though we've traveled between realms. The basement dwellers hardly ever have a reason to come up here. I flop down on one of her couches.

It's one of those comfy family couches, threadbare and lumpy in all the favorite spots, and scuffed by years of wear and tear. I rub my thumb against a jagged line on the armrest, drawn in black permanent marker. The stain looks like a lightning bolt.

Michelle sinks into an armchair. A copy of the newest game module sits butterflied over the armrest.

She checks what she was reading in the adventure before closing it, and reaches over the side of her chair to drop the hardcover sourcebook to the ground.

"This is better." She tucks her socked toes under the fleece blanket and looks at me, her head tilting to the side like a bird. In game, ravens are particularly uncanny.

"So, Art."

The way she says my name makes me want to sink out of sight into the sofa.

"So?" I avoid looking at her.

There's a pause. The silence is about as long as a round of Initiative in game — six seconds unless otherwise stated by the GM — but that's long enough.

"Well, I'm just going to come out and ask: what happened with Darcy?"

I should have expected the question, but for some reason I'm taken by surprise.

"What?"

"Seriously?" Both her eyebrows shoot up. I've seen Michelle exasperated before, but only in game and usually with our characters. Her expression is hard to absorb in real life. The heat of shame crawls up my neck.

She notices my flush, and her voice softens. "Come on, Art. I heard there was a fight and now she's not coming to Game. I can't keep stalling with side quests, and more importantly, I'm worried about her. And you, too."

Michelle's Persuasion is almost high enough to get me

talking. But I think about James, and Darcy, and about The Fight. Phantom pains throb through my split lip, which is nearly healed but still scabbed over.

I push myself to my feet. "It's nothing. Don't worry about it."

She stands with her hands on her hips. "You know why I asked if you would run Game in the new year, Art?"

"I don't know. Why?"

"Because you always do the right thing for the group."

Her words slam into me like a cartoon anvil. She notices and presses her advantage.

"You're a smart guy. You're thoughtful, you're good at mapping things out, and I love how much you invest in the story.

"But, you've been hiding from reality in game, Art. With Darcy, for the first time, I thought you were actually living, like, in real life too."

My first instinct is to deny everything she's said. I mean, what's wrong with gaming? But then I remember the fizzy cups of Witch's Brew and kissing beneath the Fairytree; the feeling of Darcy filling the space beneath my chin.

There's nothing wrong with loving Game, but of course Michelle's right: being with Darcy IRL was better, and that only makes losing her worse.

Tears splash onto my cheeks. I turn to the door. "I've got to go. Dawn will be wondering where I am."

I can't stop crying the entire way home. For once, Alex doesn't say anything.

I throw my keys and that stupid d20 keychain onto the kitchen counter. The die rolls a natural twenty, as if mocking me, and with barbarian rage I rip off the keychain and throw it across the room.

I know that Michelle's right. I know that a better person would text Darcy and try to come to a resolution. A happy ending even.

But everything hurts. I just — can't.

DARCY IRL

Mack's voice interrupts my comic strip of Art-related thought bubbles. "So, I found some interesting articles. Here."

I wipe the french fry grease from my fingers before taking the printed article from Mack. Rainbow sits beside me in the booth, with Wyatt across from her. We've moved lunch locations until further notice. After the SCC meeting, no one was very eager to return to the stage. Not that anyone really minds much. Rainbow's parents have been generous with the free fries.

There's not enough time to read the full article — a review on school policy and mental health published by the city school district — before Wyatt adds, "See, in paragraph two." He jabs his index finger at the paper. "In the city, schools can't stop us from starting a QSA. '*Students who request the formation of a QSA are to be accommodated.*'"

"I checked the school division site," Mack says. "We don't have the same policy, but if we could present to the division board, we might be able to request they adopt something similar." For the first time since we started discussing the QSA, Mack's eyes are bright. There's determination in the way they stare at me.

It's exhausting.

I set down the article. "I don't know. Would anything really be different?"

It's as if I've dumped freezing water on the fire that had been kindling in Mack. With just a few words, I can almost hear the hiss of steam as Mack deflates. Wyatt and Rainbow exchange a significant look; they don't even bother with Stealth.

"Darcy," Rainbow says, her voice soft. "We know you're in a bad place right now, but —"

"But is Arthur Bailey really a good enough reason to give up?" Wyatt interrupts. "I mean, his dad straight up sabotaged our presentation. And what did he do to stop it?"

My mouth dries. "Art's not his father."

"I agree," Wyatt says. "But isn't this bigger than your relationship status? I thought you understood that."

"That's not fair," I say. "You all didn't even want to try and start a QSA this year before I met you."

Wyatt thumps the table with his fist. "Exactly! You're the one who convinced us that going to the SCC would be the right move, but now you're ready to give up. Why? Because you can't date the boy you want to?"

I search for a response but fail to find the words. When I look up, Wyatt's eyes sparkle with unshed tears. Mack pats Wyatt's arm. "The guys in Wyatt's class haven't spoken to him since he came out. Don't you get it? We've all been heartbroken, but this is bigger than that. You're the one who said so, remember?"

Mack's words slam into me. Hard. And it hurts because they're right.

I reach across the table and cover Wyatt's hand with my own, working up the courage to look at him again. When I do, he starts to cry.

"You're right. I'm sorry. Of course we should go to the school board. Let's do it."

Wyatt squeezes my hand, then wipes his cheek with the back of a plaid flannel shirt. Somehow, he pulls it off without looking too country.

After a quiet moment, Rainbow slides the article into the middle of the table. "Darcy did bring up a good point. Even if we go to the school board, especially without the support of the SCC, it could be the same thing all over again," Rainbow says.

The wheels start spinning in the back of my head. "What if we got the SCC to support us first?"

Mack answers my question with his own. "Then we wouldn't need to go to the school board?"

I shake my head. "No, going to the board is a really good idea. If we can get them to adopt a policy like this —" I jab the article with my index finger. "Well, that would change things for any other students fighting to start a QSA. We need to talk to Marcus Bailey."

Mack, Wyatt and Rainbow stare back at me. I chew on my lip. "Look, he's our biggest obstacle, but what if there was a way to convince him to help us? He could also be our greatest resource."

"I'm sorry, I don't think I heard you right," Wyatt says, his words slow and sardonic. "Did you just suggest we buddy up with Marcus Bailey?"

"Yes."

"How exactly do you plan on doing that?"

There are only two people who have a shot at changing Mr. Bailey's mind. I look at Rainbow. "Dawn?"

"I'd volunteer her, but she's been staying with me since the SCC meeting. I don't think she wants to see him right now, not even for the QSA." Rainbow shrugs. "Sorry."

I wince. Then there's only one other person who can help us.

Art freezes where he stands, when he sees me waiting for him outside his math class. His lanky body stretches nearly as tall as the doorframe, his hair still messy, clothes rumpled.

"You're blocking the door," Alex says, then pushes Art into the hallway. That's when Alex notices me too. He glances between his best friend and me. "Oh, hi, Darcy."

"Hi."

"Hey," Art mumbles.

Hope balloons inside me. I step forward, wrapping my fingers into the hem of my sweater. "I would have texted, but I didn't think you'd answer me. Can we talk? It's important."

Alex waits for Art to nod, then shuffles sideways. "I've got to go, don't want to be late and all that. I'll talk to you later, man."

Art and I find somewhere more private to talk, a little nook next to a backdoor exit with an ancient vending machine collecting dust beside us. He leans his back to the wall, directly opposite me, and runs a hand through his hair.

"You should come back to Game. Michelle can't stall much longer, and we can't finish the quest without Poppy."

Warmth radiates through me. I've missed gaming with

everyone almost as much as I've missed Art. "You'd be okay with that?"

Art lifts his head and stares right at me. "Doesn't matter if I'm okay with it or not. It's the right thing to do. For the game, I mean."

"Right." I glance at the vending machine, his words stinging. "For the game."

Silence swells between us.

"What did you want to talk about, Darcy?" His voice is softer now, almost tender, but undercut with exhaustion.

When the QSA and I strategized, we all agreed that the best way to get to Art's dad was through Art. And the best way to get to Art was me. "Apologize, beg, seduce, whatever," Wyatt said. "Just get him to speak with his father for us."

I inch forward and brush his forearm with my fingertips. His fists clench at his sides, but he doesn't pull away. I slide my hand down to his wrist. He relaxes into the touch and twists his fingers in mine. I wiggle closer and lift my chin, eyes pleading with him.

"Art —" I try to apologize, until I'm cut off.

He kisses me.

At first, the kiss is gentle. Sweet. A whisper kiss, a reminder of what we had together. I close my eyes and kiss him back, the lockers and bad lighting spinning around us, but Art's wet eyelashes on my cheeks stop me from getting lost in the fantasy. This wasn't how making up was supposed to go. We were supposed to kiss on the football field or something, with snow falling around us like a Netflix special.

We were supposed to talk about the QSA first.

I use all my Willpower to pull back. Art's eyes are red-rimmed with tears.

"I missed you," he says.

I grip his shirt tight in my fists, not sure if I want to pull him closer or stop him from kissing me again. "Art, slow down. I need to apologize first."

Art pulls me into a tight hug. "I forgive you," he says against my hair.

My eyebrows knit together, and instead of relief or joy, confusion rattles through me. After three weeks of no contact, one frenzied kiss and half an apology, he forgives me? Just like that?

"Okay," I say slowly. "And I need your help."

"Anything."

"I —" It's now or never. I suck in a deep breath. "I need you to talk to your dad about the QSA."

And just like that, the spell is broken. Art's arms fall to his sides. When I look back up, he stares down at me, mouth open, like a husk. Wyatt's question from earlier echoes back. *What did he do?*

Nothing. The entire time. Not when Art's dad tossed me out of their home, not when his dad said we couldn't date, not even at the SCC meeting. And after the fight with James, Art just left. He avoided me for nearly an entire month, and now he'd rather kiss than talk about everything that happened?

I grit my teeth against the unexpected flash of anger. "Art, did you hear me? I need you to convince your dad to support the QSA."

"I heard you."

"He could sway the SCC in our favor, the same way he swayed everyone against us."

Art blinks. Once, then twice. "Is that the only reason you apologized? Because you need me to help your little club?"

"Little club?" My voice climbs. "Do you even hear yourself? You sound exactly like him, but unlike your dad, you know what the QSA means to me!"

Regret flashes across his face. "I obviously don't know you as well as I thought." His tone is clipped, biting. He pushes past me.

"That's not fair." I step in front of him. He falters, forced to stop or walk right into me. He takes a confused step back. "You are going to listen to me this time."

I take a deep breath. "Starting the QSA here isn't some noble quest. These are real people with IRL problems, Art! Regardless of our relationship, real people should matter to you too. Don't you get that? This is bigger than you and me, and if it were in game, you would have already done the right thing, but because it's real and because real things matter, you're running away. Again!"

"So what if I'm running away?"

"You're taking the easy way out."

"That's a bit hypocritical, don't you think? You know, because of your real boyfriend and all."

"I don't know why I thought this would work."

"You should have broken up with him, or told me about him, instead of stringing me along."

"I tried, Art! He told me he was going to kill himself! And now you're using that to justify your own cowardice, even though you have the power to change everything!"

Torn between the desire to run, and wishing he'd stop me, I spin on my heel. Then, without a backward glance, I walk away.

ART IRL

I watch her go.

The kiss burns on my lips, as does everything I said to Darcy. I hit the vending machine. Hard. A can of pop falls into the tray at the bottom.

There's no way she's right. My dad would never change his mind about the QSA because of me; there's nothing I can do.

"Oof. That was hard to watch." Dawn appears beside me. I jump, not sure where she came from. She looks over at me, rolls her eyes, then steps around me and reaches into the vending machine to retrieve the Diet 7UP that fell. She cracks it open.

"What? How?" I stumble over my words. "How long were you listening?"

"Long enough to know you're being totally unfair."

"Excuse me?" I look down the hallway to see if anyone else is eavesdropping. There's nothing but closed classroom doors, painted brick and student art.

Dawn swigs back the 7UP. "You, a cis straight White dude,

just told your bisexual ex-girlfriend that you'd do anything for her, except stand up to our super homophobic father, after she apologized to you for not knowing how to leave an abusive relationship. I'm honestly so embarrassed for you right now. Classy moves, brother."

My shoulders tense. "What? No. That's not what happened."

Dawn puts a hand on her hip and pins me with a disbelieving stare. "That's exactly what happened."

I crumble under my little sister's gaze. Buckling at my knees, I sag against the wall and slide to the floor. Dawn's words sink in and knock the wind from my lungs.

She's right. Of course she's right. And Darcy, she's right too. Shame creeps up my neck, as I realize exactly how I must have sounded to her. Now that I think about it, Michelle tried to tell me that I needed to live more IRL too. With my knees pulled against my chest, I rest my forehead on my folded arms.

"Art?" Dawn sinks down beside me. She rests a hand on my shoulder.

Tears wet the sleeve of my Henley, the pool of damp expanding under my cheek. "She hates me now."

My little sister slides an arm around my shoulder, then pulls me into a tight hug. "No. She's disappointed, heartbroken too, but she doesn't hate you."

"That's worse." I chuckle, but there's no humor in the sound. "I'm such a coward."

"You're not wrong." Dawn might be a born thespian, drawn to drama like a moth to flame, but she doesn't suffer fools. She squeezes me one more time, then let's go and leans the back of her head against the wall. "But you don't have to be. Darcy was right, you have the power to change things."

"Come on, Dawn. You know how he is, he won't listen to me."

She closes her eyes. "I'm dating Rainbow."

My head swivels to her so fast that I almost knock into the wall. "You're gay?"

Dawn's chin drops to her chest. "I'm not totally sure, but I really like Rainbow. I might even love her."

"Does —" I hate to ask, but I can't stop myself. "Does Dad know?"

Her eyes shoot to me, and she grips my arm. "You can't tell him, Art."

Dawn's fingers dig into me, as though she can coerce my response with her grip alone. The desperation in her face tugs at me. I shake my head. "Never. I wouldn't do that, Dawn."

Her fingers release, tears swimming in her eyes. "No one else knows, just me and Rainbow. Not even our friends in the QSA, although I think they've probably guessed and are too kind to ask."

"Is that why you've been avoiding the house?"

Dawn nods.

A smile tugs at the corner of my mouth. "Dad would be so pissed if he knew you'd been staying overnight with your paramour."

"God, Art! Who even says paramour?" She covers her face in her hands, but she's laughing. "You're so cringe."

When her laughter fades, I stand up and offer her a hand.

"Hey. Thank you, and —" I say, then rub the back of my neck. "And I'm sorry. No matter what Dad thinks or believes, I will always have your back. You know that, right?"

"I know." She pokes me in the chest. "Especially because you're going to talk to Dad and get the QSA approved."

...

Dad's home office hasn't changed since the house was built. The same royal blue walls, orderly bookshelves and glass desk sit exactly where they always have, when I walk in after school. Pushed against the wall is a brown leather couch where my father lies on his back with a manila file folder spread over his chest.

Even from the door, I can see the steady rise and fall of his chest. He flew home on a red-eye last night and drove straight here from the airport. The temptation to leave him and let him sleep, to avoid this whole messy conversation, makes me reach for the door handle. I'm halfway through closing the door when the hinge whines in protest. My dad blinks open his eyes, then looks at his watch.

He curses. I don't think I've ever heard him swear before.

It's not until he's sitting up, shuffling loose papers into the file, that he notices me standing in the doorway.

"Arthur?" He runs a hand through his hair. "Thanks for waking me. I shouldn't have fallen asleep."

"Yeah." I step back into the office. "No problem."

Dad stands, drops the file on his desk, then tucks in his shirt. He's rolling down his shirt sleeves when he glances at me again. "What's this? Why are you so cagey?"

"Cagey? Me? No."

He grunts. "You haven't stopped tapping your toe and you're hovering in my doorway. I may not be around all the time, but I know my son well enough to see you're nervous about something."

I stop moving. I hadn't even noticed the fidgeting in the first place. Caught under my father's pointed stare, I let out an agonized sigh. Now or never. "I was hoping we could talk."

"I gathered as much." Dad gestures to the couch for me to sit.

I shake my head. "I'd rather stand, but you can sit. Please."

He sits back down with a confused look on his face. Honestly, me too. I have no idea where to even begin. I spent most of the afternoon replaying both my fight with Darcy and my conversation with Dawn, trying to wrap my mind around all of it, instead of actually preparing for what I would say to Dad.

"Is this about that Darcy girl?"

"No!" I say with too much force. Dad nods, but I can tell by the way he leans back that he's not convinced. I roll my head away with a shake. "Well, sort of, but not totally. I wanted —" I trail off.

Dad waits, his gaze steady, without saying a word.

My foot starts tapping again. I run a hand though my hair.

"I do that too," Dad says. His voice surprises me, as does the small smile on his face. "When I'm stressed. Every time my hands went to my hair, your mom used to laugh at me."

I squeeze my eyes closed. "I want you to support the Queer-Straight Alliance at school."

At first, I wonder if I imagined saying the words, but when I finally work up the courage to peek open an eye, Dad is shaking his head.

My pulse hammers in my throat and if I don't move, I might spontaneously combust. I pace back and forth.

"Please, Dad. You were able to convince the entire SCC to table the decision, which means you can convince them to vote in our favor next meeting. If you could just —"

"No."

I stop moving. "What?"

Dad stands. "No. We've discussed this already, Arthur. You know where I stand on this issue. We don't believe in homosexual relationships —"

"You don't, but that doesn't mean that I don't," I say, but he just talks over top of me, anger flashing in his cold eyes.

"— we sure aren't going to support a 'safe space' to breed them in our high schools. That's final."

"But, Dad," I try again.

"Was I unclear? It is my job to protect you and your sister, and I will not allow you to become corrupted by some girl and her lesbian parents."

I look down. He doesn't know about Dawn. He can't know about her and Rainbow.

"This isn't about Darcy, Dad. We're talking about school and the SCC."

Dad crosses the room, his footsteps heavy, until he's standing right in front of me. Anger flashes in his eyes. "You must think I'm an idiot. I know you and Darcy were sneaking around, doing God knows what. Of course this is about her. She put you up to this, didn't she?"

Lifting my chin, I push aside all my fear. *Be brave*, I think. Be like Roman. "No. I'm asking for your help because you're my father, and this is important to me. If you want to protect your children, then start by protecting your relationship with us, Dad. Because Dawn and I are both old enough to decide if we want a relationship with you."

I watch with an unfamiliar, cool resolve, as Dad processes my words. It's a critical hit.

He takes a small step backwards. His voice dips the littlest bit. "What is that supposed to mean?"

"It means, Dawn can't look at you right now, so she's avoiding the house, and I'm starting to agree with her." My words are quiet, confident. I step forward. "It means that you're going to rethink the whole 'Pray the Gay Away' stance you've been preaching, do some actual fucking research and intro-spection, and help us with the QSA, or you're going to lose both your children."

"Arthur," Dad says. "I'm your father, you don't speak that way to me."

My jaw tightens. "You're right. You are my father, and that's exactly why I'm speaking to you this way. I didn't realize how messed up our family was until I met Darcy's moms. If anyone is corrupt, it's you. You have power. How you use it is your choice. Can you live with the consequences of choosing to prevent the QSA from happening?"

"Art —"

I spin around to leave, then hesitate at the door. I grip the doorframe. "I broke up with Darcy a month ago."

Dad's voice sounds thin, weak even. "Maybe that was for the best."

My hand tightens on until my knuckles go white. "No. It wasn't. And you know what, I'm in love with her."

I leave my father behind, and it's as if I've leveled up. I'm stronger, more confident, and suddenly I know exactly what I need to do. I have a new quest: Win the Girl Back.

DARCY IRL

The smell of cinnamon and vanilla embraces me when I get home. I kick off my boots. Monica is baking cookies. She's listening to a podcast or something because she doesn't hear me come into the kitchen. I watch her sneak a taste of the dough.

My mom finally notices me lurking and pops out an earbud. "How did it go?"

I perch on a stool at the island and lay my head against the countertop.

Monica sets aside the cookie dough. She dusts her hands on her apron and tucks her hair behind her ears. "Wanna talk?"

I groan.

"Well, Carrie is still at work —" She hands me an open delivery box. There are a couple dozen new hair pigments packed inside. She pulls one called Watermelon Sunshine. "— And I was thinking: pink is the same color as Poppy's hair, right?"

I take the dye from her and laugh. "Yeah, but how did you know that?"

"Moms know everything." She goes back to baking and pulls out a cookie sheet. "Besides, a new look is always nice after a breakup. What do you say?"

I think about Poppy, about Roman, and wonder if there's any real difference between our characters and us. "Let's do it."

We're downstairs, in the salon with a plate of snickerdoodle cookies, when Carrie gets home. Mom is wearing black gloves and brushing the pink dye onto my hair after a lengthy bleaching and toning process.

Carrie opens the French doors. Her nose wrinkles. "It reeks in here. What on earth is going on?"

"She needed a change." Monica washes dye from my forehead. Then she wraps my head in a shower cap. "Now we wait. Should take about half an hour."

Together the three of us leave the basement and make our way to the kitchen. Mom opens the fridge to grab a few ingredients for supper, but Carrie stops her with a kiss on the cheek. "Let me, darling."

Carrie chops an onion. Monica looks around, unsure what to do with herself. Finally, she settles on a glass of wine and sits beside me.

Monica swirls the red liquid in her glass. "How was work?"

"Well, I had the loveliest conversation with one of my patients. She asked if I would be her primary physician."

"That's awesome," Monica and I say at the same time.

With a satisfying sizzle, Carrie dumps the onions into a frying pan, her eyes misty. "Yeah. I thought so too. Slowly changing people's minds."

"Speaking of changing minds," I say. "I talked to Art today."

"Our brave girl," Monica says.

Carrie dabs the corner of her eyes with her wrist. "How did it go?"

I shrug, setting the table. "Not great, but it's okay. I said what I needed to say."

Monica and Carrie share a look, as if they don't quite believe me, but they don't press. "How much longer until food's done?" Monica asks instead.

"It's still going to be a bit."

"All right. Come on, Darcy," she says, already on her way to the basement. "We have to wash your hair."

We get all the way to her salon space, when the doorbell rings.

"Can you get that, darling?" Carrie calls.

Monica sits me at her sink, my head still wrapped in foil, and disappears upstairs. I pull out my phone. My fingers hover over Art's name. I hesitate, heart aching, but then I type out a message and hit send.

Michelle responds within seconds.

> I'll see you at Game this week.
> Sorry for being MIA.

> That's awesome! I take it
> things went well tonight then?

I don't have time to ask her what she means, before Monica returns with a giant smile from ear to ear. "The door's for you, Darcy."

I side-eye her. "Okay, weirdo. What's with the face?"

"You'll see," she answers in sing-song voice as she takes off my black bib.

I push out of the chair, then climb the stairs.

Mom left the door open, but I don't see anyone. I grab the doorframe and peek outside. "Hello?"

I flick on the porch light.

"You're changing your hair."

"Art?" I've been fantasizing about this moment for weeks, but after the last time we spoke, I hesitate. "What are you doing here?"

He steps out of the shadows. I burst out laughing.

He's wearing a ninja mask, devil horns and a long black wool coat. He has the foam sword and oversized die from our first date.

"Art, what's happening? Why are you dressed like that?"

He hinges at the waist, brandishing the sword like a duelist, and effortlessly drops into the voice he uses for Roman. "I don't believe I've seen your lovely face around these parts before, fair maiden."

I grab a jacket and close the front door behind me. "Are you kidding me?"

He waits for me in suspended animation.

I cover my face. This is just too much.

"Just play along. Humor me, please?"

I look over my shoulder. The picture window, which has a new sheet of glass, is suspiciously empty. Knowing The Moms, they're lurking somewhere and spying on us, but I can't see them.

I take a deep breath and slip into Poppy's familiar accent. "I do not believe we've had the pleasure, traveler."

He holds out a hand. "Perhaps we should remedy that. Pray tell me, m'lady, how can I win your favor?"

I extend a hand to him, as though I'm a fancy noblewoman

and not just a teenage girl pretending to be a hedgewitch. He kisses my fingertips. His eyes lift to mine. I can't speak so he keeps going, in character.

"Should I slay a troll? I hear there is a troublesome one nearby?"

I bite back a giggle. How can he still make me laugh when everything between us is so complicated? "I took care of that one a couple months ago," I say, tone dry.

"Maybe you need me to slay a dragon, then?"

I tilt my head to the side and take back my hand. "I can slay my own dragons."

I'm half joking, but Art's shoulders snap back. He stands and pulls down his mask. His smile is small, his gaze intense. "I know."

I look away. I don't understand what's happening. Why are we standing on the icy sidewalk? After everything?

"Darcy —" He chokes on my name. "I am so sorry. I was an ass this afternoon."

I wrap arms around my body, holding my love handles, and take a small step back. "Yeah. You were."

Art follows me, closing the distance again. The air shimmers with a gust of wind and light snowflakes dance through the night sky.

"There's more." His voice softens, his words meant for only me. "I'm sorry for ignoring you, for not listening to you, but mostly for not standing up to my dad sooner. It wasn't right."

I stare at his chest. My line of vision only comes up to the second button on his black coat.

"I talked to Dad and I gave him an ultimatum. I'm not going to pretend that I'm suddenly the hero. I know I still have a lot to learn, but I want to do the work." He hesitates.

My eyes sting but I can't bring myself to look up. He lifts my chin with a tender hand. "Say something? Please?"

"I shouldn't have lied to you!"The confession bursts out of me like a sob, then I'm actually crying, tears cold on my skin. "I don't blame you for breaking up with me. I'm the worst."

"What? No," he says, his words small and soft. He leans closer. "Darcy, no. You aren't the worst. You are fun and bold, and you make me feel like I can be brave too."

Then his lips brush mine. At first, it's half a kiss. A question on our mouths, but the hesitation is soon replaced by a familiar feeling that warms me from the inside out. I pull back before I'm swept away.

"But if I had a re-roll, if I could go back in time, I'd tell you everything. Things with James were messed up, but I should have —"

"Hey, hey." He presses his forehead against mine, as if to lend me his warmth. "I appreciate what you're trying to say, really, but you're not responsible for the way James treated you. Or the way I treated you, for that matter. You're not to blame, Darcy."

I cry harder, and in response, Art pulls me into a fierce hug. He tucks me under his chin. I turn my head, cheek pressed to his chest, and squeeze my eyes closed. "I know, but I could have told you what was going with him. I haven't been able to stop thinking about how betrayed you must have felt, and I hate that I did that to you."

"And I'm not proud of how I reacted or of how I've been acting since, trust me," he mutters above me. "But you know what? I'm actually okay with that. I want to be with you, even when we make mistakes and have to make things right again." His arms relax around me, and he leans back to look me in the eye. "You were right, you know? Real things do matter and what we have is very real."

I chuckle and wipe my eyes the edge of my sleeve. "What am I supposed to say to something like that?"

"Tell me you love me."

"Is that all?" I ask, unable to stop the smile stealing across my lips. Art waits, poised for my response. I roll my eyes. "Of course, I love you."

He doesn't miss a beat. "I know."

And I love his dorky Star Wars reference.

"I love you too," he says, capturing my lips for another kiss. This time there's confidence there. Things feel different between us now, but also familiar.

We're a party of two fighting back-to-back; we know each other's movements, the other person's pace, their strengths, their weaknesses and all their stat bonuses.

We're not the same. We've leveled up.

When the kiss ends, Art smiles. The same sly smile I've seen at the game table when he plays Roman.

His voice lowers, dark and moody. "I think I'm going to like this color on you very much."

He tucks a damp pink curl under my shower cap.

The Rescue

The fuse crackled and hissed to life as Roman ignited the explosives. Then, he barreled across the church courtyard and slid to join his friends behind cover. He shielded his ears, squeezed his eyes and waited for St. Oswin's Tower to fall.

A flash of light turned the insides of Roman's eyelids red, but no sound followed. When he peeked out from where his back pressed against the alley wall, the tower was folding in on itself in perfect silence. He stared as the steeple descended into a dark cloud, contained within a magical barrier.

With the worst of it over, Kastor groaned beside Roman. That's when he noticed the shine of sweat on Kastor's brow. The old wizard sagged against the wall. "I am getting too old for this."

Moira said something, but Roman was already halfway to the pile of rubble. He sank to his knees at the center of where the church had stood only moments before, then began unearthing the sacred fountain. The ornate basin lay in ruin, a large crack split down the middle, but where Roman expected to find water pooling forth, he found nothing.

"No!" Desperation sharpened his voice. His fingernails caught on the dry ground. He dug into the edge of the crack and heaved with all his strength, as though to tear the earth open. This should lead to the lake, there was supposed to be a stream or river, some sort of path back to the cavern, back to Poppy.

When the ground refused to yield, a sob racked Roman's body. He bent over and wept bitter tears into the dust.

"Roman —"

Moira interrupted Kastor. "Give him a moment, would you?"

"He doesn't have a moment. Roman! There's no way that's stable, if you stay there you'll —"

Roman plunged into darkness.

The air left his lungs when he hit the ground — hard — and the back of his head smacked the cavern floor with a crack. Sticky blood bloomed wet on the back of his neck. He gasped in pain.

Eyes wide, Roman tried to orient himself. The darkness yawned in all directions, and no matter how many times he blinked, nothing emerged from the void.

Nothing, but a voice. "Be still, Roman Adeleson."

Roman's body tensed. Though he'd never heard that voice before, he knew who spoke across the dark expanse: Deyja, the Promised Change, the Old Goddess of death, life and renewal.

He struggled to sit up — he refused to bargain for Poppy's freedom while lying on his back — but as soon as he rose, his head spun and forced him to curl forward or risk vomiting.

"I told you," Deyja said, a hint of amused affection in her tone. "Struggling will do you no good. Now, hold still and let me look at you."

Cool fingers lifted his chin. Roman braced for the pain but found that his head wound ceased throbbing. He blinked again, and this time, his eyes opened onto the face of a strange and beautiful woman.

She lifted him to his feet, as if he were a child. Standing a head taller than him, her shoulders were broad and straight, her arms muscular. Beneath her left eye, a white moth fanned her cheek with lazy wings. Startled, Roman pulled back.

Out of her reach, he noticed just how many of the insects clung to her. There were small wings of all shapes, sizes and colors on her hair, her collarbone, her wrists. They flickered around her as though she were a bright light. Her pale eyes softened. "You look like your mother."

His response came automatically. "I didn't know her."

"We were friends. I loved her dearly, and it pained me to watch Dietrich Sangray hold her captive for so many years. Foolish man."

"He said that you turned her into the Nixwyrm, that you murdered her."

"Murder? Arrogant, stupid man." The light Deyja brought to the void seemed to be swallowed by her anger, so that shadows were cast across her face. "Adele was my most devout priestess. She worshipped me and happily agreed to transform into the Nixwyrm, but she would have never left you so long by choice, and I am no murderer."

Roman wanted to point out that she may not be a murderer, but she was the goddess of death. Fear crawled down his spine. He dared not.

"You're frightening him, my lady."

Poppy emerged from the shadows. Her hair hung in wet clumps around her face, and instead of her medical apron, she wore a simple gray shift. Roman might have been embarrassed to see her so exposed if he wasn't already overcome with relief. She opened her arms to him, and he crashed into her embrace.

"I thought I'd lost you," he said, lips pressed into the crown of her head. "I thought I'd never see you again, never get to tell you how much I love —"

Poppy kissed him. And unlike back at her clinic, this kiss held joy and life and celebration. He pulled her off her feet and spun her around until he felt her smile against his lips. They laughed into one another until Roman released her to cradle her face. "We thought — we — I saw you die. You transformed. How? What?" Roman's thoughts scattered as he tried to understand. "Are you okay?"

"I'm fine, Roman." Poppy's eyes met his, fierce and steady. "I'm here."

"But how?"

She looked to the goddess.

"She's being modest," said Deyja. "She did, in fact, die, and your eyes did not deceive you. She is the Nixwyrm now and she will be until the mantle is passed on to another acolyte. That's the truth of it."

Water dripped from a stalactite somewhere beyond Roman's vision. He tucked Poppy beside him and held her hand against his chest. "I won't let you keep her."

The moths surrounding Deyja took flight when she began to cackle. She laughed, until Poppy's voice interrupted. "I'm not her prisoner, Roman. I made her a deal."

He blinked into her green eyes. "A deal?"

"Your sweetheart swore to protect the river, Roman Adeleson, in exchange for her life, and I accepted. She's not a high priestess like your mother was, which has always been tradition, but I understand that my children have been forced into hiding. Exceptions had to be made."

"But the legend. I thought only women murdered in your name became the Nixwyrm, like your daughter. The Nixie?"

Beneath his palm, Poppy tensed. The goddess' face grew hard. "The Nixie was the first river guardian, but she wasn't murdered. She chose to be mortal, she wanted to live the rest of her days with her ferryman. I begged her not to, but she always had a mind of her own. She was cunning, like her father, and she bargained with me.

"She wanted to grow old and die with her lover but promised to fulfill her divine duties and purify the river forever after — a river that leads to Aaderhall will always carry death, after all — and I was foolish enough to agree. I could see no way for her to fulfill her end of the bargain, and I assumed that she would regain her immortality upon her death. Clever girl bestowed her powers on her daughter. And her daughter, onto the next daughter. Over time the rules have varied but there has always been a Nixwyrm, and the river has always been purified of death. That is, until Dietrich Sangray locked your mother under that tower."

"She saved my life," Poppy said. "The goddess — I heard her call to me, and she offered to save me, if I became the Nixwyrm."

"But you're still human."

Poppy smiled. "And I'll remain human for all but one night, each year."

"The Nixwyrm only travels down the river each spring equinox," Deyja said. She lifted a finger to above her head and a silver month landed. She tilted her head as if to listen to the creature. "Time to go already?"

Roman sputtered, his head swinging between the two women. "My mother told me that I'd have to free Poppy and bargain for her life! She said that you'd only spare her if I swore an oath of service."

"Adele did love her dramatics." Deyja's physical form shifted, moths fluttering to life where the hem of her skirts brushed the ground; the goddess was both taking wing and dissolving before their eyes. She laughed again. "No, Roman, I won't press you into a life of service, especially when it appears that your loyalties clearly belong elsewhere."

The goddess vanished before Roman could thank her.

From above, rocks slid down the cavern wall. Roman pulled Poppy away from the small landslide, as light pooled against the stones. When Roman looked up, three faces peered over the edge of the hole.

The end of a rope dropped down.

Sun sparkled off the now clean river, and Bearpuncher squeezed Roman's waist hard enough that he heard a pop in his spine. Pressed beside him in Bearpuncher's wide arms, Poppy chuckled. "We'll miss you too," she said.

"Are you sure you two can't come with us?" Moira asked from the deck of the *Baroness*. Behind her, Penn showed Kastor the spells that would propel the river barge.

Bearpuncher set both Roman and Poppy down. Finding his footing on the dock, Roman rubbed the back of his neck. Poppy slid her fingers into his free hand. He glanced down at the gold signet ring resting on his littlest finger, glinting in the sunshine.

"You know we can't. There's work to be done here," she said.

"But we expect you to return each spring," Roman added. "The Nixwyrm will never again be locked away, but that doesn't mean I'll leave her vulnerable. I'll need the best hired guard money can buy."

The barge only pulled away from the dock after two more spine-crunching hugs from Bearpuncher. Roman's friends were in the middle of the water when Poppy pointed. "Roman! The reward!"

"Almost forgot," he said, then he unhooked a purse from his belt. He threw the heavy bag at the *Baroness*, where there was a loud thud on deck. "Courtesy of Baron Blackwood and Deyja's Path! For all your service!"

Roman and Poppy watched until the river barge became small in the distance.

They had lots of work ahead. The rubble from St. Oswin's Tower had mostly been removed from the square, but there were still reconstruction efforts, and Roman was still fighting with nobles who refused to acknowledge his appointment as the new baron. He couldn't even begin to think about the new freedom of religion edict that he'd passed without developing a headache.

Among the common people — his people — Roman found tremendous support, but if he had any hope of avoiding an assassination within the next year, he'd need to secure more allies.

Poppy leaned her head against his arm and, for the moment, his worry evaporated. Roman turned to her and swept into a bow. "My Lady."

She scrunched her nose, but took his offered arm nonetheless. "My Lord."

ART IRL

My breath puffs from my mouth in little white clouds. Darcy knocks on Michelle's door. My girlfriend doesn't wait for a response before she pushes inside. A wave of warmth and yellow light greets us in the wintry evening.

"Hello! Happy New Year!" Darcy shakes flecks of snow from her pink hair. A month ago, she had this startling, Candy Crush-pink head; now, the color has faded and is almost pastel. She's very concerned about her dark roots showing, but I kinda like it.

I follow her inside, a box of brightly wrapped Christmas gifts in my arms. Kicking off my shoes, I juggle the box while Darcy hangs up her coat.

Michelle appears in the entrance. "Long time, no see!"

Behind her, everyone is huddled around, looking at Alex's phone. He waves us over. "Have you seen this?"

We climb the short landing stairs and pass through the kitchen into the dining room. "What?" Darcy and I say at the same time.

She laughs. Funny: I'm not nervous around her anymore. "Check out this article from the *City Observer*." Alex shoves his phone in our faces.

I squint. "I can't read when you're holding your phone like that."

"So much for your Perception." Alex hands his phone to Darcy. I put down the box of gifts and read the headline. *Rural School Division Committed to Safe Spaces.* Below there's a picture of Mr. Elliot shaking the hand of a man in a suit. Standing behind him, just to the left, are Darcy and her moms.

She reads the rest of the article and gives Alex his phone back.

"Turns out there's a school division policy in the city that says if a student asks for a QSA, the school must comply. The Moms helped the QSA draft a letter and we sent it to our division office," Darcy says.

"It was either this, or go to the press, and for some reason the bigwigs didn't like that idea," I add. "They invited us to a meeting the next week."

Dad didn't try to stop me from attending the school division meeting with Darcy, her moms and the rest of the QSA, but he's still refusing to help us with the SCC. In the end, we found a workaround and went above his head, but things have been tense at home since. Dad's new "Don't Ask, Don't Tell" policy and our uneasy truce won't last forever. And the worst part is that he doesn't even understand just how much harm he's causing. Thinking about how my sister must feel around Dad, I cringe and push aside the now familiar disappointment. As Darcy's reminded me every time I start to rant about him, I can't do the work for my father. I can't change what he doesn't want to change.

"So what now?" Michelle asks.

Darcy rummages around through a variety of bright bags. "Now, we have a game to play, but first, happy holidays!"

She hands a bag to each person in the dining room, and soon the crinkling of tissue paper is everywhere.

Alex gets his present open first. He holds up the five-by-seven-inch framed illustration of Kastor.

"Is that?" Alex points at the frame, then to himself. Alex has the same zany smile that stretches across Kastor's bearded face.

One by one, everyone pulls out a piece of custom character art. Drawing and writing were my only escape during the break, with Dad home on holidays and Game on hiatus until tonight. That and spending as much time as possible at Darcy's place.

Robert laughs and flexes his arms just like Bearpuncher; Tyler sets his art on the table, Moira smiling amiably from the frame; and Michelle cackles as she unwraps the inked sketch of her wearing a wizard hat and holding a globe between her hands, floating dice in the background.

"There's more!" Darcy says.

Alex shakes his bag and something rattles inside. He pulls out a set of rainbow dice.

Darcy bounces on the balls of her feet. "Charity dice!"

She was intense as we picked gifts for Game. Hours of research went into finding these dice.

"Fifty percent from each set is donated to queer game developers," I explain.

Michelle cradles her portrait and dice to her chest. "Thank you so much!"

Everyone has something to share after our two-week break. We take forever to catch up, before we go downstairs. Finally, Michelle sits down. "You ready?"

We are all in our usual spots, except for Michelle and me. I'm in the GM's seat now. I've spread out my notes, books and new rainbow dice. I also have a great view of what everyone else is doing, including my girlfriend, who winks at me.

I blush, then double-check my notes. "I think so."

Behind the GM screen, I run a hand through my hair.

"All right. You find yourselves in a dusky tavern. Please roll Initiative."

The End

POPPY LE FEY

Class & Level: Warlock 12 · Background: Acolyte
Race: Standard Human · Alignment: Chaotic Good

STR: 11 (+0) · **DEX:** 13 (+1) · **CON:** 13 (+1) · **INT:** 14 (+2)
WIS: 18 (+4) · **CHA:** 20 (+5)

SAVING THROWS: Str 0 · Dex 1 · Con 1 · Int 2 · **Wis 8** · **Cha 9**

SKILLS: Acrobatics 1 · Animal Handling 4 · **Arcana 6** · Athletics 0
Deception 5 · History 2 · **Insight 8** · Intimidation 5 · **Investigation 6**
Medicine 4 · Nature 6 · Perception 4 · Performance 5 · Persuasion 5
Religion 6 · Sleight of Hand 1 · Stealth 1 · Survival 4

OTHER PROFICIENCIES & LANGUAGES
Language: Abyssal, Common, Old Common, Infernal · **Armor:** Light Armor
Weapon: Simple Weapons

Armor Class: 11 · Initiative: 1 · Speed: 30 · HP: 73

PERSONALITY TRAITS
I remember the Old Ways and use
my folk magic to serve those who
have been lost or forgotten.

IDEALS
Balance. There can be no life without
death, no peace without war. We are
called to restore balance to corrupt
systems of power.

BONDS
I walk Deyja's Path; all I do is in Her
service.

FLAWS
I lack boundaries and give too much
of myself in pursuit of justice, to
the detriment of those I love.

BACKSTORY
When her grandmother, the healer Lisbet le Fey, died, Poppy wasn't
prepared for the family secrets she would uncover in her grandmother's
recipe book. Spells. Runes. Words in Old Common so ancient and familiar
it was as if they sang to her. All of it carefully written next to salves for
burns and remedies for the common cold.

At first, she was angry. When she realized what they were, what they had
always been and what her grandmother had kept from her, Poppy tossed
the old book in the very back of a wardrobe and resolved to forget she'd
ever discovered the horrid thing. But once she knew, her magic knew, and
after being ignored for nearly eighteen years, the power in her would no
longer be denied.

Poppy le Fey belonged to the Old Gods, to the oldest of the Old Gods, and
Deyja had plans for the young hedgewitch.

ROMAN

Class & Level: Thief 12 · Background: Noble
Race: Standard Tiefling · Alignment: Neutral Good

STR: 12 (+1) · **DEX:** 20 (+5) · **CON:** 16 (+3) · **INT:** 12 (+1)
WIS: 14 (+2) · **CHA:** 20 (+5)

SAVING THROWS: Str 1 · **Dex 9** · Con 3 · **Int 5** · Wis 2 · Cha 5

SKILLS: Acrobatics 13 · Animal Handling 2 · Arcana 1 · **Athletics 5**
Deception 5 · **History 5 · Insight 6** · Intimidation 5 · Investigation 1
Medicine 2 · Nature 1 · **Perception 10 · Performance 9 · Persuasion 13**
Religion 1 · **Sleight of Hand 13 · Stealth 13** · Survival 2

OTHER PROFICIENCIES & LANGUAGES
Tools: Thieves' Tools · **Language:** Common, Infernal, Thieves' Cant
Armor: Light Armor · **Weapon:** Hand Crossbow, Longsword, Rapier,
Shortsword, Simple Weapons

Armor Class: 16 · Initiative: 5 · Speed: 30 · HP: 95

PERSONALITY TRAITS
After a lifetime of being trapped by
my father's expectations and noble
birth, I am finally free, and will not
go back.

I believe in freedom for all.

IDEALS
Atonement. I will make amends for
the harm I've caused and swear my
fealty to the common folk.

BONDS
I have found my true family and
would do anything to protect them,
even expose my greatest regrets.

FLAWS
Shame both compels and consumes
me; I am trying to outrun my past
and my father's legacy.

BACKSTORY
All of Durgeon's Keep knew of the Baron's son, though few had ever
laid eyes on him. Whispering nobles and visiting merchants speculated
wildly about the mysterious heir — he was a bastard, a monster, he was
a myth. Roman heard it all from the shadows, from his place behind his
father's throne, and the truth was much worse. For a man who spent his
days collecting information and secrets about each of those nobles and
merchants, he hadn't realized his father's true nature, the nature of his
family's wealth, until it was much too late.

And rather than confront the true monster in Durgeon's Keep, Roman ran.
His truth was that he'd been a fool, a fool and a coward.

DARCY LAROCQUE-EVANS

Medium, Human (Teenager)
Armor Class: 10 (Looks That Slay)

STR: 10 (+0) · **DEX:** 14 (+2) · **CON:** 11 (+0) · **INT:** 17 (+3)
WIS: 16 (+3) · **CHA:** 14 (+2)

SKILLS: Insight 5 · Perception 5 · Persuasion 4

Languages: English · Challenge: 1 (200 XP)
Proficiency Bonus: +2

TRAIT
Loyal — Darcy is fiercely loyal. She will do anything in her power to protect her loved ones.

ACTIONS
Take a Stand.
Once per long rest, in the presence of allies, Darcy gains an additional +5 armor class and one inspiration, which she may use herself or bestow on an ally.

Sarcastic Eye-Roll.
Melee Weapon Attack: +4, Reach 10 ft, One target
Hit: 3 (1d6) Psychic damage
Darcy may use her body language to deal small amounts of psychic damage to a single target each turn.

On a successful hit, target must make a WIS saving throw. If they fail, the target takes 1d6 psychic damage until they roll a successful save.

ARTHUR (ART) BAILEY

Medium, Human (Teenager)
Armor Class: 10 (Cinnamon Roll Energy)

STR: 11 (+0) · **DEX:** 16 (+3) · **CON:** 12 (+1) · **INT:** 14 (+2)
WIS: 14 (+2) · **CHA:** 16 (+3)

SKILLS: Insight 4 · Performance 5 · Religion 4

Languages: English, High Geekery · Challenge: 1 (200 XP)

TRAIT
Unassuming — Art is quiet and modest. He has a nonthreatening demeanour and makes others feel safe in his presence.

ACTIONS
Moved by the Muse.
Once per long rest, Art can call upon his Muse and apply profiency to one of the following skills: Deception, Intimidation or Persuasion.

Level-20 Nerd.
Art may cast "Disguise Self" as a cantrip when playing an RPG of any kind. This spell lasts the duration of the role-play.

ACKNOWLEDGMENTS

No one tells you how to do this part, and finding the right words to thank everyone who supported me, my writing and this book may as well be a boss fight on Nightmare mode. And I'm a casual play girly.

That being said, I'm also a fangirl through and through, and I can't miss the opportunity to gush, squeal and celebrate everyone who made *Who We Are in Real Life* possible.

First, *Who We Are* wouldn't be in your hands if not for the vision — dare I say, *magic* — of my editor, Emma Sakamoto. Emma, you have a gift, thank you for sharing it with me. Alongside my editor, I would like to thank the publishing team at Groundwood Books — Karen Li, Michael Solomon, Lucia Kim, Kirsten Bassard, Fred Horler, and by extension Alison Strobel — who poured their skill and labor into producing this project. I am grateful to be one of your authors!

A very special thank-you to Bhavna Madan, the cover artist who saw my characters better than I ever could. I straight up cried when I saw those early sketches. So. Many. Feels.

Thank you to my writing community, who have invested in me

in so many ways, for so many years. To the EWG — Andrea, Ashley, Betty, Jeremy, Kyle, Laura, Maggie, Maureen, Nicki F., Nikki W., Rhonda and Shauna — you all believed in me before I believed in myself, and I want you to know that this publication wouldn't have happened without our writing group. To the fantastic folks at the Sage Hill Writing Experience, particularly Micheline, Tara, Tariq and Wayne, thank you for not one, but two fantastic retreats. And to Merilyn Simonds. I can't thank my writing community without honoring just how much you've shaped the ways in which I write. Merilyn found me and my writing before I even finished the first draft of this novel. She mentored me through draft after draft and assisted me with the submission process. Her friendship with Shelley Tanaka, who also deserves my sincere gratitude, put my manuscript in front of the right eyes. Merilyn, you're my real-life hero and I am so grateful for our friendship. Thank you for seeing me and for investing in my work, every step of the way.

I couldn't write a book about tabletop role-playing games without all the gamers in my life.

Thank you to my OG *D&D* crew — Adam V., Logan, Nathan, Ryan, and of course, our fearless Dungeon Master, Jocelyn. I hope you enjoy the little nods to our Raven Queen campaign, because if you recognize yourselves, then that's probably done on purpose!

To Darren, Karly, Mark, Sarah, Steph and Zack, thank you for sticking with me as I developed my storytelling skills as a DM and for becoming part of my gaming family along the way. Thank you to all the adventurers, to Adam N., Cullen, Justin, Lora and Tristan, who joined me for games, snacks and straight up vibes.

Also, thank you to the geeks and nerds who have, in some way, influenced my creative work. Thank you to the team who brought us *Dragon Age: Inquisition*, and to anyone who wrote and posted Solas fanfiction on AO3. For real. Special thank you to Sam Maggs and

Rainbow Rowell, who both wrote books about fandom and made me feel that I have something worth sharing too.

To my non-gaming friends, Ciara, Haleigh, Jayce, Jesse, Marina and Martina, thank you for being your fantastic selves and for listening to me either talk about TTPRGs or this book.

To the students and staff in our WCS Queer-Straight Alliance — you know who you are — thank you for giving me a reason to write this story. And to all the adults out there in rural areas trying to make the world a little more kind and a lot safer for students and families like Darcy and her mothers, thank you from the bottom of my heart.

Thank you to my father, Michael, for playing *D&D* with a six-year-old girl who just wanted to cast magic spells (and maybe sacrifice her sister to a dragon along the way). To my mother, Sheena, thank you for telling me stories and listening to mine. Thank you for writing a book first, so I grew up knowing this dream could come true. To all my grandparents — Muirhead, Murakami and Koops — thank you for loving me and everything I do in the way only grandparents can love.

I come from a large, loud family, full of stories and I want to thank my aunts, uncles and cousins — Andrea, Janet and Ian, Kellen, Lanelle, Neve, Angela and Brian B., Ivan, Dominique and Emora — for always being the first people to ask about my writing.

Thank you to Tonya and Brian M. for being my second family. To my siblings-in-law and my darling nephews, to Chris, Cody and Aidan, Deandra, Zack and Bennett, Nicole and Tyrone, I love you all.

My sisters, Megan, Arwen and Moira, are freaking out right now because they haven't read their names yet. This was intentional; I love to see them squirm! But in all seriousness, if you are lucky enough to have femmes in your life as amazing as these three, then your party is complete. Adventure forth!

Megan, I couldn't ask for a better sister-friend and I am so honored to count you among my nearest and dearest. Thank you for checking in on me and being so incredibly excited about all my passions. Arwen Dawn, you make me want to be brave. Thank you for living boldly, for letting me tell you stories late at night, thank you for inspiring me and lending me your name for Art's little sister. And Moira, I am lucky to have found my twin soul in you. Thank you for being my mirror, for challenging me and listening to me in equal measure. Thank you for the hours and hours of fangirling late at night and for helping me untangle plotlines long before I wrote anything down.

Thank you to my little family. To Tyler, my partner in all things, I love you. Thank you for all you've sacrificed to believe in my dreams, for taking on overtime so I can afford to write, for giving me space to create and for loving me so completely. And to our Edith — you can't read yet, but this book is for you. All the play, all the stories, all the conflict and reconciliation, it will always be for you. In my books and also IRL.

And finally — FINALLY — thank you to the readers. May you find your own heroic self in these pages and know that I am grateful you picked this book, these characters, and stuck with us for the entire adventure. You are not alone.

Game on!

Victoria Koops never stopped playing make-believe and often writes while wearing a tiara. She writes stories full of epic adventure and swoony romance that navigate social issues through the power of fandom and geek culture. *Who We Are in Real Life* is her debut novel. Victoria is a practicing counselor in Treaty 4 Territory in Saskatchewan, where she lives with her family. Victoria loves to sing off-key, tease her sisters and pretend that she'll choose a different romance the next time she plays *Dragon Age: Inquisition*.